AS THE CURRENT
PULLS THE FALLEN UNDER

AS THE CURRENT
PULLS THE FALLEN UNDER

A Novel

DARYL SNEATH

N_1 O_2 N_1
CANADA

*Publisher's note: This book is a work of fiction. Names, characters, places and
incidents are either the product of the author's imagination or are used
fictitiously, and any resemblance to actual persons living or dead
is entirely coincidental.*

Library and Archives Canada Cataloguing in Publication

Sneath, Daryl, 1975–, author
As the current pulls the fallen under : a novel / Daryl Sneath.

ISBN 978–1–988098–36–4 (softcover)

I. Title.

PS8637.N43A88 2017   C813'.6   C2017–904635–7

Printed and bound in Canada on 100% recycled paper.

Now Or Never Publishing
#313, 1255 Seymour Street
Vancouver, British Columbia
Canada V6B 0H1

nonpublishing.com
Fighting Words.

We gratefully acknowledge the support of the Canada Council for the Arts
and the British Columbia Arts Council for our publishing program.

for Mr. (Richard) Borek
&
for Ethan, Penelope, & Abigael
&
for Tara

'Everywhere the ceremony of innocence is drowned.'

—Yeats

'Tell the truth—but if the truth doesn't tell the truth lie through your teeth.'

—Karl Knotold

FREEDOM STARTS HERE

STEPHEN & SERRA'S: HERON RIVER, ON

After they took Max away I went to live with Stephen and
Serra on the river. There were canoes, including the one
they gave Rayn on her fourteenth birthday, fishing rods and
tackle, a vegetable garden I helped with, a tractor I learned to
drive in all seasons with a bucket and a tiller and a snowplough
and a deck that cut five-foot swaths, two snowmobiles and an ice
hut Stephen spent the evenings of January and February in.
There was the store they'd had since 1968: Down to Earth. I
worked there after school and in the summers which I didn't
mind and at times actually liked. Three years went by in a flash
and besides the obvious I lived a normal teenaged life.

In the summer I often paddled the river in the mornings as
the sun came up. I used Rayn's canoe and the paddle she'd won.
To those who didn't know any better—which was everyone,
even Stephen and Serra—riding the river in Rayn's canoe was a
sentimental thing to do: a son holding onto the memory of his
mother, attempting to stay connected in some earthly way. I overheard Serra tell one of her friends that she thought it was nice.
Beautiful, really, and sad. A child without his mother. Poor soul.
But there was nothing sad or beautiful or sentimental about it.

Before leaving for BC I struck out in the canoe one last time,
four years to the day after Rayn died. As I came through the
cedars and rolled the boat from my shoulders to my thighs to the
ground the great blue heron perched on the stump on the far
shore in line with our dock lifted and pumped its wide wings in
slow low-sounding thwumps against the air. It lifted and soared
and I watched it land downriver on another stump amidst the
long grasses and it became still again and part of the landscape. I
dropped the canoe in the water off our dock and climbed in. The
air was cool and smelled of river water and earth. A temporary

lunar coolness succumbing to the August sun. I reached forward, dropped the paddle in, and pulled. Fell into the rhythm of moving. The silent wake. The underwater sounds of the boat cutting through the surface. Of the paddle being dropped in and drawn. Wooden. Dull. Quiet.

And then there she was in the bow. Smiling. An occasional hand through her hair. A look and a smile. Forever the way she was the moment she left this world behind.

'So,' I began. 'This is it. I'm off to a place called Quest University. An old-fashioned liberal arts sort of place. They accommodate athletes, aspiring Olympians.

'Had my last session with Dr. Carl the other day. To be honest, he's one of the reasons I'm leaving. I don't mean he encouraged me or guided me in any way. I mean he's one of the things I have to get away from. Not to mention Baron. I've always felt like I was his product, his creation. Like I belong to him. Everyone thinks he's the reason I've managed to do what I've done on the track, that he's got the magic pill. I finally told one coach who wouldn't stop badgering me about my so-called 'program' that the key was to have his runners sleep in three hour chunks and do five hard workouts a week at two in the morning with half an apple and thirteen raisins ten minutes before the workout, a peanut butter sandwich right in the middle, and three room temperature beers afterwards. I told him to be sure to record the 50 metre splits for every rep—accuracy is vital—and have them run counter-clockwise every other set for balance, both physically and psychologically. I told him for the three-a-week 50 click easy runs he should drive alongside the group with a megaphone out the window yelling things like, 'Grass grows faster than you slugs run.' Negative refrains can be great motivation. Oh, and once a week make the trek into Toronto to do some free running through the city streets. If you can survive an honest session of hardcore parkour you can survive anything. Plus it's great for the, well, core. You should have seen him. Feverishly writing down every word. He asked me to repeat the part about the post workout beers. What an idiot. The world seems full of them.

'So I leave tomorrow. Stephen and Serra are seeing me off. They've been so good to me. When I told them I was going they gave me your journal. They said you wrote in it all the time. They said you never showed it to anyone. Not even Max. They said you'd want me to have it. I haven't read it yet. To be honest I don't know if I can.

'Anyway, I should be getting back. Stephen and Serra are throwing a little going-away party. Baron'll be there. A few friends from school. I'll miss them I guess. But not really. Not the way I miss you and Max. I figure whatever happens in my life one thing I can be sure of is that I've been trained well for loss.'

And then she was gone.

I turned the canoe around. The great blue heron lifted from the stump among the long grasses and glided on the air above me, making her own return home, I could only assume, as I made mine.

Clippings (1)

(taken from "Freak Summer Storm to Hit
Central Ontario": weatherwewatch <app>)

"Chance of snow overnight: 100%. 5 – 10 cm. With
Toronto at the centre of the storm, the radius will
stretch east to Peterborough, west to Hamilton, north to
Barrie, and South across Lake Ontario. Temperatures
will drop to between −5 and −10 °C. Expect flash-freez-
ing conditions. Black ice on the roads. Ponds and small
lakes and slow-moving rivers will crust over with 5 – 10
mm of ice. Animals will be confused. Especially migra-
tory birds. Temperatures will rise quickly throughout
the morning, reaching seasonal norms by noon. Most of
the affected regions will have recovered by 5 pm EST
and summer will have fully re-emerged by 10 pm EST."

~

*If I were a numerologist (or a praise-be-to-God born-again literalist)
it wouldn't have taken much to convince me the weatherwewatch forecast
meant something more than cold and snow. All those 5s and 10s.
Coincidence was no explanation. It was the earth telling us something.
God on high (praise Jesus, Hallelujah, let's get high on God) talking
down to us (as he's wont to do), warning us in forecast code that the end
is nigh. Prepare thyself. Pray, purge, plead for forgiveness. Love one
another one last time. Embrace each other, brothers and sisters. Put your
hearts together. Feel them thump-thumping through. Feel the love. Feel
the beat. Clap hands. Embrace God. Embrace Jesus. Oh, Mary, mother
of God, pray for us sinners. Say goodbye to all earthly evil and welcome
in all Godly goodness. Bye-bye Beelzebub! Hey there, Heavenly Father!*

Jesus, take me home! Sing Hallelujah! Hallelujah! Hallelujah! Raise your hands to the heavens! Open your arms, open your hearts, let the good Lord of burning brimstone in. Let him judge, the big bully. Let him cast away the castaways. Let him pick his team. Let him flip his coin. Let the ascent of angels begin. And let the rest of us good honest souls— the non-believers, the undecideds, the oops-missed-the-judgement-day-deadline-begging-for-an-extension-so-as-to-cover-our-asses converts—fuel the bubbling terra firma fire that warms the dangling toes of the rising heaven-bound 5th and 10th Airborne Divisions of the Army of God chosen few. It's the least we can do.

I jest, but honestly, all it takes for some of the most devout apocalypse-chasers are a few number patterns in weather or dates to get the ball rolling on a good old-fashioned Armageddon campaign.

I think I'd love to have the job of writing anonymous app reports. There could be a series: weatherwewatch, windwewatch, waterwewatch, whaleswewatch, warwewatch, weaponswewatch, westwewatch, westernswewatch, westernerswewatch, watcherswewatch. Instead of phones, users would get the feeds through a device they wear on their wrists, make it look like an old school timepiece. Call it the weeW. A classic chrono font uppercase W on the band. Choice of colour: silver, black, or gold. Get good old good-for-a-malapropism Dubya himself to self-deprecate in the ads: 'I don't go nowheres without my wee dubya.'

I wonder, will an old-fashioned liberal arts degree from Quest University properly prepare me for such ambitions?

It was late. The party was still going but people had begun to leave. They shook my hand and wished me luck, people I'd never see again unless in passing on a return visit home. Many of them still looked at me like the boy who'd lost his mother. Which I suppose I was. Their closed-lip grins and empathetic eyes. Out west no one would know about Rayn or Max or any of it and I wouldn't tell them and they wouldn't look at me with sad faces. Life would be normal.

Normal. Whatever that was.

The snow had started and I snuck outside. The three Chrises—Chris, Kris, and Criss (short for Crissy, short for Christina)—who I'd hung out with quite a bit in school, were outside already. I told them if we didn't want an audience we should head down to the river. And so we did.

In the midnight summer cold in our shorts and sandals we stood on the dock and listened to the listless black water lap lightly against the wood and we watched the strange snowfall in the light of a full August moon, passing one around.

'Jesus Aged Christ but it's cold. Isn't it cold?'

'It's snowing, Kris. Yes, it's cold.'

'But it's summer. It's summer and it's snowing. Isn't that odd?'

'Yes, Kris. It's odd.'

Criss took a pull, exhaled, and corrected Kris.

'It's H you know.'

'What's H?'

'Jesus H Christ.'

'No, I think you're wrong.'

Chris backed her up. 'No, Kris, she's right. It's H.'

'Really?'

'Really.'

'I always thought it was Aged. You know, like wine.'

'It's H.'

'Huh.'

'Mind-blowing, I know.'

'What does it stand for?'

'What does what stand for?'

'The H.'

'Harry.'

'Hmn.'

'She's messing with you, Kris. It stands for Holy.'

'Oh. But isn't that a little, uh, what do you call it when a word isn't necessary?'

'Unnecessary?'

'No, no, no. More than that. Vec—what do you call it when a word isn't necessary?'

'Redundant. Unless it's intentional. Then it's tautological.'

'Redundant. That's it.'

'By that logic, Jesus is redundant.'

'Don't say that.'

'Why not?'

'Well, I mean, Christ, you never know what could happen.'

'I never pegged you for a religious man, Kris.'

'I'm not, but still.'

'Still what.'

'Still, you never know.'

'Yes. You do.'

'Well, I don't.'

'Anyway. I didn't mean Jesus the man is redundant. I meant Jesus the name is.'

'That's okay. I guess.'

'There's only one person with the name Christ, so what's it matter if you call him Jesus or Harry or Buck?'

'Like Madonna.'

'Yes, Kris. Like Madonna.'

'I like her. She's good.'

Criss chimed in. 'Nothing against Madonna, Kris, but someone like Gandhi might be a more suitable comparison.'

'Gandhi. Is that a band?'

'Never mind.'

'Nirvana, right?'

'Jesus, Kris. Are you that high?'

'What.'

'Nothing. I'm heading in. Criss?'

She nodded and followed. Kris called after them.

'Hey! You two. Wait for me.' He ran after them. 'Christ, it's cold all of a sudden. Isn't it cold?'

(I miss those three.)

They met Baron as he emerged from the cedar trail. They nodded, he nodded, and they carried on. I thought about catching up but it was too late. They were gone. I'd been trying to avoid him all night and had been successful until now. Chris had passed me the joint when he left and I was standing there on the dock holding it like a pro.

'So. There you are.'

I nodded and took a pull.

'Celebrating?'

I nodded again, held the smoke in, exhaled.

'Mind if I join?'

He stepped onto the dock and extended a hand, thumb and index finger in the receiving position. He took a hit and coughed, a disruption to the night. I heard the great blue heron on the opposite shore lift and take her leave. I should have done the same.

He returned what was left of the joint. 'So, kid. You got a plan?'

I watched the black river water like it was a fire. 'Not really.'

'I can send you workouts you know. No problem.'

'Yeah. Sure. I don't know.'

'Olympics in three years, Vec. Gonna take some kind of regimen to get under 3:30. Which is what it's gonna take to win.'

I nodded. I didn't care. At that moment I really didn't.

'I can help. Email, Skype, Facebook, Twitter, Instagram. All of it. It'll be like you never left.'

I shrugged.

'Who you gonna train with? There's that Durn kid. Second behind you at Junior Nats. He's fast. Tough. Gritty. Like you.'

'Maybe. I don't know. I'll look him up.'

'I'll contact his coach. I know him pretty good.'

I shrugged again.

'Give'm your cell and whatnot. He's a good guy.'

'Yeah. Sure. I don't know.'

'We made quite a splash, you and me. Records'll never be touched. Not for a hundred years.'

'I appreciate everything. Really.'

'Don't sell yourself short. I was just the architect. You did all the heavy lifting.'

He laughed. I didn't.

'We'll team up again one day, kid.'

'Yeah. Sure. Maybe.'

'No, really. I've got it on good word I'm in the running for the Olympic team.' He grinned like an idiot. 'No joke. I'm going to be national distance coach.'

I looked at him.

'Olympic gold, kid. Ours to lose. Like I always said.' He put his hands out. 'Hey, have I ever been wrong?'

I took a pull, held the smoke in, exhaled.

'So. Listen. I gotta ask. Why the big move all of a sudden? I could see if you were going south. That would make sense. I coulda got you in anywhere. Full ride. All the bells and whistles.'

Let's be clear. *I* could have gotten me in anywhere. *Me*.

'I just don't get it. All the way out west. And such a small school. No track. No nothing far as I can see.'

I shrugged. 'I don't know.'

'You don't know? Jesus H, kid, if you don't know, who does?'

I decided I liked Jesus Aged better. Right or not.

'To get away I guess.'

'What's wrong with Toronto, London, Windsor. They're away.'

I shrugged again. 'I like the idea of the ocean and the rain.'

'Shit, well, you'll get lots of that. It rains when the sun shines out there.'

'I need to put some distance between myself and a few people.'

I looked at him. He nodded. Idiot.

'Dr. Carl, for one.'

He nodded some more.

'And Max.'

He blew out a bunch of air and shook his head, like he really understood. 'Yeah. Crazy. I don't know if I ever told you how sorry I was about all that.'

No. You didn't. And I'd appreciate it if you didn't start now, especially if you're going to use insensate dismissive phrases like *all that*.

'Can't be easy still.'

I took a pull and held it in, shut my eyes and wished him away.

'Listen. I gotta ask, Vec. Now that you're leaving. Now that we're having this little heart to heart. Now that's it been a while. I gotta ask. Did your mother ever tell you about me?'

I opened my eyes. 'What?'

'Your mother and me. Before Max. We were pretty close.'

I flicked the roach into the water. I don't know why I didn't hit him.

As I left I pictured the great blue heron returning, swooping low over the dock, knocking him with a powerful thwump of her wide wings into the water. I imagined him flailing, splashing, choking, helpless, calling out. And it gave me pleasure.

'Hey, kid. Wait. Come on. Don't leave like that. Vec. Hey, Vec.'

I walked through the cedars and up the hill, breathing in the anomalous cold.

Jesus Aged Christ.

Right then I swore I'd never speak to Charlie Baron again. A vow I'd break only once. Three years later to the day.

Clippings (2)

(taken from "Oh, Canada! Sorn Stays in
Country for School," runnerspace.com)

"Heron River native and middle-distance phenom
Vector Sorn is set to continue his running career in
Squamish, BC, home to the forward-thinking liberal arts
and sciences university, Quest. When asked why he was
staying in Canada, Sorn told us he did not want to
become the workhorse of some title-seeking school
south of the border. He was, to quote, 'wild and
untameable, not to mention allergic to apples and straw.'
On a more serious note, he told us he was attracted to
the 'academic rigour and freedom' Quest has come to be
known for. 'It's the perfect place for me. I have no idea
what I want to be or do,' he said with a wink, 'and they
seem to welcome, if not celebrate, that kind of uncertainty.' Sorn will be one of only a hundred new
Canadian students at Quest this fall. Highly selective in
their admissions process, it is an institution which
accepts not only the best and brightest but the most
intellectually curious and creative. Apparently Mr. Sorn
is as quick between the ears as he is fleet of foot. All the
best in the west, Vector, and keep on running!'

~

*Just for the record, I didn't come out west to continue my so-called
running career. A 'career' (not to state the obvious) is an occupation—a
trade, a craft, a vocation, if you will—which spans the better part, or at
least a substantial chunk, of a person's adulthood garnering financial*

stability and personal satisfaction. To note, I'm barely an adult. I'm certainly not in the hood part of being one. Also, to be clear, I have made no money as a runner and although I have experienced some success on the track, I am always left feeling—like most elite runners I know and have read about—that I can do and be better. Satisfaction is fleeting at best. Apart from a discussion on how the latter has an etymological connection to the former, the words 'running' and 'career' have no business sharing the same phrasal space.

Had I been asked point blank (and had I been honest in response), the three reasons at the time of departure I would have given for venturing west were, in no particular order, these: to free myself from Max, to get away from Baron, and to escape the real and foreboding presence of Rayn. I feel bad for mentioning her as one of the reasons, but it's true. I suppose I should have been thankful. I should have held onto every moment. How fortunate I was. How most people would give anything to feel and see someone they'd loved and lost the way I continued to feel and see Rayn.

I told Stephen and Serra about it and they said there were times they believed they could see her too. Stephen nodded and Serra hugged me and said Rayn would always be with me. In their own way I suppose they understood. But not really. It was like I could touch her. Like she was alive. But not. I could not understand it then and I cannot understand it now. She'd be there walking beside me and then not. On the edge of my bed when I woke and then gone. In a chair across from me at the table and then, whsshh, into thin air. I told this to Dr. Carl, pseudo psycho simian that he is. He gave me some psychobabble explanation of how our memories of the dead are our way of holding onto those who have passed. That was his phrase: 'those who have passed.' He said there was real evidence of late supporting the claims of mediums. Those among us who had access to the other side. Some people, and I might be one of them, he said, have a gift. He actually believed this. I could see it in his eyes. A doctor for christ sake. A true ambassador of wisdom, that Dr. Carl. A living embodiment of the excellent foppery of this world.

I think it's clear by now but I'll mention it just to be sure: I'm not a religious man. I have no delusions about an afterlife. We are here and then we are not. That's it. I should note too that I don't consider myself a spiritual person either, as some of the secularists might say. I don't have *a wind-in-the-trees connection to nature. The wind in the trees is the wind in the trees. I believe in science, reason, and the explanation of things based on knowledge and discovery. I strive to understand what happens to me and around me. Art is an important part of that striving (hence this little project I'm writing). In all its forms art allows for an intuitive understanding. It speaks a language we feel rather than one we comprehend, which is an essential part of knowing. Feeling is a type of knowledge we cannot yet articulate but know for certain is present and true and real.*

.   .   .

It's true. I didn't want to be anyone's workhorse. Which is one of the main reasons I didn't go south on scholarship. I got offers from all the Ivy League and Big-10 schools. They sent recruiters, paid for flights and accommodations to visit their campuses, treated me like royalty when I went, assured me I'd receive the best education, the best coaches, the best programs, the best labs, the best roads, the best tracks, the best fans, the best sunsets, the best food, the best water, the best beds, the best coffee if I drank coffee, the best beer if I drank beer, the best music, the best books, the best people, the best women, the best men if that was my thing, the best nightlife, the best morninglife, the best life period.

The best the best the best. The best of the best. The number of sentences I heard that began, 'I assure you, we have the best . . .'

I took all the free stuff they offered and said, all earnest and nodding, shaking their extended and over-eager hands, 'You know, it's funny. I don't know. I like it here. I really do. This could be it. This could be the place for me.'

What a prick I was. I never considered going south. Not once.

.   .   .

I heard about Quest listening to the Sunday Edition on CBC radio. A place where you did one course at a time. Complete subject immersion. Courses like Fate & Virtue, Reason & Freedom, Democracy & Justice. In the same year I could choose to study the Neurobiology of Learning & Memory, Forensic Geology, and Evolutionary Psychology. There were

courses with names like Testimonials, Narrating Murder, the Limits of
Knowledge, and Asymmetry, a course premised on the question of
whether there was really such a thing as left and right.

And they accommodated elite athletes.

It was perfect.

I told Stephen and Serra about it and they said Rayn would have
been in the seat next to me on the plane. Stephen shook my hand and
said I'd do well wherever I went. Serra hugged me and wished me luck.
When I said there was no such thing she grinned and said in the history
of the world no one has ever been more his mother's son.

Air Canada, Flight 510:
Toronto to Vancouver

Pickups always seemed out of place to me on the highway. But even more than out of place, Stephen and Serra's pickup was anachronistic: the two-tone brown, the open box with the worn spare tire up front and two concrete slabs for weight at the back, the hand-powered windows, the clunky wipers that moved out of time, the lack of head room, lack of leg room, lack of air conditioning, the temperamental heater, the primitive speedometer (the needle bouncing somewhere between ninety and one hundred), the fuel gauge that never moved from three quarters full, the AM/FM dial with its vertical red line that floated across station numbers as you manipulated the knob requiring the hands of a surgeon to locate certain channels, the absent USB ports, blue tooth, sync system, satellite, the fact that there wasn't even a CD player or a tape deck. There was the strange absence of any type of button or computer-dependent mechanism, the outside modern frenetic world limited to what you could see through the windows and the few unsophisticated and imperfect sounds of the radio. But more than anything it was the smell. The smell of rubber boots and hay and country air and river life and cellar dampness, the smell of a time that did not belong to me, the smell that never failed—whether I wanted it to or not— to bring back Rayn.

We said very little on the drive to the airport. We didn't have to. Risking the ticket, Stephen stopped outside gate 18 and we all stepped down from the truck. I reached into the uncovered box for my one suitcase and shook Stephen's hand which was warm despite the cold. I said thanks and he nodded and told me if I ever needed anything they were only a call away. I hugged Serra and she held onto me longer than I expected. I stood there for a moment, the suitcase at my side. Part of me wanted to stay. Part of me wanted to ask them to come. But neither were really options. It was the nervousness surfacing, the uncertainty. At the sliding doors I looked back and saw them standing there: Stephen, stalwart as a man half his age, one arm about Serra's shoulders, strong, squeezing her close, and Serra, settling into him, her head against his chest, watching me go, semi-smiling, her sad-happy eyes looking on, the truck exhaust like dry ice rolling at their feet in the unseasonably abnormal cold. It was a picture I would remember. They reminded me of what Max and Rayn might have looked like had they reached an age of grey hair and forgotten freedom. But 'remind' is the wrong word. It suggests a remembering and I cannot remember them the way I remember Stephen and Serra. I would never know them as old. One day, should I make it to that age, they will in memory be younger than me, their son, and it will be strange to picture them with less life in their faces than the one looking back from the mirror in that distant hard-to-imagine morning as I wake one more time and wonder (as I have come to do in my singular obsession) why we do what we do and, more selfishly, what the many things of my days might have been if the one thing on that particular day had not.

·   ·   ·

As the plane ascended I watched the city shrink and go quiet. The towers and skyscrapers became chess pieces. Roads became maps, the designs of men long dead revealed. Lakes became depthless and crayon blue. Outside the city all land was green or brown or yellow, boxed and neatly partitioned as though parcelled out long ago by some ancient unnameable king. There was no sound and no movement save for the miniature vehicles inching silently along. There were no people anywhere that I could see. It was so easy, at times, to imagine the end of things.

I squeezed my eyes shut. This was to be a fresh start. All it takes to change a mindset is a decision to do so. Like changing a shirt. By the time the attendant came around with her cart I was feeling excited again, mischievous even. The seat next to me was empty and so I had no audience but her. I asked for a vodka martini and gave her my library card for ID. She could have easily rolled her eyes and said there was a whole cabin-full of people to serve if I couldn't tell and so she had no time for little boys and their games. But she didn't. Instead she grinned and folded her arms which I appreciated and interpreted as permission to continue.

'See, this card lets me borrow books like *Beautiful Losers* and *Portnoy's Complaint*. Not to mention the boozy tomes of Bukowski and Richler. The way I see it is, if I'm allowed to read about it I should be allowed to do it.'

She put the pink eraser-end of her pencil to her chin, nodded, and said I may have a point but by that logic she should be allowed to wear her uniform unbuttoned just enough to encourage tips and tuck a Glock .45 into her ass-tight pants so that she might reach back and pull it on anyone who seemed suspicious or gave her flack about the speed of service or tried to use a library card for ID.

'Elmore Leonard.' I pointed. 'Let me guess. You're an actress.'

'Let me guess.' She pointed. 'You're a director.'

I slid the library card into my wallet and grinned.

She took a glass and a silver shaker from the belly of the cart and did her thing. Her hair was platinum blonde and pulled neatly back, a thin streak of pink down the middle, mostly hidden. I imagined a tattoo, something Asian, hiding beneath the short navy scarf she wore, tied off to the one side of her neck. The uniform was androgynous: navy pants and a collared navy shirt, neither of which revealed anything of the body beneath. The standard name tag below her left lapel read Valerie.

She set a napkin down, the martini next to it, and asked if I wanted anything else. I said a cigar would be nice and she said that she was sorry but since we were living in the early twenty-first century and not the early twentieth century we weren't allowed to smoke on planes anymore. Maybe I'd noticed the signs and the clean air. I said I was pretty sure there were no commercial airlines in the early twentieth century. Everybody travelled by train or by ship. And the air, just so she knew, is not as clean as people think it is. Just look how many kids have asthma these days. She said history had never been her strong suit but she knew for a fact that the air Canada (she paused for me to tally the pun) had to offer was some of the best air in the world, particularly the air in BC, which is where she was from, if I cared to know, but nevertheless, if I really wanted a cigar I should head to Gastown when we landed. A place called The Irish Heather had a whiskey room in the back called Shebeen where it was rumoured you could get a fine cigar and Scotch from God's own reserve.

We talked twice more on the flight but only briefly: once when she brought the meal (Pacific salmon on wild rice) and a second martini (which I hadn't asked for, and, to note, was virgin like the first), and once when we landed. When she brought the salmon and the faux martini she placed another napkin down with a black arrow drawn across the bottom. When I flipped the napkin over I saw a name and cell number. She was serving the seat in front of me when I looked up. I raised my glass and she smiled. When we landed she was one of two attendants standing at the exit issuing the standard 'Thank you for flying Air Canada' goodbye. The exitway was narrow and somewhat awkward in its limited space and so as I inched by her I was close enough to see the tiny hole in her nose where the ring she wasn't allowed to wear while in uniform would go, close enough to smell the mango shampoo she used, close enough to touch her though I didn't, close enough for her to touch me which she did, furtively squeezing my hand, which stopped me for a moment and made my heart go and hastened me to say, 'No—thank you,' which I felt immediately stupid for but she smiled again and said, 'Careful of your step, Mr. Sorn,' so the feeling of stupidity dissipated and as I walked the corridor to my new province I felt the way I imagine someone who believes he's been born again feels the moment he realizes his new path: driven and confident and good, eager to begin, humming with too much excitement.

Clippings (3)

(taken from Twitter)

Danny Mann @d_man   32m
totally mucked @vanval's latest project. youtube.com/watch?v=
dmko. had it coming the little fucker

Valerie Argent @vanval   23m
You're such a man, @d_man.

Danny Mann @d_man   22m
least I dont fuck little boys @vanval

Valerie Argent @vanval   21m
The wit, @d_man. How I miss the intellectual stimulation. God
knows there was never any other kind.

Danny Mann @d_man   21m
@vanval bitch, slut, fuckin whore

Valerie Argent @vanval   20m
Oh, the daggers @d_man.

Danny Mann @d_man   11m
how much his mommy paying u anyway @vanval, xtra for dia-
per changes & bedtime stories?

Valerie Argent @vanval   10m
Make that up all by your lonesome, @d_man? If only you knew
what a good bedtime story can do. Oh wait, you're not very
good with your tongue. I forgot.

Danny Mann @d_man   8m
why dont u f.o.a.d @vanval he's lucky I didnt do worse the little
fucker next time I see him I'll kill'm I swear

Valerie Argent @vanval   6m
Just so everyone reading this is clear, @d_man: he's not the little
one—you are. And I mean that (pinky finger wave) in every
possible way.

~

*So much for the fresh start. More than four thousand kilometres from
home and in town for less than one full rotation of the earth and already
I had a good old-fashioned bounty on my head.*

*Dr. Carl would say @d_man was suffering from a classic case of
heartbreak and that I didn't really have anything to worry about. It was
natural, Dr. Carl would explain, expected even. Pounding his gorilla
chest, kicking at the dirt and snorting like a bull, sounding the lion's roar,
relying on his evolutionary instinct to reassert himself as the alpha male.
He was lifting his leg and marking his territory in solipsistic tweets.*

*I wasn't what you'd call twitterate enough back then to fully com-
prehend all the details of a tweeted tête-á-tête. I had an account but never
really used it. The fact that the conversation was waiting for me like a
message when I woke up meant only one thing: that she—VA—had
gone into my phone and had a thirty-minute row on my dime. At the
time I didn't even think about it. I simply read what was there and interpreted @d_man's final words as a real and present threat against me:
'next time I see him I'll kill'm I swear.'*

*Some might feel violated by a cellphone intrusion. Not me. I don't
keep anything I care about inside that mash of synthetica. If I lose it or
spill a coffee on it or it stops working for some other reason I go out buy
a new one and move on. Had she gone into my suitcase and leafed
through my journal (or Rayn's), on the other hand, then I would have
been upset. Those are real and private and undisclosed to the world.
Untraceable, undownloadable, unfollowable. Actual physical pages filled
with thought-about, written-down words. But then again how would I
ever know if she read them? They're not locked. There's no 'search*

history' detectable anywhere, no control panel, no virtual depths to mine. There are fingerprints, I guess, but even if I was that neurotic the only thing fingerprints would prove is that she touched the books, not that she read them. The act of reading itself is essentially unprovable.

I clicked on the YouTube video of @d_man's one-shot TKO of yours truly (one of his friends must have been recording it). How could I not? It was laughable really. We were both swaying in the wind in the parking lot behind Shebeen. I held my fists up way out in front like I was mocking the whole thing (which I wasn't—I was scared shitless to be honest), like I was one of those black-and-white sped-up silent-film pugilists from the 1920s. Danny Mann stood a good two strides away, opposite me with his fists at his sides, like an ape. Karl Knotold provided the commentary: 'Good evening, fight fans, we're here in Gastown in the back parking lot of Shebeen and Danny Mann is about to defend the honour of his unrequited love who is standing here with me now, our lady Bond, Scotch in one hand, cigar in the other. Calm, cool, collected.

'So, Miss Argent, the fans want to know, who are you rooting for in this epic man-against-man battle for love?'

'Oh, Karl, don't be silly. This is not about love and even if it were, love isn't something a man should have to battle for. Didn't your mother ever teach you that?'

'Well, there you have it, folks. Slice your hearts out. The cold hard truth from the oh-so sensuous lips of our Lady Bond as she stands here sipping her single malt and puffing her Romeo y Julieta. No irony intended.'

One other thing. Upon looking more closely at the feed, it seems the last tweet VA thumbed into my phone was posted mere minutes before I read it. It was probably the door clicking shut on her way out that woke me. She likely shut it loudly on purpose. I'm sure if I'd gone over and looked out the window I would've seen her leaving the hotel. She would have paused and looked up. She would've smiled—like in the movies— and walked away.

Victorian Hotel: Vancouver, BC

I was just waking up. The side of my face ached in the shape of a fist. It took me a moment to realize where I was exactly. I sat up in bed and looked around the room. It felt like something from a home reno show. The fake flowers on the breakfast-nook table matched the colours of the walls and the accents in the bedspread and pillows: creamy white, rusty red. The hardwood floors complemented the antique desk and dresser drawers: distressed and aged and used, evocative of other lives. The alarm clock on the antique bedside table said 10:55 which I read as *loss*. I picked up my phone and read the Twitter feed waiting for me there. My head hurt. I shut my eyes and when I did the night began to return.

. . .

Standing outside Vancouver International an hour after landing, I was alone in the big city as the sun was going down. Like Holden Caulfield, only older and Canadian and not exactly down on my luck.

I took the napkin from my pocket and unfolded it.

Valerie Argent. 778.786.7867.

I thumbed the number and sent a text.

—So I asked a woman walking by if she knew where's Shebeen. She said of course she knew where she's been but what the hell was it to me.

—Ha . . . vodka martini . . . I'll meet you out front.

Through the window of the cab I watched the city hum. As we got closer to Gastown and the harbour behind it I could smell the ocean air. Different from the lake and river air of other towns I knew. The people, as diverse as in Toronto or Montreal, seemed a little different somehow. Friendlier maybe. It was hard to tell at first but they seemed less hurried. Like they'd been rained on a lot and were okay with it.

The cabbie pulled up in front of The Irish Heather. I paid him, took my leave, and stood out front facing the pub, suitcase hanging at my side. A group of six or seven barhoppers walked by, abuzz and laughing. I looked into the street and breathed deeply in through my nose. This was the place.

Without notice I felt someone behind me. I turned and there she was. Valerie Argent. Zippered, calf-hugging, black leather boots to her knees. Lowrider designer jeans like they'd been painted on. A thick black belt hugging her hips and a silver buckle. A thin silvery shirt, lowcut and midriff-revealing. Two silver bangles on her left wrist, a small silver ring in her nose. She wore no makeup. Her hair was pulled back but not as severely as it had been on the plane. There were loose strands, like they'd escaped, like they'd been freed. Deliberately casual. The pink streak was no longer narrow and hiding. She had the kind of relaxed confidence politicians often go for but never quite attain. She had a highball of Scotch which wouldn't have been allowed outside the pub. (One of the first things I learned about her was she cared very little for rules.) There was a smirk on her face and she raised one eyebrow which lowered the other and made her eyes look a little evil. Everything about her shimmered.

She sipped the Scotch. 'Nice suitcase. My grandparents have one just like it. Only newer.'

I'd borrowed the suitcase from Stephen and Serra. It was two-tone brown, like the truck, hard-shelled, and had two lockable buckles that flicked open with a spring-loaded snap when you thumb-slid the buttons away from the centre.

'Funny. So do mine.' I raised the suitcase a little and looked at it. 'At least they did.'

She grinned and when she turned around she paused. Like on a catwalk. I'd been right about the tattoo beneath the scarf. An Asian symbol just below and behind her right ear. There were two others. One between her shoulder blades in the space between the two clear straps that held up her shirt: the stylized words Silver

Light. And one in the small of her back, half hidden by her jeans: a pair of Queens, hearts and spades, fanned out like someone had laid a winning hand there and somehow it had stuck.

When she stepped toward the door of The Irish Heather she moved like she was in control of every single muscle in her body and I followed like she'd somehow tapped into every single one of mine.

The Heather was a long narrow place, rich-looking and dark. The people inside all had a glow about them, well-heeled and sure of themselves, having landed in early adulthood on the right side of life, and my own confidence grew somehow the further I moved in.

Valerie slid right through the place and drew the eyes of everyone there. The bartender raised his chin when we walked by. In typical filmic fashion he was drying a glass with the end of a towel draped over his shoulder and he was wearing a white shirt rolled to the elbows. I felt him staring at me even after we'd passed.

'Hey, Val.'

Until now she had not looked back. She paused at the door to the backroom, the sign above which read SHEBEEN, and turned. She could have said I was carrying a bomb in my suitcase and proclaimed us holy soldiers of God, sent by our heavenly father to put an end to all earthly debauchery and sinful Satan-led ways and I'm sure they'd have all dropped to their knees, every single one, pleading for forgiveness and mercy. Further to her blatant disregard of the rules it was clear from the outset that Valerie could make most people—especially men—do anything she wanted them to do. And she knew it.

The Bartender: 'Looks like Little Red Riding Hood's lost his way.'

She looked at me in the hoodie I was wearing and shrugged. 'He works for Google. All IT guys under forty dress like they have no money.'

The bartender crossed his arms. 'Google. This guy.'

She flashed him a smile. 'He's cool. I served him on the plane.'

'First class, I'm sure.'

'Coach actually. He's a leftist. Doesn't even own a car. Bikes everywhere.'

'I wondered who had the Red Rider Special parked outside.'

She put an arm around me and pinched my chin. 'He's got a youthful face. That's all.' She spoke looking at me. 'He's a man. Trust me.'

The bartender stacked the glass he'd been drying and started on another. 'I'd like to say you're lucky, son—'

I didn't like the 'son' bit.

Valerie was opening the door to the backroom when she stopped and spoke over her shoulder. 'Watch what you say now, Paulie.'

He held the glass up and checked it in the light. '—but a lucky man doesn't need another man to tell him about his luck.'

Inside Shebeen I followed her to a table for four where there was only one empty seat. She sat and I stood, suitcase still hanging at my side. The man at the table—Karl Knotold, I'd come to know—coiffed and good-looking and sure of himself, in his late twenties, early thirties I guessed—though he had the kind of face that made it hard to tell—was in the middle of a story about a cougar. He was sitting on the edge of his chair, leaning across the table. The two women opposite him, dressed like Valerie and beyond beautiful like her, in their twenties, too, I guessed (though they could easily have been my age), were also on the edges of their chairs, shoulders touching. Engrossed. Eyes wide.

'So, there I am, walking innocently along, inside my head trying to work through a problematic ending for a story I was writing, the sun going down, the temperature dropping just enough to be pleasant, blissfully alone on a quiet trail in the middle of the woods, ruminating, when all of a sudden, BAM.' He smacked the table and the two girls jumped and laughed despite themselves. 'It came to me. There is no ending. And that's the point. Problem solved. Story done. Genius. Prize-winning for sure. Relieved and eager to get back to my laptop to delete the unfinished ending and pour myself a celebratory finger or two of

Johnny Walker Blue, I stopped, about to turn and head back, and there she is, two maybe three strides in front of me, this wild, lithe-looking cat, staring me down. So what do I do? What are my options here? Run? There's no way. Play dead? A lot of good that would do should she decide to pad over for a pre-prandial sniff and nibble. Scream? What if that excites her? Enlivens the blood in her veins? So there I am. Stuck. Nowhere to turn, nothing to do. You always, always have a choice, say the pundits of free will. Well, not me. Not this time. Not at that moment. I was truly and utterly optionless. Frozen. Cock stiff.'

He leaned back and sipped his Scotch, glanced at Valerie, who was sitting beside him, and grinned. The other two girls looked at each other, then at him. One of them tapped her feet under the table like she were sprinting and hunched her shoulders, tucked her chin and held her face in her hands.

The other leaned forward and slapped the table with two open hands. 'Well? What happened? What did you do?'

Karl glanced at Valerie again, then up at me. He winked.

'I approached with caution and asked her not to bite.'

The table-slapper furrowed her brow. 'You approached a cougar and spoke to it.'

He shook his head. 'I was mistaken. Turns out she wasn't a cougar. Only thirty-eight.'

Valerie, leaning back in her chair, snickered and sipped her Scotch. The other two smiled and shook their heads.

Karl crossed his arms, took in the suitcase I was holding, and looked up at me. 'So. What's your story, Paddington Bear?'

I set the suitcase down and pocketed my hands. 'I'm a runner.'

I don't why I said that.

'Well. Pull up a chair, runnerboy. If you're with Val you must be the gold standard best.'

I stole a chair from the next table and sat. I felt like I should be presenting something. An entrepreneur pitching an idea to a table of potential backers. Four sets of eyes on me, waiting for me to speak.

'Mr. Sorn here is an original.' This was Valerie.

Karl nodded. 'Is that so.'

'He used a library card for ID on the plane.'

'Did he. And how did that work out for you, Mr. . . ?'

I answered. 'Sorn.'

'Sorn. What an unusual name.'

'Vector Sorn.'

The table-slapper scrunched her nose and repeated my name, nodded and sounded her approval. 'Vector Sorn. Cool. I like it.'

What would it have meant, I wondered, if she hadn't?

Karl: 'So. Vector Sorn. Back to my question.'

I looked at Valerie. 'I'm here aren't I?'

Karl nodded. 'That's true. You are here. Here is where you are.' He clasped his hands and leaned towards me across the table. 'And why is that, Vector Sorn. Why are you here, exactly?'

'Ooh, ooh, let me guess.' This was the toe-tapper.

Karl leaned back and presented her with a hand like he were introducing an act. 'Mr. Sorn, let me introduce Miss Veronica Redhill. Clairvoyant extraordinaire.'

Veronica sat straight up, closed her eyes, stuck her elbows out like wings, and touched her temples with the tips of her index fingers. She opened her eyes and looked right at me. 'You're trying to get away from someone. More than one. I can see them. There's a group, only they're not really a group. One's a teacher. The other's a—oh, I can't quite get it—a doctor or something. And, oh. Oh, no. I'd better not say.'

I could feel my heart going.

Karl: 'Come on now, Ronnie. Don't hold back. Vector's all right, aren't you old boy?'

Karl looked at me, I shrugged, and he urged Veronica on.

She sighed and put her hands together, touched the tips of her fingers to her lips like a woman at prayer. She sighed again and stared at me as though she were in pain. 'The one you're really trying to get away from is—your father.'

Karl, the table-slapper (whose name I still didn't have), and Valerie all looked at me. I nodded.

Karl clapped. 'Oh, she's good. Isn't she good?' He pointed at her. 'You're good.'

I agreed with Karl, that indeed she was good, but I wondered out loud if she wasn't just a little bit lucky too. I mean, really, he had to agree, most eighteen-year-olds leave home to get away from their parents for one reason or another.

Karl nodded and looked around the table. 'He has a point.'

The table-slapper: 'What about the doctor and the teacher?'

'Yes, Vanessa.' Karl pointed at her, then at me. It was like he had money invested in Veronica's clairvoyance. 'Yes. The doctor and the teacher. What about them?' He leaned in and waited.

'Well,' I said, 'there was a psychiatrist and a phys-ed teacher. A coach.'

Karl clapped once and held his hands together. He stood and bowed toward Veronica. He sat again and looked at me. 'Let me guess. The coach was abusive and the psychiatrist blabbed about it.'

I shook my head and looked at Veronica.

She closed her eyes. 'I'm not getting anything particularly strong for either one.'

I nodded. 'That sounds about right.'

Valerie sat forward and looked at me. (I'd have done anything she wanted.) 'I don't think there's anything interesting about the lap counter or the shrink. They are what they do. What I want to know is what the father did to make our man here want to leave.'

Our man. I wasn't sure about the accuracy of either word.

Karl took the thick black frames that had been resting on the top of his head and slid them into place. He looked like Clark Kent, only more stylish and confident. 'Miss Argent, right for the jugular.' He rubbed his hands together. 'But before we get any further on the father I think we need to replenish our rhenish. Vector, name your whiskey, old boy. It's on me.'

'I'd be lying if I said I knew.'

He rubbed his hands together again. 'Pick a letter.'

I looked around the table. 'V.'

Karl checked the high ceiling and cracked his knuckles. 'Nothing on the list starts with V. And there's nothing from

Canada or the States with a V in it. Nothing from Ireland either. From the World selection we have Australia's Sullivans Cove. From Premium Blends, Chivas Revolve. And from Scotland, the one true heaven on earth, we have four. Glenlivet, Balvenie, and Convalmore. All from Speyside. And from the Islet of Islay, Lagavulin.'

He looked at me, grinning, and waited.

I was careful not to shrug. 'I like the sound of the last one.'

'Lagavulin. Excellent. And I promise.' He shoved the centre of his thick black glasses with an index finger. 'She'll be gentle.'

He was gone and back again, it seemed, within seconds with a tray of highballs and five cigars. 'Balvenie for the Redhill sisters.' So they were sisters. 'Johnny Walker Blue for yours truly. And two Lagavulin. One for our lady of the sky and one for her lad in the making.'

Lad in the making. I'd remember that.

He raised his glass and the table followed. 'With the running I wasn't sure if you'd partake but I brought you one in case.'

He offered me one of the cigars and I took it, smelled the length of it, held it in my teeth, struck a match, and puffed until it burned.

'Not your first time, I see.'

'Special occasions.'

Karl was holding a lighted match for Valerie. Looking at me, he asked what made this particular occasion special. Vanessa Redhill slapped the table and said it was my birthday. I shook my head and looked at her sister who closed her eyes and touched her temples again. She nodded, looked at Valerie, smiled, and said it was love. Love made this occasion special.

I felt the blood go to my cheeks. 'I was thinking a fresh start.'

Valerie puffed her cigar and looked right at me. 'Yes. The father. We all want to know.'

I looked at her. 'I'm not sure you do.'

Karl broke in. 'Trust me, old boy. She knows what she wants.'

I drew on the cigar and let the smoke out slowly. 'Well. He's a murderer.'

I said it like he was a teacher or an engineer or the policeman that he had been.

Like someone about to reveal a secret, Valerie unfolded her arms and leaned across the table. 'Really.'

I nodded.

'Who did he kill?'

I drew again on the cigar and spoke in the tone of someone talking about the weather. 'My mother.'

I don't know why I said that. Maybe I believed it on some level. He could've convinced her that day to let Baron give us a ride. He could convince her of anything. If he had she'd still be here.

'Jesus.' This was Karl.

Valerie leaned back and said nothing.

The Redhill sisters looked at each other and Veronica told me she was sorry. I said she had nothing to be sorry about and I felt calm. I had given them something they hadn't expected and for the moment I had command of the table. Yet what I'd said didn't affect Valerie the way it did the other three. I could see it in their faces: awkward sympathy, discomfited reticence. With Valerie, though, there was the kind of smirking reserve found in the countenance of villains. Indifferent, nearly, to the events of others' lives. Impervious to the sadness. Compassionless. Solipsistic. Ever-concerned with the present and what comes next because nothing can be exhumed from the past but ghosts and bones. And she had no time for either.

As though on cue, in walked the man she had, I would soon learn, most recently excised from her life.

Relieved and elated to move on, Karl Knotold grinned and stuck out his hand to the man standing behind me. 'Danny Mann.'

I resisted the natural urge to turn and look at him and yet I knew he was big. Weightlifter, t-shirt busting, alpha male big. I could sense his heft. Like an ape. I hated him instantly.

I watched Valerie to see how she would react. I watched her because I couldn't not.

'Val.' He paused, like he was really thinking about his next line. 'It's good to see you.'

She checked her nails. 'Like, wow-what-a-coincidence-it-is-running-into-you-like-this good to see me? Or, You've-been-stalking-me-like-a-pathetic-fucking-nutjob-creep-for-two-weeks-and-can't-stop-jerking-off-to-the-hundred-pictures-you-take-of-me-a-day-coming-out-of-my-building-doing-laps-in-the-pool-leaving-the-gym-the-grocery-store-the-library-sun-bathing-on-my-balcony-and-oh-I'd-love-to-get-a-copy-of-the-candid-zoomed-in-close-up-pics-you-take-standing-across-the-road-looking-up-through-my-floor-to-ceiling-loft-window-at-night-while-I'm-belting-out-Bon-Jovi-ballads-to-the-street-below-in-my-stripper's-thong-and-bra-because-I-know-people-are-watching-and-I-like-that-they're-watching-and-because-I-know-you're-watching-and-it-tortures-you-and-I-like-that-it-tortures-you-but-you-do-it-anyway-because-you-convince-yourself-that-if-you-set-the-camera-to-multi-shot-you're-bound-to-get-one-where-my-head-is-back-a-little-and-my-eyes-are-slightly-closed-and-my-mouth-is-open-like-I'm-coming-and-my-lips-are-at-the-edge-of-the-invisible-microphone-I'm-holding-as-though-it-were-your-cock-in-my-hands-like-it-was-in-your-Hummer-that-time-we-crossed-Lions-Gate-Bridge-and-I-loved-that-it-was-in-your-Hummer-by-the-way-or-like-it-was-the-first-night-we-met-and-I-brought-you-here-to-Shebeen-and-I-blew-you-in-the-back-parking-lot-because-I-felt-like-being-dirty-and-found-you're-hulkiness-lip-licking-ly-attractive-and-your-roughly-hewn-edge-and-diminished-intelligence-and-lingual-inferiority-charming-however-unintentional good to see me?'

Karl Knotold clapped. He clapped slowly and shook his head, grinning but not. The Redhill sisters rolled their lips in and pressed them together. I felt Danny Mann leave. Vanessa slapped the table and Veronica toe-tap-sprinted on the spot beneath it, both erupting in laughter. I turned and watched him go, What could he do? What could any man do? I felt for him then, this man whose face I'd yet to see, this man who would in less than an hour call me outside and drop me with a single drunken punch to the side of the head, this man who had not long ago in the grand scheme of things been where I was now and was now where I would eventually no doubt be.

Karl: 'You have a heart of stone, Miss Argent, and a tongue of forged steel.'

She grinned and puffed on her cigar. 'Why, thank you, Mr. Knotold.'

He looked at me. 'And you wonder why we never got involved.'

All of this—all of it—was fair warning.

Out of nowhere but not awkwardly the Redhill sisters said they were sorry but they had to be going. No one asked why. They hugged Karl, told me it had been nice to meet me, and, finger-waving to Valerie, said they were sure they'd see me again.

After a moment of not saying anything, Karl poked a thumb over his shoulder and said he had to go, too. Valerie raised her brow a little and shrugged. When Karl vacated his spot in the booth, she looked at me, sipped her Scotch, and tapped the leather seat beside her. I got up and sat down as directed.

'So. Vodka martini. Tell me. What is it you're willing to lose?'

CLIPPINGS (4)

(taken from personal email)

Vector Sorn:
Your quest, should you choose to accept it, begins now. More accurately, it begins tomorrow evening, but for the sake of weighty moments—

Who:	You & Us.
What:	Meet & Greet
Where:	Main Hall.
When:	Ten days hence – 5:30 post meridian – an indeterminate but eventual end
Why:	You tell us: your first assignment

In anticipation & with curiosity,
The Faculty at Quest

~

This was the place for me.

#305 36 WATER STREET, TERMINUS BUILDING: VANCOUVER, BC

I hadn't seen her in ten days. I felt like Arturo Bandini. Only I wasn't poor and she wasn't a waitress and I couldn't return to where she worked whenever I felt like it. A man can't just walk onto a plane in the middle of the sky whenever he feels like it and have a cup of coffee. Or a virgin vodka martini.

We were in her loft. The bedroom. It wasn't really a room. More like a space. There was a half-wall you could rest your elbows on and look over, like a balcony, which I tried when she took me upstairs.

I was supposed to be making my way to Squamish to 'accept my quest,' as The Faculty had put it, but now I found myself pleasantly and willingly helpless beneath her. She cuffed my wrists with her hands.

She whispered and her voice felt like a ghost's in my head. 'You don't really have to go, do you?'

I couldn't speak. Like a spider on its prey she wrapped me up and sank her lovely teeth in.

I woke from a dream of her cooking my flesh. Thin slices of thigh sizzling in the pan, peppered and curling at the edges. The cutting board and the knife beside it were bloody. I could see myself seated at the table, shirtless, my right leg wrapped in white gauze, the red seeping through, like a wounded soldier. I was wearing a bib. I held a knife in one fist and a fork in the other. Stunned, I was watching her. She flipped the meat and pressed it into the pan which made me wince and salivate at once. She looked over her shoulder, grinning. Which is when I woke, sweating, and bolted upright in the bed reaching for my leg.

I dressed and went to the bathroom sink and brought hand-
fuls of cold water to my face. My eyes widened and I breathed
deeply in. Coming out of the bathroom I saw the clock by the
bed. It was six minutes after five which I read as *sob*.

I took the top of the half-wall in my hands like a rail and
leaned over the side. I couldn't see her. There was music I
recognized but couldn't name. I could smell and hear something
cooking in a pan. I tried to think of a joke about the dream I'd
woken from but nothing would come, and when I turned with
the intention of going to find her she was already coming toward
me from the top of the stairs, a glass of red wine in each hand.
She offered me one and I took it. Her legs and feet were bare and
I saw how perfect they were. I noticed another tattoo on her
right ankle which I'd missed somehow until now. A bird of some
kind. A pterosaur. She was wearing an oversized t-shirt like a
dress with the saying 'Love is Overrated' printed across the front.
She leaned a hip against the half-wall and crossed her feet, ran a
hand through her hair. The shirt lifted and I saw she was wearing
nothing beneath it. I wondered if the shirt was something she had
purchased that size on purpose or if it was something some other
guy had left behind. I looked at her and tried to think of something clever to say but again nothing would come.

'You're alive.'

'It feels that way.'

She sipped her wine and I did the same.

'Hungry?'

I nodded. 'Starving.'

She turned to descend the stairs and I followed.

The wooden table in her dining room was four inches thick
and heavily lacquered. Everything looked expensive: the art on
the wall, the furniture, the plates, the cutlery, the flowers in each
of the rooms, the silk sheets and pillows on the bed, the bottle of
wine sitting on the table between us.

'So. What do you think?'

I looked around and nodded. 'I love it.'

She grinned, poked a scallop with her fork, held it up like a
head on a spit. 'I meant the food.'

She reached across the table and fed me the catch, watched me chew, and waited until I swallowed the morsel down. 'So?'

I sipped the wine and nodded.

'You don't know what it is, do you.'

I shook my head.

'You often put things in your mouth you can't name?'

She came around the table, put her hands on my shoulders, and climbed on as though my lap were a saddle. She put my hands on her waist, moved them up her body, and slipped out of her shirt like a magician.

She moved her hips and I felt the heat through my jeans. She whispered for me to carry her upstairs and I did—she weighed almost nothing—and told me to lay her on the bed. She directed my head, moved against my mouth with an unrelenting purpose and energy. When she came I felt her whole body go off and I wasn't entirely sure what had happened. She drew me up, kissed my mouth, and bit my bottom lip as I moved inside her. She took my face in her hands and told me to look at her. I did and she kissed me, eyes open, and it felt somehow like I was making a promise, a vow I could not articulate. Before she rolled me away she bit my chest hard enough to leave a mark. She patted the impression her teeth left and made a little laughing noise that bordered on evil.

When she returned from the shower I was lying on the bed, sheets drawn over me, nearly sleeping again. She stood at the foot, naked, drying her hair. I sensed her and opened my eyes.

'Didn't you say you had to go?'

'No. Well. Yes.'

She pulled on her thong like a stripper after a dance and put her hands on her hips. 'We'll have to work on your clarity.'

I smiled. 'I really should go.'

She went to the armoire in the corner and spoke with her back to me. 'Should's not a very good way to live.' With the hanger hooked on a finger and the uniform draped over a shoulder, she turned and did a catwalk strut towards me. 'Want is much better.'

There was no doubt in my mind she had taken everything she had ever wanted.

'Okay. Well, I can't say I want to go because I don't. What if I said I have to go?'

She gave a little shrug. 'It's more immediate but it sounds too desperate.' She took the uniform from the hanger and put it on. 'How do I look?'

I tapped my neck and the side of my nose.

'Right,' she said. 'My secret identity.'

She opened a drawer, pulled out a short navy scarf, and waved it in the air. She sat on the edge of the bed, her back to me, and asked me to do the honours. She bunched her hair and held it up with two hands. I drew the scarf around her neck and began to tie it.

'Not too tight now.'

She sounded like Curly's wife talking to Lenny in the barn. A tee-heeing sexy sort of voice with a hint of apprehension, completely affected.

She stood, looked at me, and removed the ring from her nose.

'I have to ask—'

She corrected me with her eyes.

'I mean, I want to ask. What's it mean? The tattoo on your neck.'

She shrugged like it didn't matter. 'Something like power or control.'

I nodded. 'Fitting.'

'So I've been told.'

Shirtless, I stood and stretched my arms above my head. 'So let me get this straight. When I said I *should* go you say I should've said I *want* to go.'

She nodded.

'Because we should always do what we do because we *want* to do it?'

'Close. There should be no should.' With a finger she examined the bite mark she'd made on my chest. 'You don't seem eighteen.'

'So I've been told.'

'Cute—why is that?'

I shrugged. 'Grew up in a hurry.'

'Right. The father.'

I hesitated. 'Yes. The father.'

'When I talk about you I'm going to say you're twenty-five.'

So she planned to talk about me.

'If I'm twenty-five I'd have to have a job.'

'If you were twenty-five you'd *want* to have a job.'

'Right. So what do I do?'

'You're an IT guy. Google. Remember?'

'Right. I forgot.'

She looked at my chest again and swept her fingers over the mark as though to wipe it away. 'We need to get you a tattoo.'

She turned me around and drew invisible marks on my skin as she spoke. 'First, an old fashioned arrow. Right here. A steel-looking tip. Quills at the base. Then the letters B-I-D-M to the left of the shaft and E-R-U-N to the right.'

She tapped a period at the end and spun me back around.

'Why an arrow?'

'Because. You're a vector.'

'And what do the letters mean?'

'You don't know?'

I shook my head.

'You said you're a runner.'

'I did.'

'I assume you're also here for school.'

I nodded.

'What are you studying?'

I shrugged. I really didn't know.

'Well, whatever it ends up being, be sure to get some Shakespeare.'

She said Shakespeare like it was sleep. Like it was something as easy to get, as inevitable and necessary, as rest.

It fit. I could see her on stage. A female Prospero. A gun-slinging Cordelia.

She handed me my shirt and I pulled it on. Then my jeans and my socks and she fastened my belt. I pocketed my hands and looked at the floor.

"Seriously, I really should—'

'Careful now.'

She tapped my chest, went on her toes, and kissed me, eyes open. 'Don't worry. Duty calls for me, too.' She dangled a set of keys. 'Here, you can drive. After you drop me off you can take the car. Go wherever it is you want to go and when I get back in a few days you can pick me up.'

'You want me to take your car.'

'You sound surprised. You didn't think this was a one-off encounter I hope.'

'Two-off, you mean.'

She grinned, touched my face, and tilted her head to the side. 'Oh, Vector. Nothing happened that first night. We kissed a little. I iced your wounds. You passed out. That's it.'

I looked confused, I'm sure.

'Tell me this wasn't your first time.'

I didn't say anything.

She bit her bottom lip. 'It was. Well, if it makes you feel any better, I couldn't tell.'

I had never felt any better in my life to be honest.

'Anyway, there are two things you'll want to know about me.'

Her word again: want.

'One: this—' She drew an invisible line back and forth between us. '—won't be forever. I don't do forever. There's no such thing. And two: I don't do one-night stands. I decided the moment you handed me your library card on the plane that I was going to keep you for a while. You see, Vector, we're only at the beginning.'

ALL I CAN SEE

From the Journal of Vector Som

It's been four years since Rayn died. As many days nearly as there are metres in the race I run. Though the distance from then to now is far greater than any physical measurement. There is no forgetting but the remembering changes. The event shifts from an immediate reality to an archived truth, a personal truth, which is a paradox, I suppose. There's a movement from *the happening* to *the story of the happening*. Scenes arise. Selections are made. Unintentionally and by design. Truth is liquid, as alterable as the container that holds it.

If only Max had said no—which he would never do—but if only he had. If only he'd suggested waiting or made some joke about her insatiable appetite which he could do without being offensive. He had a way of making everything he said to her sound like love. Because it was.

If only he'd scanned the subway station like he was trained to do. If only he'd seen the pusher standing like a spectre by the column of Osiris: the dishevelled hair, the glassy eyes, the saliva pooled at the corners of his mouth, the wicked grin, the finger-nails bitten to the quick, the ratty woollen sweater despite the summer swelter, the beltless bloodstained kneetorn pants, the bare feet, six strides away and zeroed in, the indiscriminate hate in his eyes. The underworldness of him.

There were so many signs and he saw none which is what would do him in. Knowing that he could have prevented it. Knowing with tortured certainty that it wasn't inevitable or as the pundits of death say 'her time.'

I can only guess how he felt. For a year I witnessed the unravelling. Regardless of how close you are to someone—what you are witness to—you never really know how another person feels. Feeling, I've come to learn, is not about knowing.

Let me be clear. I have no defence for what he did. Nor do I have any judgement. I've never understood the point of judgement, and even if I did, what right would I have now?

I stood beside the pusher like we were together waiting for the train. I stood there and did nothing. I watched her get to her knees like some final parody of prayer. Our eyes met the moment before impact. She smiled. She smiled at me to say everything would be okay when I knew there was no way in hell that it would. There was time for her to get to her knees and smile at me and I didn't even reach for her. Looking back I see a boy whose instincts tell him to step away from the edge of the broken ice when someone ahead of him falls through, a boy who watches, dumbfounded and useless, as the current pulls the fallen under. What kind of instincts tell us to step away from the person who loves us most the moment she needs us, the moment she needs us to step forward—despite all our fear, despite whatever else that's in us to cause delay—and reach out our hand? How difficult it is when it matters most to reach out a hand.

All I can hear is the screeching of the train. All I can see is her smiling and me stepping away.

I don't know why we do what we do. But we do.

CLIPPINGS (5)

(taken from "Local Legend in the Making,"
Heron River Review)

"Grandson of local business duo—Stephen and Serra
Down—Vector Sorn did his hometown proud winning
gold at National Track Tourney [sic]."

~

*Stephen and Serra clipped all the articles I was in the way Rayn
used to and continued to paste them into her book which they gave me
when I told them I was leaving. They said I should continue it, that
she'd want me to. In a way, this keystone project I'm writing—this collection of stories, these clippings from my life—is Rayn's book continued.*

*Heron River is my hometown because Rayn wanted it to be and
Max wanted what Rayn wanted, even if it meant three hours of com-
muting for them both every day. He would've done anything she wanted.
He loved her inarticulately. They had the kind of love that predates
speech. Sprung from the sea of awakening. I witnessed it every day for
more than fourteen years. To me Heron River is simply where I grew up.
I don't mean to sound dismissive or arrogant but I really don't know
what it means to do a place proud.*

Clippings (6)

(taken from "Swift-footed Canadian Youth Takes National Title in World Best Time," iaaf.org)

"Reminiscent of a young Sebastian Coe, Canadian Vector Sorn stakes his claim on the future of the metric mile taking the National Youth title in an age-group world best time of 3:43.43."

~

The only thing I'd ever staked was a tent in the backyard and at the time I'd never even heard of Sebastian Coe. 'A claim,' as it were, on anything, had never entered my head.

CLIPPINGS (7)

(taken from "Veni Vidi Veci: a Champion's Story,"
Globe & Mail)

"His greatness weighed, his will is most assuredly his own, and the athletics world waits with bated breath for the next act."

~

As for my will, I suppose it is as much my own as it is for anyone. I'm not bound or governed by any sort of real obligation. I don't run because I have to or because I was meant to or because I love it (because I don't) or even because I'm good at it. I don't run because Rayn wanted me to, although her desire to see me excel does have something to do with why I continue to do it, if I'm being honest.

Clippings (8)

(taken from "Sorn Soars to Vectory," TorontoStar.com)

"As though propelled by the sandals of Hermes himself, young Vector Sorn flew around Varsity Stadium in a performance which brought the capacity crowd roaring to their feet."

~

I remember when I first read this article. Rayn used to call me Herman, a play on the god's name only she and I and Max knew about. Coincidence I guess. But I'm certain words like coincidence exist only because things occur we cannot explain, like accidents, which are something Rayn believed in the purposefulness of, which is in turn why what looked like an 'e' instead of an 'i' on my birth certificate paperwork stuck and I became Vector.

Clippings (9)

(taken from "Sorn: Born to Run," Toronto Sun)

"Not too many of us knows [sic] from an early age what we're born to do. At fourteen, Heron River native Vector Sorn knows he was born to run."

~

At fourteen I didn't know much. At twenty-two I don't know much more, but I do know this: I certainly wasn't born to run. No one is. Running is an evolutionarily developed and inherited activity which has helped sustain us as a species. But it's not a purpose. Such a notion suggests a belief in a preordained, preternatural reason for being. Which is silly and egotistical. Not to mention I believe in very little.

CLIPPINGS (10)

(taken from "A Rare Vector," nationalpost.com)

"A rare Vector of seismic magnitude and unwavering direction. A god in mortal's clothes. Daunting, mythical speed. An athletic artist. A heart of golden fire."

~

If my heart was ever made of fire it burned out long ago.

NATIONAL YOUTH CHAMPIONSHIPS:
VARSITY STADIUM, TORONTO, ON

From the Journal of Vector Sorn

We were at the start, the twelve of us. We looked like we'd been punched from a mould on a factory line. Tall, lanky ectomorphs. Springy. Sinewy. Like gazelles. One guy was short. Another, overmuscular for his age and looked more like a sprinter. One had a beard already. For the most part, though, we were physically the same. We'd been engineered to do this. Not by choice or by happenstance but by evolution. Every anatomically equipped human being can run—opposite arm, opposite leg, one foot after the next—but we were among the few whose muscles fire at a greater rate over time, whose hearts pump more blood more efficiently, whose bodies can withstand more pain because of a brain more willing to push. We were the rats in some god's science lab.

In the early days the worst part was the waiting. My stomach turned and I yawned.

We stood behind the line and the announcer went through the list. So and so from such and such. Provincial champion A, provincial champion B. Returning silver-medallist. Member of the national cross-country team. Defender of this. Winner of that.

We stood there shifting from one foot to the other, shaking out our legs, our hands, staring down the track, rolling our heads from shoulder to shoulder, feigning calmness, pretending to be relaxed and indifferent to the mounting intensity, the amplified sensation of our hearts thumping in our ears.

'And rounding out this field of fine young distance runners—' Say my name, I thought. Just say my name.

'—the youngest of them all, Vector Sorn, who has made an assault on the record books this season, breaking the provincial and national records an unprecedented nine times in nine successive races. Let's see if he can do it again today.'

Sure. Why not. Let's see.

There was applause from the packed stands across the track. Rayn and Max were there somewhere. I could picture them. Rayn standing when they announced my name, hands like a megaphone, yelling something like, 'Come on, Herman,' even before the race had begun, oblivious to and unconcerned with those around her, unembarrassed, genuinely excited and nervous and proud. When she sat again she'd slap Max's leg three times like it was a drum. 'That's our son,' she'd say. 'Our son.' Sitting back in the bleachers, legs crossed at the ankles, Max would smile behind his aviators, a program rolled in one hand, the other free to touch her arm. His way of letting her know he was proud and excited too. His way of saying, 'Just so everyone knows, she's with me.'

They were the kind of couple everyone noticed. Max was six-four and Rayn was five-eleven. They were both fit, put together, confident, relaxed, and unerringly happy. Max was a two-time Olympian. He won silver medals in the hundred metre fly at Seoul and Barcelona, out-touched both times for gold. Rayn had the fastest C-1 in the country for six years and could've been competitive on the men's side. Had there been women's paddling in the Olympics she'd have stood atop the podium. She would've been the flag-bearer. There was no doubt.

Max and Rayn met at the zoo of all places. There was a monorail accident, serious enough but no severe injuries. There was a lot of standing around: Max was one of the boys in blue, Rayn one of the women in white. The first thing he said to her was, 'You look like an expert. I've always wondered, if man came from monkeys, where did women come from?' She smiled and folded her arms. 'The future. We came back out of curiosity. What a mistake.'

They loved to retell the story and when they did they made it sound like a movie. They could've been in the movies. The camera loved them. They made a lot of money doing commercials on the side. They were the couple on the beach in ads for island vacations, the carefree newlyweds at the casino, the tired parents savouring their morning coffee while playful chaos ensues in the background (I was one of the screaming kids—my big debut). Max was the F-150 guy in dusty jeans and workboots. Rayn was the lakefront runner clad in Nike from head to foot, an iPod strapped to her arm. Anytime the Toronto Police Department needed one of their own for a photo op they called on Max. Decked out in his uniform he looked like he'd been cast for the latest cop film. Rayn was forever on the cover of the magazine and brochures for the zoo: in her lab coat (arms crossed and smiling), bottle-feeding a baby bear, leading a group of zoo-goers through a pavilion.

Their faces were everywhere.

People couldn't take their eyes off them. Every time we were in the city someone asked for their autographs, not knowing who they were exactly but knowing they had to be somebody. They'd write 'Cleopatra and Marc Antony' or 'Jesus and Mary Magdalene.' One time someone held the pen out to me and without hesitation I took it and signed 'Superman.' I was ten. Rayn couldn't stop laughing. Max started calling me Kent. Vector Herman Kent Sorn, lone progeny of Max Sorn and Rayn Down, sole beneficiary of their singular and collective greatness.

I was never the kid who begged his parents for a baby brother or sister. I knew why I was an only child and so I never mentioned it. I can't recall now how I found out. I've known for as long as I can remember. I'm sure I overheard them talking. I listened at the top of the stairs a lot. The gist of it is the doctors strongly recommended they stop with me. Rayn nearly died in labour, which is almost unheard of in this part of the world nowadays, I know, but it's true. It was close. She haemorrhaged badly. There was a lot of damage. Not irreparable. But still. It would've been risky to have another child. Imagine living with the knowledge that your mother almost died giving birth to you. Rayn wouldn't like it if she knew I thought this way, but I can't help it. Sometimes the truth is the truth.

After the gun all I heard was our spikes tearing the track away beneath us. The sound of a torrential downpour. Halfway down the back straight I was already ten metres ahead. At the line I heard someone say, 'Three to go,' and I saw the digital clock go from :42 to :43. I was in a rhythm. I felt like I could go on forever, which is always the way in the beginning. Around the track again and I heard, 'Two to go.' The clock looked exactly the same except for the 1 in front. There was a symmetry about it I loved. I could hear the crowd and I glanced up on my third pass but it was impossible to make anyone out or hear individual words. My breathing was heavy now and I could feel my heart in my ears.

If you froze time and pulled me from the track at that moment and sat me down somewhere like in a talk show and shoved a mic in my face and said, 'When you're out there running and you're ahead by so much, what is it in you that won't let up? What makes you push so hard to the end?' I wouldn't know what to say. 'Being the best,' maybe. 'Setting the record.' 'Because I can.' But none of these are good reasons. One day they won't be reasons at all because they won't be true. One day I'll lose. I know that. As naïve as I was at fourteen about the permanence of some things, I knew that one day I would lose. Max had been the best and he had lost the biggest race of his life—twice. So it had to be something else. To be honest it was the only way I knew how. Really, it's the only way any competitive runner knows how. It certainly wasn't unique to me. I saw the way the guys behind me drove the line, arms about each other's necks some of them, faces full of agony. We all ran the same way: to exhaustion, beyond any reasonable effort, to the point where our whole bodies hurt and we couldn't see straight, like our lives depended on it and the eternal footman was at our heels, taunting us. It's absurd, I know, but true.

Three hundred metres to go and my body was screaming. Had my muscles the independence to get at my brain they'd have strangled it. Everything burned. As I hit the final straight I closed my eyes and Rayn was right there beside me, her voice strained and full: 'Come on, Herman.' My heart was about to explode: the exquisite pain of it. I can never remember the last fifty metres, all ache and relief and elation. I broke the line and collapsed. Hands on me instantly, hauling me up. Arms flung around the shoulders of strangers.

In the emergency tent, they stretched me out on a table. I closed my eyes and went after silence. Baron was there shouting numbers, predictions, assurances, claims of greatness. His voice, like the others, seemed distant.

Eventually I opened my eyes and my breathing settled.

'There,' someone said. 'He's alright. You're alright.'

Like anyone could know.

My brain and mouth were in sync again but I said nothing and nodded. Someone pulled me to a sitting position and gave me water.

Baron's hands on my shoulders. Like I was his. Like he created me. 'See? I told you. He's fine. What a run. What a god damn run, Vec. National champ. National record. World best time. Can you believe that? A world fucking best time. And this is just the beginning. You wait. You'll see.'

I looked at him. He was beaming.

I closed my eyes and moved to lie down again.

The emergency people stretched out my legs and lowered my head. I gave them my weight and let them manoeuvre me. Eventually everything passed, like a storm, and I felt normal again.

Normal. Whatever that was.

CLIPPINGS (11)

(taken from "Police Investigate Domain Ride Accident,"
Toronto Star)

"Police have confirmed there was nothing suspicious
with respect to the cause of yesterday's monorail accident. 'It's just one of those inexplicable misfortunes,'
maintains junior officer and former Olympian Max
Sorn. 'Thankfully no one was seriously hurt.'"

~

*The accompanying picture in the Star is of Max directing uninvolved
lookers-on away from the accident site. He appears serious and effective.
If you know the story and look closely enough you can see that his attention is not fully on those he is directing but on Rayn who is in the background in her lab coat, arms folded, looking in Max's general direction.
They used to joke about how it was the perfect picture to accompany the
story of their meeting (a story I heard so often it feels like a memory):
Max seeming to be in control while Rayn quietly waited for him to summon enough chutzpah to approach her.*

Metro Zoo: Toronto, ON

The area around the station had been cordoned off with police tape. Zoo-goers formed a crowd. They stood on their toes and craned their necks to see.

The sun was high and hot. Behind his aviators Max was calm and cool. Impressive, intimidating. He stepped up to the crowd, hands in the air. 'Keep it moving please.' He walked back and forth along the line of lookers-on, edged them back and onwards. 'Paramedics coming through.'

The ambulances blipped and nudged their way, parting the throng the way a whale moves through a school of fish.

With one hand Max directed people aside. With the other he ushered the ambulances in.

Rayn watched. She stood in the background in her lab coat, arms folded. Someone else in a lab coat was talking to her.

Later, Max entered a building marked Information. He needed a signature. He leaned on the counter and just as he did a door opened and out she walked in her lab coat, pencil behind an ear, eyes full of blue light and wonder.

'You look like an expert,' he said. 'I've always wondered, if man came from monkeys, where did women come from?'

She smiled and folded her arms. 'The future. We came back out of curiosity. What a mistake.'

By the end of the day they were Max and Rayn. One would never be whole without the other again.

CLIPPINGS (12)

(taken from "A Down-pour of Paddle Power,"
Heron River Review)

"The 'Rayn' came a-pouring 'Down' yesterday at the hundredth annual Paddle the Heron funraising [sic] event when fourteen-year-old daughter of Stephen and Serra Down—owners of Down to Earth and main sponsors of the event—outclassed the fifty boat field, including five-time winner Stephen Down himself (second to his daughter this year), by over a minute. Rayn is the youngest ever victor of the century-old race and the first ever woman. She is pictured here showing off her spoils: the coveted Heron trophy and the handcrafted paddle donated by her parent's [sic] store. In all, the event raised four hundred and seventeen dollars to be put toward the Heron River Conservation Project. A great day was had by all."

~

If drive and spirit are genetic I get them as much from Rayn as I do from Max. You can tell from the picture. The energy in her smile, the grip she has on the trophy and the paddle, the urgency in her eyes.

She would've excelled at any sport—especially the individual ones—but it was paddling she put all her time and effort into. She spent two or three hours a day on the river from ice-out in April to the first crust-over in November. For ten years.

There was no money to be made, no professional circuit to dominate, no fame to be had (beyond the pages of the inglorious Heron River Review and the few features in Canadian Paddler), no chance for the

Olympics, no World Championships. But none of that mattered to her. What mattered was being in her canoe on the river. The near noiselessness. The solitude. The power and speed she had complete control over. She loved it unapologetically, unwaveringly. Which is rare and enviable.

THE 100TH ANNUAL PADDLE THE HERON: HERON RIVER, ON

It's called 'pursuit.' Every thirty seconds another boat is sent off downriver. Save the first who has no one to chase and the last who has everyone, each paddler becomes both the hunter and the hunted.

At dinner the night before the race Serra looked across the table and told Stephen she'd heard there was an up-and-coming solo paddler who might give him a run for his money this year. Trained two, sometimes three hours a day. Strong. Tough. Relentless. Technically proficient. Smart too. Knew the river like it ran through her veins. Even slept with her paddle if you can believe it.

Rayn looked up from her plate. *She* slept with her paddle.

Serra raised her glass and motioned for Rayn and Stephen to do the same. 'To a daughter in pursuit of her father.'

Rayn leapt from the table and threw her arms around her mother so hard they fell together to the floor. The two of them lay there, laughing.

Stephen buttered his bread. 'Imagine you'd told her about the new boat waiting for her in the garage.'

Rayn sat up and looked at him. He grinned and held up his glass. She turned to her mother who nodded and smiled. Rayn looked at her father again.

'Happy Birthday, Ray.'

She looked at her open hands in her lap, paddle-calloused and a little shaking, a welling in her throat. She was the happiest fourteen-year-old burgeoning solo canoeist in the history of the world.

Her father finished his wine and wiped his mouth. 'Go see how she feels.'

Stephen and Serra stood at the kitchen window and watched their daughter emerge from around the corner with the canoe on her shoulders.

Stephen folded his arms.

Serra touched her head to his chest. 'She might beat you tomorrow, you know.'

'She might.'

'And if she does?'

'I'll say I let her win.'

She bumped him with her hip. 'You will not.'

'I'll say it was the boats. Hers is new and light and fast. Mine is old and heavy and slow.'

'You mean you're old and heavy and slow.'

He put an arm around her and squeezed. 'If she's as quick as her mother I'm in trouble.'

'Seriously. What will you do?'

He pictured the image before he said it. 'I'll swing her up to my shoulders like she was four again. I'll parade her around the docks. I'll say, Hey everybody, this is my little girl, Rayn Down. Fastest paddler on the Heron. Ain't she something? Ain't she something?'

CLIPPINGS (13)

(taken from "Sorn Settles for Silver," *Toronto Star*)

"Gliding into the wall one one-hundredth of a second slower than superstar American swimmer Matt Biondi, Toronto's Max Sorn, who the country was banking on to win gold, had to settle for a silver medal yesterday in the men's hundred metre fly. When asked about the loss shortly after the race, Sorn didn't know what to say. Poolside, he stood dripping, hands on hips, chest heaving, and shook his head."

~

I've seen the video of the race a hundred times. Biondi holds half a body length on Max for the first fifty, and after the turn Max inches his way even. Three strokes from the wall it's like they're swimming in unison. The finish was so close they had to go to the tape to determine the winner. If Max's middle finger was an inch longer, he would've won.

This is for certain: there was no gliding and he didn't settle. Max never settled. Put anything in slow motion and see how easy it is to point out faults.

Fortunately, what wasn't caught on video is what Max did that night in Seoul.

The Olympic Games: Seoul, South Korea

After he cooled down he gathered his things, said very little to his coach and teammates, and left the Aquatic Centre. He donned a solitary disappointed look so no one would bother him. He didn't want the consoling, the conciliatory congratulations. He didn't want to be talked to about it. He had bore the weight of a nation's expectations and he'd failed. That was it. The race was over. There was nothing else to say.

At the time, he believed he was finished. There was no way he could start another four years of training. What would be the point? The hours upon hours of pulling himself back and forth through water in a lane that never changes. A two-by-fifty metre cell. Eyes on you all the time. Relentless.

I remember him telling me he wanted to disappear after Seoul. Get lost in the desert or fly to the moon. Somewhere without water and expectations. But as it turned out he only took three weeks off before returning to the pool. He said it was the scholarship that brought him back. There are far worse ways to make money, he assured me, than swimming a few laps a day.

A few hundred is more like it.

But I don't think it was the scholarship. I don't think it had anything to do with money or obligation. I could tell by the way he talked about it. He felt lost without it. I don't think I'll feel lost without running when the time comes. But who knows? It's so much easier to identify a thing after it's gone.

Anyway, before the return to training—before the completion of his Psychology degree at Michigan State and his year at St. Clair College for Police Foundations, before Barcelona and the second silver medal, before his life with Rayn, before me— there was the one inglorious night in Seoul, South Korea.

. . .

It was after ten when he left the Aquatic Centre and climbed into the front seat of a cab.

He slapped the dashboard.

'To the place where the beer flows freely and the women are wild and willing.'

As a rule Max never drank more than the occasional blood-friendly glass of red wine. Indulgence conflicted with training and his commitment to a clean lifestyle. Ahead of his time, he knew about post-workout protein requirements and electrolyte replenishment before the existence of protein bars and Gatorade. He knew the approximate sodium and saturated fat contents of foods before products had bare-all biographies printed on their sides. Health conscious before it was trendy. In tune with everything.

But that night in the centre of the South Korean capital he was on a mission: total debauchery. He needed a release.

The cab driver looked at him, wide-eyed.

'English not good. Tell again. Slow.'

Max recalled a little of the 'survival' Korean he had studied leading up to the Games.

'Na-nun mek-ju yuh-ja gamnida.'

His accent was far from native and his grammar was broken. He'd managed to say, 'I beer woman go.'

The cab driver squinted.

'Once more time.'

'Mek-ju. Yuh-ja.'

'Mek-ju. Beer.'

Max snapped his fingers and pointed.

'You got it, my man. Beer.'

'Yuh-ja. Woman. Sexy woman.'

'Yes, god damn it. Sexy woman.'

'Ahhh, you go Itaewon. Red light district.'

Max clapped once. 'Itaewon. Let's go.'

'Gamshida. Let's go.'

'Gamshida. Gamshida. Gamshida.'

They laughed together in a moment of borderless fraternity, these two men who knew nothing of each other or the type of life the other lived.

In Itaewon, just past the Hamilton Hotel, the stretch affectionately known as Hooker Hill, it wouldn't take Max long to achieve his goal. He entered the first bar he saw and sat down at a table with three American soldiers who were well on their way. He bought a few rounds and in less than an hour he'd thrown back half a dozen beer himself and a few shots of soju. For good measure, he took two or three healthy pulls on the joint the soldiers passed around, inexperienced as he was, and mimicked the way they held the smoke in. He exhaled and fell back in his chair, grinning, arms limp at his sides. After one more round, he got up from the table, tipped an invisible hat to his fellow tokers, and stumbled outside into the throng. The street was a river of the inebriated and staggering and it roiled with their slurry song. Every man was every other man's brother and they had all lost their way, left to wager on the comfort they might find in oblivion.

Max clapped strangers on the back, joined in the wailing, and, taken by the moment, stood imbalanced in the middle of the road, teetering, arms spread wide to the night, eyes closed to the moon. 'Second fastest flyer in the world, god damn it. So what's wrong with that?'

When he opened his eyes, he marched on with intention, mumbling *gamshida, gamshida, gamshida* as he went.

He swung himself through the door of the first place he found with a barbershop pole out front, and in the sour, sweaty darkness he felt damp hands on his body and lips at his ear almost instantly. Classical music played softly in the background.

'Oooh, so strong man. So sexy man.'

The stranger kissed his mouth, ran her hands over his body, moaned.

'Oooh, sexy. Mmm. Sexy, sexy.'

He put his hands on her like a blind man feeling his way.

'Mmm. You rike. Mmm-hmn. You rike, yes?'

His eyes were closed and he nodded. She took him by the wrist and led him to a room with a beaded curtain for a door, a muted light beside a jar filled with bills on a table in the corner. He could see her face, but barely, and didn't want to. She sat him down on the squeaky cot, straddled him, and spoke as plainly in English as she could.

'Ten dollah hand. Twenty mouse. Pipty inside.'

He slipped a crisp American hundred from his shirt pocket. 'What do I get for this?'

She stretched the bill to the light and her eyes widened. 'For this, I fuck you rike God.'

She stood and peeled her silky slip, went to her knees, pulled him out, stroked him with the money in her hand, took him in her mouth and moaned, slid him between her tiny breasts, slapped him against her skin, slipped her lips around him again and devoured him, moaning with the effort, and then like an artist intent on a line drew the tip of him from her mouth and with it traced a slow wet snaking brushstroke down the length of her body and held him there at the edge, throbbing in her hand, against her teasing heat.

She slid down the length of him and he fell back on the bed with the rush of it.

'God,' he muttered. 'Like God.'

He woke on a bench by the River Han with a woolly mouth and a thumping head. Every heartbeat hurt and squeezing his eyes did nothing but bring back the night. Joggers went by with purpose and the ten-lane road behind him hummed with its hurried, unwaning traffic.

He stood, teetered, stuck out his arms like a tightrope walker, and crossed the path to the rail. He gripped the cold metal with both hands, for balance at first, then leaned back and loaded his body as though he were on the blocks at the start of a race. He breathed deeply in and at the imagined sound of the starter's horn hurled himself over the rail into the cold coffee-coloured swill. He swam the width, climbed out the other side, and stood there, hands on his hips and nose to the rising sun like some kind of hero. Then he fell to his knees and emptied his stomach into the river. Relief and punishment at once.

By the time he returned to the athletes' village the place was beginning to buzz with the day's competitors. When he entered his room his roommate groaned, sat up, and rubbed his eyes. Said if he'd woken up and Max wasn't there he was sending out a search party. Max sat on the edge of his bed and told the room-mate he'd had quite the night but he was fine now. He went on to explain how he'd left the pool after the race wanting to clear his head. He went for a jog. Navigationally challenged as he was, he joked, it didn't take him long to get lost. A right turn here, a left turn there, and the hum of the city was behind him. He should've known better. Everywhere he looked looked the same. There were no signs and no one he encountered spoke English. Soon it was dark. He kept running and turning down random streets trying to get back to the recognizable city but it seemed every turn took him farther away. At one point he was jumped from behind by four men wearing black bandanas and black leather wristbands. He was able to fend them off for the most part but they managed to hold him down long enough to liberate him of his money and his athlete ID.

'You were mugged?'

Max shrugged and nodded.

'Jesus. You okay?'

'I am now.'

The roommate shook his head. 'That's fucking crazy, man. You're lucky they didn't kill you.'

Max opened his eyes wide. 'I know.'

The roommate yawned and stretched. 'So why the fuck are you all wet?'

Max stumbled a bit but not noticeably. 'Didn't the storm hit here?'

The roommate shrugged. 'Couldn't tell you. I was sound asleep.'

'Oh. Well, after my little encounter with the black bandanas. I found a park and curled up on a bench.' He shook his head. 'I can't believe I slept on a park bench. Anyway, I woke up to the sky pouring down on me. By the time I climbed into a cab I was soaked.'

Satisfied, the roommate nodded, dropped his head to the pillow, and closed his eyes.

'Glad you're all right, man.'

'Thanks. I should grab a shower.'

Which is what he did and that was the end of it.

Until twenty-five years later when Max found himself sitting in an armchair by a window in the psyche ward of St. Joe's, slippered and medicated, telling me—his seventeen-year-old son, who he claimed not to recognize—the story of his Olympic debauchery, a story that sounded true but was so out of character it was difficult for this once worshipping son to believe.

At the end of the visit I asked him if he needed anything. Without thinking I called him Dad. By then I knew better.

'How many times do I have to tell you, kid? I'm not your fucking dad. You must be stupid or something. Wait. That's it isn't it. You're a retard. The doctors must have had a brainstorm. Hey, the retard and the whack job might get along. Let's put them together and see what happens. Nice. Well fuck them. And fuck you, too.'

I spoke calmly. 'Nobody put us together.'

'Oh, I see. You chose me. Is that it? You're a fucking con then. I know how it is. Get close to the nutbar and maybe he puts you in his will. Big score. Well, I don't think so, sonny-boy. So why don't you just fuck off and leave me alone.'

'I'm not going to do that.'

'Okay. I know what it is now. They caught you with your hand in the cookie-jar and this is your punishment. Sit and listen to Mr. Loonie-Tunes an hour a week. They think it makes us feel good, to have someone to talk to. Well, I'll tell you something. It doesn't. It makes us feel like fucking charity cases, you want to know the truth. No one in here has anyone who cares. That's why we're here. So come if you have to. Serve your sentence. Do your Jesus work. Whatever. I'll play my part. But don't call me your fucking dad. You hear? Don't call me your fucking dad.'

I lost them both that day in the underground. The difference was that some of Max remained. I often thought it would've been easier if he were completely gone. I don't mean dead, just gone. Whatever that means. Each time I went to see him I went with the fleeting hope that more of him would return but it never did. At least with Rayn the image was fixed. In my mind she never changed. She was forever sunbright and smiling, forever proud. I picture her reaching for my hand as the train comes screeching in. She smiles and her eyes say, Vector, don't worry. Everything will be okay.

LIKE SOME KIND OF HERO

CLIPPINGS (14)

(taken from "Evil Underground:
Man Pushes Woman to her Death," TorontoStar.com)

"Museum Station was the site of a tragic, unspeakable scene yesterday afternoon when a man described by one witness as 'crazed-looking' pushed an innocent bystander onto the tracks as a train was approaching. Another witness said the pusher then 'stretched out his arms, threw back his head, and called out, *Jesus, take me home*' as he threw himself in front of the oncoming train. The woman's son and husband were with her at the time of the incident. The name of the woman and her alleged attacker have not yet been released. Investigations continue today."

~

I've tried to forget his face but I can't. I wake up at night and he's right there looking down at me. He taps me on the shoulder when I least expect it and whispers, 'Boo.' He sits across from me in restaurants, superimposes himself onto the bodies of strangers in crowds. He's the tattooed girl with blue hair in Starbucks who hands me my grande every morning. He's the garbage collector. The bearded homeless man asking for change. The bus-driver. My Fundamentals of Energy Sustainability Tutor. He's my father. He's the image of God in my dreams.

I want to run into a hospital screaming, 'There's someone trying kill me—inside my head—he's right here, see?—someone please catch him by the throat and haul him out—shoot him, stab him, cut him free and burn him to ashes—please, someone help me—help me, please,' and if the surgeons can't do anything then maybe they'll send me to the psyche ward and lock me up like Max and serve me trays of gourmet pills. That might be enough. That might do it.

The reporter's witness (two too many people removed from the source to capture any sort of truth for me) said he was 'crazed-looking.'

Jack Nicholson poking his head through an axed door announcing the arrival of Johnny is crazed-looking. The sonofabitch who pushed Rayn to her death was not crazed-looking. He was human waste. I wish that's how I'd described him to the police. Stinking, wretched, vile, repulsive human waste.

That black and white grainy mugshot from The Star online grows in my head at times like a camera zooming in. Those glassy, bulging, dead animal eyes. That nefarious little grin. Like someone just punched him in the stomach and he liked it. Like he's about to laugh and say, 'Ooh, fuck yeah, that hurt, do it again, do it again.' That greasy, matted, slicked-back blonde hair that's the result not of careful combing but of aggressive, obsessive flattening.

To note: it wasn't an 'incident' and calling her an 'innocent bystander' doesn't make calling him an 'alleged attacker' any less offensive. There was nothing 'alleged' about it and he didn't 'attack' her. He killed her. He's a murderer. A sick twisted fuck the likes of which evolution has fallen terribly short of eliminating. In the future it would be nice if 'survival of the fittest' referred not to physical strength or any type of dominance of one kind over another, but to simple unselfish decency. Survival of the civil. That would be an improvement. That's the sort of evolution we need now.

Clippings (15)

(taken from randomacstofviolence.com/
smokedbyatrain/comments)

'Fuckin shame . . . tightest ass I ever seen
hammer4hire

> I know right . . . she musta been a model or sumthin
> *redsoxsuck*

>> i reconize her to where she from
>> *teeohbro*

>>> Just found her. Nike ad. Here's the link:
>>> nike.com/running/lakefrontrunner
>>> *vulcher*

>> awsum u da man vulcer thx
>> *teeohbro*

>>> np
>>> *vulcher*

Check out that fuckn body
hammer4hire

> Really to bad she bit it
> *redsoxsuck*

>> Got her name. Rayn Down. Searching for naked pics.
>> *vulcher*

ahh yee-ah vulsher let us no bro
teeohbro

I tell you what I wish she'd bit
hammer4hire

Good one hammer
redsoxsuck

yo wait a sec rain down she a porn star?
teeohbro

You're thinking of Rain Storm.
vulcher

yo right thx.
teeohbro

Fuck ya I'd a ruin'd her
hammer4hire'

~

When I googled 'Toronto woman killed by subway train' the video came up on the first page: 22,341 views. A number nearly equivalent to the population of Heron River. Not exactly viral but enough to make you wonder how there are so many people interested in watching someone else die. If not interested in, then indifferent to, and I don't know which is worse.

A few common reactions to a photograph or video that captures a moment of human terror: 'Why didn't the guy with the camera do something to help? How could he just stand there and watch it happen? How could he record it?' These are easy judgements to make.

But really, what's a cellphone videographer supposed to do? Be a hero? Step in and mediate? The pusher had spent the last six years of his life immersed in therapy. It's safe to say he was sick of talking. So what's the witness supposed to do, save the victim? Run and push the *stranger to safety so that he himself may be the one thrown to the tracks and killed? All with perfect timing?*

When asked the hypothetical question, 'What would you do if you came upon a burning house and heard the cries of the trapped inside?' most people feel a swelling in their chests and say something like they'd do their best to help those who were trapped. Which means they would run inside the burning house—despite the threat to their own safety, despite their physical limitations, despite their being human—and ferry the helpless outside. No one says, 'I'd be frozen by the awe of it and so I'd stand there and watch, useless.' No one says, 'I'd thank my lucky stars it wasn't my house burning down.' No one says, 'I'd pull out my phone and record the whole thing—you know the kind of dough they pay for footage like that?'

No one says these things but people do them all the time.

Often there's someone who dons a cape and flies in for the rescue, claiming in the five-second evening news soundbite that he just did what anyone else would have done. But he's wrong. No one else did. Most people don't. Most people stand and watch. Shocked and immobilized by the horror of the scene. Some people point a phone and hit record. Most shake their heads sympathetically, quietly thankful it wasn't them. All human and understandable reactions to have.

I'm not surprised by the comments attached to the video. I've been used to those kinds of reactions to Rayn for a long time. Most men who saw her walking down the street took mental snapshots of her, I'm sure. Many leered at the ads in magazines and commercials on TV, I have no doubt. Objectively speaking she was beautiful. Beyond beautiful. A goddess, most would say. I remember as early as grade seven guys in my class calling her a milf right to my face. Your mom's a fucking milf, dude, you know that right? I'd shrug and say, Whatever. What was I supposed to do? They weren't trying to insult her. Or me. The opposite actually. In their awkward hard-on driven adolescent way they were complimenting her. And me. I think at times I was accepted only because I was her son.

Having sexual thoughts about a stranger is completely natural but there's nothing natural about the likes of hammer4hire et al. They are sick, pathetic, insensate jerkoffs who need psychological help. It's understandable for a guy to be curious and tentatively click the play button on potentially salacious or disturbing links, checking over his shoulder even though he knows he's alone (I've done it myself—I'm sure as hell no saint), but it's quite another thing to take the time to comment on, engage in a virtual conversation about, and repeatedly watch a video in which someone is killed. There are those who spend their lives trying to forget and erase the unending reels of terror they've had the misfortune of being witnesses to and here these senseless necrophiles are discussing the subject of the footage like she's the latest pornstar sensation.

Fuck them.

I have fantasies about drawing them out of their seedy little dens of iniquity and unleashing on the lot of them a Bruce Lee inspired spinkicking fists of fury asskicking that would leave them unable to utter their own names. If only evolution would step in and alter the biology of such specimens so that every time they had a tug at themselves the potential for procreation diminished exponentially. Even better, there should be a built-in trigger in the brains of the inalterably fucked-up that cuts off the production of seed entirely. Sterility should be directly related to depravity.

So, Dr. Carl, what do thoughts like these make me?

I can't figure out why the police needed a description of the pusher. They had a picture of him. It's right there online. And anyway, who cares what he looked like? It's not like he fled the scene and they had to hunt him down. He jumped to his own death calling on Jesus.

I wish I'd pushed him. I fantasize about pushing him. It's easy to imagine because in the competing worlds of 'what happened' and 'what didn't happen' the result is the same. I've learned there's no sense in dreaming something that alters the outcome of the past. Truth may be difficult to nail down but it knows itself and it's impossible to erase or change in any major way, regardless of the effort or desire to do so.

I've tried. I've tried to save her a million times in my mind. Lying on my stomach, reaching into the cold dark endless space between us, waiting for the feeling of her hand that I know will never come. Sensing the tips of her fingers. Her face. Smiling up at me. The scream of the train. The inevitable impact.

So I stand and I push him. I load my two hands like the double hammer of a gun and drive them into his back with everything I have. His head snaps back and I stand there—chest heaving, fists clenched, tears welling—and watch him lose his fight for balance just as the train comes screeching into the station. I can actually sense all of it if I think hard enough. My hands on his back, the thud of his body being hit by the train. It's like a rush of water washing over me. Cold and jarring and good.

Then the truth comes sweeping in. The pusher spreads his arms and dives to his own death asking Jesus to take him home. I hate that he had that moment, whatever it meant to him. I hate that he had control and was given the chance to choose.

Museum Station: Toronto, ON

Outside Varsity Stadium on Bloor the city moved on. Hundreds of people coming and going. Everyone seeming to have a destination or purpose in mind: students, suits, joggers, bikers, couriers, shoppers, parents with athlete-children wearing National Championships hoodies. Throngs moved in and out of Varsity Stadium. Teams with equipment bags. Coaches with lanyards around their necks. Press with badges. TV cameras and over-keen interns who held microphones under the chins of exhausted teenaged runners asking stupid questions like, 'How do you feel?' People walking by noticed and nudged each other. The potential sighting of someone important, someone famous.

Max and Rayn drew the stares and nudges of passersby. People turned their heads. Someone, as always, approached and asked for an autograph.

Max shifted the aviators to the top of his head, took the pen and paper, scrawled a name, and returned the stationery.

The stranger looked at Rayn. She ran a hand through her hair and obliged. When she was finished she handed the pen and paper to me and said, 'But here's the real superstar.' Smiling, Rayn bumped me with her hip.

The stranger: 'Really?'

I shrugged and mumbled something about running.

Rayn looked at me—half smiling, half sighing—and shook her head. 'What he meant to say is he's just become a National Junior Champion.'

'Cool. You must be, like, really fast.'

To keep from rolling my eyes I looked at the paper Rayn had given me and I noticed for some reason she and Max had written their real names this time and legibly. There was something lasting about it: Max Sorn and Rayn Down. They even sounded famous. I wrote my real name too and returned the paper.

'Thank you. And hey, good luck with the running.'

I felt Rayn's elbow.

I rubbed my arm. 'Yeah. Okay. Thanks.'

The stranger turned, held the paper over her head like a trophy, and ran back toward her group of friends. They would pass the paper around and thumb our names into their phones. Eventually they would pull up the Nike ads Rayn had done. My name would show up on a track site somewhere. They would get hits of Max in the Olympics, pictures of him in a Speedo, a towel around his neck. They would scream and post the pictures on Facebook. They would tweet their star-sighting: just met superhot swimmer #MaxSorn & his supermodel wife #RaynDown & their supercute runner son #Vector—I'd do them all (ha ha). They would have a story to tell. Which is, when it comes down to it, all anybody is really after.

We carried on. Max and Rayn holding hands and me a step or two in front. Our standard formation. I grew up thinking happiness was a natural state.

Our plan was to get Chinese, eat in the park, and drive to the zoo. It was how we celebrated. It was tradition: birthdays, promotions, commercial shoots, report cards. The zoo was our favourite place to go. Especially in the late afternoons when the crowds started to thin out. Sometimes we'd arrive even as they were locking the gates but because of Rayn we could still get in.

I loved watching the cougars. My heart would start to go as we approached the cage. I'd stand there and watch the muscular pacing, the patience, the unblinking eyes fixed upon me as the animal moved back and forth, the low rumble in its throat, all a declaration of my impending doom were it not for the bars between us.

Without notice Baron came running up from behind. He grabbed me by the shoulders and shook. 'We've got to celebrate, Vec.' He drummed my chest with both palms. 'National champ. We did it, man. National fucking champ.'

He couldn't stop smiling. He put me in a headlock and I let him. He was happy and he deserved to be. We'd spent a lot of time together over the past year and he'd invested a lot of thought and effort in the individual design of my short and long term training. There was no doubt he knew what he was doing. By the end of the previous November he had laid out all the steps, the overlay and progression within and throughout each of the micro and macro cycles, each phase clearly defined, every major and minor race leading up to Nationals carefully chosen, and just to further exhibit his confidence in me (and himself), he predicted the time I'd run in each race. He was always within a second. He told me there was no doubt in his mind I'd be the first Canadian in Olympic history to win gold in the fifteen hundred.

He spoke in absolutes. He spoke quickly and confidently and most of the time it was difficult to get a word in edgewise.

'So what do you say? You name the place. My treat.'

Rayn pulled herself close to Max.

Baron pretended not to notice.

'Awful nice of you, Charlie,' said Max. 'But we sort of have plans.'

'So break them. Come on, Max, baby. Let's celebrate.'

He shadow-boxed Max, dancing on the spot. *Huh-huh. Huh. Huh.*

'Thing is, it's sort of a family thing we do.'

Baron put his hands up, still smiling. 'Say no more. Another time then.'

He looked at Rayn. His face went serious. 'I'll let you be.'

I broke in. 'Listen, Mr. Baron. Thanks for everything. Really.'

He ducked and weaved and tossed a couple of shadow punches my way. 'Don't mention it kid. Hell of a run. What'd I tell you? Sky's the limit.'

Max shook Baron's hand. 'Thanks, Charlie. Really.'

I thanked him again, too, and as the three of us turned to leave he stood there by himself with his hands in his pockets.

We were already gone when he ran up behind us again. 'Let me drive you back to your car. I've got the van.' He looked at Rayn. 'Least I can do.'

Rayn sent her eyes to the sky and squeezed Max's hand which made him look at her. I watched myself kick a stone.

Max tried a grin. 'Thanks, Charlie. Really. We're okay though. We like the adventure.'

Baron nodded and put his hands up again. 'Suit yourself. Thought I'd offer.'

'Thanks. Really. We'll do something next time.'

'Right,' he said. 'Next time.' Baron put a hand in the air, took one step backwards, turned, and walked away.

Max kissed Rayn's hand and on we went, me leading, and soon we were underground.

'Osiris was an Egyptian king. Merciful God of the dead.'

We stood there, Max and I, listening to Rayn. Like the station itself was a museum and we were alone, the three of us, in a great room with a statue.

'His brother, Set, killed him and usurped the throne.'

A train rumbled in like thunder and screeched to a stop. The doors slid open. People spilled out, filed on, an underground violinist busking in the background: a mournful song of human longing and heartache.

'Undeterred, Osiris's wife, Isis, managed to revive his body long enough to conceive a child.' Rayn touched the white column as she spoke and moved around it. 'She had a son named Horus who overthrew Set and became the god of light.'

The train doors slid closed, the brakes sighed release, and the train slipped away.

Rayn touched my face with both hands. 'We had a son who overthrew them all and became the god of speed.'

She leaned in, kissed my forehead and smiled, then turned and took Max's hands, looking up at him like a child. He brought one of her hands to his mouth and kissed the palm, felt on his cheek the coolness of the ring he'd finally been able to persuade her to wear.

'Let me guess.'

She closed her eyes, set her head back, and breathed in through her nose. 'The smell is killing me.'

He nodded and fished a few coins from his pocket, checked with me before going.

I shook my head.

'Hot peppers?'

She went on her toes and kissed him. 'Hot as they come.'

He smiled and kissed her back. A few strides away he spoke over his shoulder without stopping. 'Don't go anywhere.'

Twice he turned fully around as he moved away from us toward the vender, pointing to his eyes with two fingers and then to us. The second time she ducked behind the column of Osiris, waited, then stuck her face out so he could see her. He shook his head, smiling, and she laughed. Their playfulness never seemed odd to me or made me feel uncomfortable. It seemed normal. Everything about them seemed normal although almost nothing about them was. They were, when I think about it, extraordinary in every way.

The next train rumbled in and screeched to a stop. This is where I wish I could jump in and hit the edit button. File new. Ctrl-alt-delete. Undo. Undo. Undo. But there are no such functions in the mind. The memory of certain moments is inalterably permanent, and as much as the printed word has the power to recreate, by its very nature there is nothing it can do when it comes to erasure. What happened happened and it keeps happening in my head. Even as I write this now nothing changes. Instead it becomes more fixed. Each word like a spike driven into the earth, pinning down the truth. The details, if anything, become stronger. The sounds clearer. The colours brighter. The impact more impactful: harder, driving, crushing, like a ball-peen hammer to the skull.

Rayn takes five steps toward the tracks and I take them with her. I count them even as I try to stop them: one, two, three, four, five. She's wearing the blue Nike Frees from the last ad she did. Light as air. Blue as sky. Like walking barefoot. Like walking on clouds. Shoes that don't make a sound. The slogan: freedom starts here.

I don't know why I watched her feet. Maybe I didn't but that's what I see now. That's what I remember. Dr. Carl said it's because her feet symbolize the potential for escape. But as I've already said, Dr. Carl's an idiot. There's no potential in something that's finished. She can't escape and I can't escape her not escaping.

Etymologically, the notion of potential has to do with strength but not real strength, only possible strength, which isn't strength at all, and when you think about it, no one wants to rely on the possible. I suppose even the existence of God is possible but what good is that to me now? What good was it to her then?

The sessions with Dr. Carl were mandatory, although they didn't phrase it that way. They said 'highly recommended' and then appointed someone from CAS to pick me up and accompany me to Dr. Carl's once a week. They figured I'd become suicidal or irreparably repressed or psychologically damaged by the incident if I didn't see someone professional. *Incident*. Fuck them. It was no incident. Besides, who they should've been worried about was Max. All they had to do was look at him.

I went to the sessions because the men in ties and the women with sad faces told me they had my best interests at heart. I believed them. They seemed earnest and I knew it would make them feel better, like they'd done their jobs, like they'd saved the child. And really, I had nothing left to lose. Rayn was gone and Max, though still in shock and yet to show obvious signs of his destruction, was irreversibly on his way. The life went out of him the moment the pusher's hands made contact. When I pause the reel in my head and do a panoramic sweep of the station I can see Max reaching out for her, the distance between them insurmountable—he's falling—like he tripped or lunged forward in a futile attempt to catch her, the vender dog he'd gone to get suspended stupidly in the air. He looks like a cartoon. Like he's been shot from behind. Dead before he hits the ground. Zoom in and you can see there is no life left in his eyes. He knows even as he reaches he cannot save her. The blessing, as though there were such a thing, is that he can't see her on the tracks from where he is. The angles won't allow it. He can't see her getting to her knees. He can't see her smiling at me as the train comes screeching in. If he knew the truth I'm certain he would've closed his mighty hands around my neck long ago and squeezed the life right out of me. Of that—and of nothing else—I have absolutely no doubt.

From the Journal of Vector Sorn

Looking at my fourteen-year-old self now it's easy to see I was suffering from shock, which is a real and dangerous state to be in. Even Dr. Carl knew that. What I find truly mystifying is the seemingly natural inability to recognize the condition we're in when we're in it. If only we knew danger without doubt. Or wrongheadedness. Or love. Or happiness. If only we knew these things instantly. Why should we have to think about them? How can we not recognize these conditions as they happen? Where's the evolution in doubt and reflection? Why do we need to confirm what we know? What good are our brains when they get in the way of instinct? Thought will be our end. Man will take his last breath while teetering on the brink, finger to his chin, thinking about it.

I've read that it's exactly our ability to reflect and think deeply that makes us human and so it is that very ability which will continue to save us.

At times I disagree. At times I know, without thinking, it will be the thing that buries us.

Back to the point in the reel I cannot stop. The old-fashioned projector in my head clicking away. The shadows and light of those final moments. Her feet—the blue Nike Frees—stepping toward the tracks. Five steps. I count them slowly: one, two, three, four. I try to stop the last one from coming. I slow it right down but no matter how slow I make it I cannot stop her foot from touching down and as it does I sense the presence of the pusher upon us. His shadow. His ugly weight. His breathing. His stench. The irreversible instant. I turn as his hands—his filthy, contemptible hands, those nail-bitten bestial paws—make contact. There is the breath that leaves her and that is all. I try to force my hand. I try to make my body do something. But the truth of my inaction is too powerful to overcome. I can't even pretend to change it. I just stand there.

If only Toronto were Venice and we were standing by the Grand Canal waiting for a boat to take us home instead of a train. If only it were that simple. I imagine us there in that faraway place, a faraway time, Rayn in the stern, smiling. Max standing in the bow with the long pole, pushing us home. Me between them, elbows on the starboard gunwale, eyes closed, face to the Venetian sun.

But we're not in Venice. We're in the Toronto underground and there is nowhere to go. She is trapped on the tracks and there is no time. Only the light of the train and the thundering metal bearing down. The final certainty. The utter awareness of the end and the acceptance that nothing can change it. Not even her own son who is right there: staring, stupidly, stepping away. Don't worry, her eyes say. Everything will be okay. Behind me somewhere is Max. Hands above his head. But it's too late. There is nothing he can do. There is nothing any of us can do.

CLIPPINGS (16)

(taken from "Speed Kills," nationalpost.com/thebeat)

'Like a scene from a Cormac McCarthy novel, Bloomington Sideroad and Warden Avenue, a normally quiet stretch of near-rural driving north of the city, became the site of an inexplicable and terrifying act of violence last night. Because there's an Elementary School nestled in and easily missed at the bottom of the hill, police often set up a speed trap to help slow traffic through the quarter-mile school zone. Commuters often get caught in the trap and are stung with hefty tickets. But little did Lyle Govern know when veteran officer Max Sorn signalled him over to the shoulder and approached his pickup as the sun was going down that he would be issued far more than a fine for speeding.'

~

Lyle Govern. Not much more than a name in the story to me. If it wasn't him it would have been someone else. I don't mean to be callous. I should feel sorry about what happened, but what good is sorry? Don't get me wrong, I recognize the senselessness of what Max did. I neither condone nor defend it in any way. But to me all the name Lyle Govern does is remind me of the end of Max. The end of my father as I knew him.

Soon after Max approached the truck he discovered that Lyle Govern had no family, that he was a Chartered Accountant, and that he was in therapy. People always opened up to him. It never took him long to discover the essentials. Physically Lyle Govern fit the bill too. Same height, same weight. Same slicked-back blonde hair. The clincher was the date. A year later to the day. Why they had Max scheduled to work that evening I do not know. Maybe they hadn't. Maybe he'd snuck in and taken a cruiser without telling anyone. Maybe he'd planned the whole thing. Whatever the prefacing details, what remains the unfortunate truth for Lyle Govern is that he became in my father's eyes a surrogate for Michael Norman Boon. The man who pushed Rayn to her death.

Michael Norman Boon. Mike Boon. As a kid, Mikey no doubt. As a teenager, Booner. His beer-league hockey nickname: Mike 'the Goon' Boon. A jersey with 'Goon' written across the back, double zero beneath. His professional name before the mental illness: Michael N. Boon, CA. Etched on a goldplated nameplate on his desk. On his office door. Michael after his father's father, Norman after his mother's. By all accounts a seemingly normal childhood, normal adolescence, normal adulthood. Normal Norman. Nothing to indicate the psychological trouble which lay ahead. Michael the angel. Norman the Norseman. Blue-eyed, blonde, big. According to the police reports, what went wrong remains a mystery. There was the suggestion of schizophrenia but with little evidence. Simply put, and in the vernacular of centuries past, he was a man gone mad. An upwardly mobile, highly successful, single man approaching middle age who was astute enough, the records say, to recognize a calamitous shift in his own mental health and so commit himself to hospital before he might cause any damage to himself or to anyone else. The question is, what made him want to escape? Can it even be called 'escape' if he was there willingly? Was he allowed to come and go as he pleased? Was there a schedule of 'out' time? If so, how did they know it was safe for him to leave during those hours? Who decided? Did someone go with him? Did someone follow him just to make sure? If he did escape, what was it that made him want to leave the security of the very place he had sought out himself? His 'condition', whatever that was? Were there voices in his head? Did Hyde finally defeat Jekyll? And why that day? Was there significance in the numbers? Was he a believer in gematria? Did something happen in his past on that day that acted as a trigger? Was it random? Were there warning signs? Did someone fall asleep on duty? Did someone lose him? If so, why no red alert? Why no consequences? Did he have help? Was there a Chief Brombden? If so, why didn't the Chief (staying true to his character) snuff him out in the middle of the night in an act of mercy? Why did he end up where he did? Why Museum Station? Why not College or Queen's Park? Why not Union?

Did he have a purpose? A plan? Why was he wearing a sweater in the middle of summer and no shoes? Were they even looking for him? If so, how could they not have found him? His appearance made him stand out like a full moon in a clear night sky. Why didn't Max see him? He was trained to see people like him. Why didn't I see him? Why didn't Rayn? Why didn't anyone? Why did he zero in on her? Did he think she was someone else? Did he pretend she was someone else? Did he intend to kill himself from the outset? If so, why didn't he just jump? Why did he have to take her with him? Why wasn't it someone else? Why wasn't it me?

Michael Norman Boon. Michael Norman Boon. Michael Norman Boon.

His name is like his face. Permanently there. Inescapable. Whenever I hear even a part of it—a Michael or a Mike or a Norman on the street, at school, online, on TV, the radio, wherever—the whole comes screaming in. Michael Norman Boon. I've written his name out a thousand times and burned it. I've scratched it into rocks and hurled those rocks into rivers. I've built effigies in my head with his name written all over them. I've imagined hanging those effigies from trees, beating them, straddling them on the ground, stabbing them and choking them, ripping the stuffing from them. I've tied them in my dreams to the back of Stephen and Serra's truck and dragged them over country roads until the gravel rips the cloth open and I imagine it's his skin. I imagine it's his body bouncing back there and I take pleasure in it. I've pissed on them. Set them up and shoved them in front of oncoming trains. I've sat them in chairs and talked to them. I've asked them why and shut my eyes as hard as I can, waiting, waiting for an answer.

Not long before I had my last session with Dr. Carl and moved out west for school I went to visit Max one last time. I didn't know when I'd see him again. To be honest I didn't know if I wanted to. He was in one of his storytelling moods. I had never asked him about what happened—I didn't want to know, really—but for some reason that afternoon he told me about the night he pulled Lyle Govern over for speeding.

Like I said before, I neither defend nor condone what he did. But who am I to judge and what right do I have?

Warden & Bloomington:
Whitchurch–Stouffville, ON

Lyle Govern was on his way home. It was past nine. Had he not stopped at the bar he would have missed Max and his life of long hours, money, and casual sexual encounters would have carried on. By all accounts he was a happy man and he would have continued to be so. There was the therapy, but he didn't really need it. He went mainly for something to do. He looked at it as entertainment. Plus he'd discovered it was a great place to meet women. The trick was to make your appointments in the middle of the day and show up half an hour early. There were two or three shrinks in the same office and so potentially two or three women waiting to tell their life stories. All you had to do was smile and show a little interest and before you knew it you found yourself nodding away, asking questions like the shrink himself. From there it was something like, 'I've got to get back to work after this, but I'd love to hear how that all turned out. My office is just around the corner and I know this great little sushi place. Do you like sushi?'

Max got all this from Lyle Govern in the first couple of minutes. He had a way about him. He put people at ease. They opened up as soon as they met him.

'So, hey. You seem like a pretty decent guy. You're not really going to give me a ticket, are you?'

'Mr. Govern. You said you stopped at the bar after work.'

'Yeah, for a quick pint. Check the scene, you know?'

'I'm going to have to ask you to step out of the truck.'

'Come on. Really? It was one pint, man. I'm sober as a judge.'

'It's protocol.'

'You can make an exception, can't you? I mean, really, I don't see why it's—'

'Mr. Govern. Please step out of the truck.'

Lyle Govern put his hands on the wheel and stared out the windshield. Whether he was thinking about it or not, it looked like he might drive the pedal to the floor and speed away.

He nodded and undid his seatbelt.

'Okay. What the hell. You're just doing your job, right?' He laughed. 'It'll make a great story. Hey, you'll never guess what happened to me last night. I'm driving along, minding my own business, going a little fast through that speed trap on Bloomington, but nothing crazy. Anyway, there I am driving along when all of a sudden the cherries light up and the siren goes and I'm hauled over by that famous Olympic swimmer cop.' As he pulled the door handle, Lyle Govern stopped and looked straight at Max. 'Didn't think I recognized you, eh?'

Max said nothing. He stepped back to allow Lyle Govern space to exit the truck. The door swung open and he hopped down. The truck dinged incessantly. The lights were on and the key was in the ignition. The door remained open.

Lyle continued: 'Yeah, I follow sports pretty close. When the Olympics roll around, man, I'm glued to the couch. Seoul. Barcelona. Two silvers. That must've been something. Bet you were a little bummed though. That close to gold twice.'

Max furrowed his brow but only slightly and only for a moment. 'Do you mind shutting your lights off and pulling the keys out of the ignition, Mr. Govern.'

'Yeah, sure.' He reached inside the truck and the dinging stopped. He closed the door.

Lyle Govern turned to face Max. They were the same height, close to the same age. Their features were not entirely dissimilar. In another life they might have been brothers.

'Say, what about an autograph after you do your thing here?'

'I'll need you to face the truck, put your hands on the hood, and spread your feet.'

Lyle Govern laughed. 'Yeah, right.'

Max didn't say anything. Lyle Govern shrugged and did what was asked of him.

'Man, the story's getting better by the minute. Hey, you should've seen him work me over, I'll say. Christ, I was shaking. Man, I didn't think I was going to make it out of there alive.'

Max didn't say anything. He stood behind him. Patted him down from head to foot.

Lyle Govern looked over his shoulder and down. 'You know, usually someone buys me a drink first.'

Max stood and took a step back. 'You can turn around now.'

Lyle Govern turned around. 'So am I clean?'

The sun was low and the day's light had all but died.

Max held a notebook and a small flashlight in one hand. He was writing in the notebook. 'Do you ever ride the subway, Mr. Govern?'

Lyle Govern shrugged. 'Yeah, sure. When I'm in the city I ride it all the time. Pretty good pool to fish in, to be honest. I've done alright on occasion.'

Max continued to write. 'Have you ever boarded at Museum Station?'

'Shit, I don't know. Maybe. Probably.' Lyle Govern drove his hands into his pockets and lifted his chin at Max. 'So what are you writing there, Doc? What's the diagnosis?'

Max looked up from his notebook and closed it. 'Do you pay attention to the news, Mr. Govern?'

'Depends how hot the anchor lady is.' He snickered.

Max didn't move. He didn't speak. He waited.

Hands still in his pockets, Lyle Govern shrugged. 'Yeah, sure. I listen to the news. I like to be, you know, *abreast* of what's happening. Heh heh.'

'Mm-hmn.'

Lyle Govern crossed his arms and shook his head. 'Man, tough crowd tonight.'

'There is no crowd here, Mr. Govern. You may have noticed.'

Lyle Govern looked around. It was dark and they were alone. He was nodding when Max turned and walked over to the police car. Max placed the notebook on the dash, retrieved a magazine, and returned to where Lyle Govern was standing beside his truck. He hadn't moved.

'Mr. Govern, do you recall what happened a year ago today at Museum Station?'

'A year ago.'

'Yes. A year ago. One year ago today.'

Lyle Govern touched the back of his head. 'Listen, man, I can't even remember the name of the last chick I banged.'

'Your sex life is not news, Mr. Govern.'

'Neither's what happened a year ago.' He laughed. His laughter had changed. 'Am I right?'

Max nodded. 'Yes. You are right.' He unrolled the magazine he'd taken from the police car, flipped open to a page, and held it in front of Lyle Govern's face. 'Have you ever seen this woman?'

Lyle Govern folded his arms and looked at the picture. 'Shit, only in my dreams, man.'

Max closed the magazine, rolled it, and held it with both hands the way a man would an ancient scroll. 'So given the opportunity you would fuck her.'

'What?'

Max spoke slowly. 'I said given the opportunity you would *fuck* her.'

Lyle Govern put his hands up. 'Listen, man, this is getting a little weird for me. If we're about done here I'll just get in my truck and mosey on home. Okay?'

He took a step and pulled the handle on the driver's side door. Max put an open hand on the window and drove the door shut again. 'Step away from the vehicle, Mr. Govern.'

Lyle Govern's eyes widened. He nodded and did as Max said. He pocketed his hands.

'Have you ever been in a fight, Mr. Govern?'

'No. I mean, yeah. I guess. One or two maybe.'

Max nodded.

Lyle Govern scratched the top of his head. 'Listen, I really do have to get home.'

'No. You don't.'

'I don't.'

'No.'

'Okay.'

Lyle Govern looked down and shook his head.

'Look at me, Mr. Govern.'

He continued to stare at the ground but eventually he looked up and Max's eyes held him there. Like a magician.

'I'm going to give you two opportunities to escape.'

'Escape.'

'Yes. That is what I said.'

'Look, I've got five hundred dollars in the dash of my truck. What's say you let me get it for you and we never met.'

Max flicked the snap on his holster like an old-fashioned gunslinger. 'I'm not interested in money.'

Max unholstered the gun and pointed it at Lyle Govern who threw his hands up and stumbled backwards. He tripped and fell.

Max stepped forward and trained the gun on the fallen man before him. 'Stand up.'

Lyle Govern scuttled like a crab, put a single hand up, and turned his face away. 'Fuck, man. Don't do this. Why are you doing this?'

'Stand up.'

Lyle Govern stood and batted the dirt from his pants.

Max didn't say anything. He held the gun steady. Like holding someone at point blank was as common for him as shaking hands.

'Listen. What about putting that cannon away?'

Max shook his head slowly. 'I don't think so, Mr. Boon.'

'What?'

'You really didn't think I'd recognize you?'

'Jesus. I don't know what you're talking about.'

'Every bit of news I read said you jumped. But I never believed them. I knew you were still alive.'

'Listen, man. I'm just a fucking accountant. I've never done anything newsworthy in my life.'

'They were just trying to protect you.'

'Protect me. Protect me from what?'

'They hid you well.'

'They who? Who hid me?'

'But here you are. Out on a day pass. Looks like I got lucky.'

'Out? I was never in. I don't know what you're fucking talking about.'

'I don't like your language, Mr. Boon.'

'Sorry. I'm sorry.'

'Mentally ill or not, you're a cold-blooded murderer.'

Lyle Govern put his hands on his head and looked to the sky. The stars had begun to reveal themselves and the moon was out, a sliver of light in the hot summer darkness.

'Hah. This is funny. A murderer. Hah. You're funny.'

'I'm not laughing, Mr. Boon. You may have noticed.'

Lyle Govern covered his mouth with a fist and sucked a mouthful of air deeply in. He held the breath a moment, puffed his cheeks, and pushed the air out. He looked over both shoulders and across the road where there was nothing. Ignoring the gun, he walked toward Max and past him, held a hand up to his brow like a visor, turned, and walked back to where he had been standing. He put his hands on his hips, nodded, spoke as though there were hidden cameras.

'Okay. Okay. You got me. You can show yourself now. You win. Go ahead and laugh. Everybody laugh at old Lyle Govern.'

'As I said, Mr. Boon, we are alone.'

Occasionally a car drove by but Max knew enough about angles and shadows that he had kept himself and Lyle Govern hidden from passersby.

'I said I was going to give you two chances to escape—which is two more than you gave her.'

'Listen. I don't want to escape. I don't want anything.' He took two deep breaths. 'I just want to go home.'

'And home you shall go, Mr. Boon, should you be able to escape.'

Lyle Govern heard the last part of the sentence as a question. His breathing became shallow and quick. 'I don't know. I don't know if I should be able to escape. I told you, I don't want to escape. I don't want anything.'

'You said you want to go home.'

'Yes. Yes. I want to go home. Please.'

Max flipped the gun upside down so that his hand cradled the barrel and the grip was skyward. 'Take the gun, Mr. Boon.'

'I don't want to take the gun.'

'Take it. If you want to go home, take it.'

Lyle Govern crossed his arms and shook his head.

Max struck him with the butt of the gun and he stumbled back. Lyle Govern touched his face and looked at his hand. There was blood.

Again, Max held the gun on offer. 'Take it.'

Lyle Govern did what he was told. When he took the gun he squeezed the handle between his thumb and index finger and held it at his side the way he would a piece of garbage or a dead animal.

Max positioned himself in front of the police car. 'Good. Now let me explain opportunity number one. I want you to point the gun at me and pull the trigger three successive times. That will be enough to cause someone in the subdivision over there to call my colleagues.'

He gestured north and Lyle Govern looked.

'Here's where your opportunity to escape comes in: when you point the gun, aim it at my head or at my heart.' Max pointed between his own eyes and then to his own heart. 'Hit your target and you're free to go.'

Lyle Govern shook his head. 'This is fucked. You're fucked.' Lyle Govern threw the gun in the long grass and crossed his arms. 'I'm not going to shoot you.'

Max shook his head and tsked. He reached out and slapped Lyle Govern, seized him by the back of the neck and squeezed, moved him like a puppet and shone a flashlight into the long grass where the weight of the gun had pushed it down. 'Pick it up.'

Lyle Govern shook his head.

Max struck him with the flashlight. 'I said pick it up.'

Which he did.

Max retook his position in front of the police car where he produced another gun and trained it on Lyle Govern. 'Now. Point the gun over here and pull the trigger three times.'

'I don't. Want. To shoot you.'

'Aim at the car then.'

'I can't.'

'Mr. Boon, if you do not point that gun over here and pull the trigger three times like I said, I will shoot you in the face. It's that simple.'

'I—'

Max cocked the gun and stepped toward Lyle Govern.

'I can't. I can't do it.' He was crying.

'I will count to three.'

'No. Please.'

'One.'

'Listen. Stop. Stop.'

'Two.'

'I'm not him. Jesus. Fuck.'

'Three. Goodnight, Mr. Boon.'

When Lyle Govern saw Max's index finger begin to squeeze the trigger his eyes widened. He raised the gun and fired three successive shots. He never blinked. All three shots hit the police car. The windows shattered. The shots boomed and echoed in the distance. There was no mistaking them. What wasn't clear was whether the misses were intentional or not.

Lyle Govern dropped the gun at his feet. His lips were pressed together and tense. His chest was heaving. His hands were fists.

Max tossed his gun and Lyle Govern was forced to catch it.

'Hard to tell these days when someone's faking.' The weight and look of the replica were perfect. 'In my fifteen years I've never drawn and fired a weapon.'

Lyle Govern looked at the gun and then hurled it like a rock at Max. He missed. The fake gun went through the broken window and landed in the back of the police car.

'That's it, Mr. Boon. That's the sort of rage I'm looking for.'

'I'm done. I'm leaving and you can't stop me. You sick twisted fuck.'

Lyle Govern marched over to his truck and climbed into the cab.

Max let him and followed. 'Earlier you asked what I was writing in my notebook. I'll tell you. First I made note of the colour, make, and year of your truck. And the license plate of course. Very distinct by the way. GVRN CA.'

Lyle Govern was about to turn the key. He stopped and looked at Max.

'Then I noted the hostile deportment you displayed when I first approached your vehicle. Not to mention the distinct smell of alcohol on your breath.'

Lyle Govern nodded and stared out the windshield.

'When I was finally able to calm you down the results of the breathalyzer were astounding. Three times the legal limit. Automatic suspension. Seizure of your vehicle. Twenty thousand dollar fine. Potential jail time. Community service. Safe driving course at your expense.'

Lyle Govern, hands on the wheel, turned and looked at Max. 'I had one beer.'

'Well, Mr. Boon, that's your word against mine. The numbers I wrote down say otherwise. And to note, I am a highly respected officer of the law with an unblemished record.'

Lyle Govern drove the door open. The edge caught Max on the nose. He stumbled back and put a hand to his face. When he checked his hand he saw blood.

He smiled and looked at Lyle Govern. 'Excellent. I think you're going to like opportunity number two.'

Lyle Govern stood there, raging.

'I want you to hit me as hard as you can.'

'Sicko. You're a fucking sicko.'

'If you fight and win, you are free to go.' Max went to the police car and retrieved his notebook which held said evidence against Lyle Govern. 'Here.' He held up the book. 'You win, it's yours.'

He tossed the book on the ground and without pause Lyle Govern swung at him. The swing was clumsy and wild but he managed to make contact.

Max took the hit and rotated his jaw. 'Good. Again.'

Lyle Govern was shaking out his hand. He leaned into it this time and drove his fist clean into Max's nose. There was a pop and Max's head snapped back. Blood ran from his nostrils and his eyes watered. He'd taken up boxing in police college. He'd fought for St. Clair College during his tenure there and had done quite well: ten and two, four by TKO. His nose broke easily now and the pain was nothing. He shook his head, wiped the blood away, and clenched his fists. 'Excellent, Mr. Boon. And again.'

Max took one more hit. His one eye was beginning to swell, his nose was crooked, and his bottom lip was cut. Sufficient cause for him to defend himself.

The next time Lyle Govern swung, Max drew his head back and to the side, a deft little move which caused Lyle Govern to pitch forward. Max used the momentum to throw Govern against the side of the police car. He went down with a thud and groaned.

'Get up.'

Lyle Govern sat against the cruiser, legs outstretched, and held his left arm. 'My arm is broken. I think you broke my arm.'

Max hauled Lyle Govern up by the shirt collar and punched him in the stomach. He buckled over and moaned. Max grabbed him by the hair and delivered a thunderous blow square on his nose. He felt and heard the pop. Max stood back and grinned. Lyle Govern teetered and with hands like weights at his side— unready for the fall, eyes gone shut—he toppled like a felled tree.

Had there been a ring the ref would have stepped in with the count. Max would have bounced from foot to foot, gloves at his side. The imminent victor.

But there was no bell to ring and there were no rules to follow. There was no one to step in and Max was not fighting to raise a champion's hand in the air. He straddled the unconscious Lyle Govern and swung at his face with everything he had. Right, then left, then right. A hypnotic, pulverizing, vicious rhythm. There were no sounds of pain. No sounds at all but for the pornographic smack of skin against skin. The face beneath his fists turned to clay. As though he were a sculptor making pliable the substance of his craft. The eyes of the face he pounded, unrecognizable now, swelled shut. Contusions surfaced and turned the dark colours of blood pushing out against skin. The orbital and cheek and jaw bones cracked beneath the blows. The skin split and bled. The mouth dropped open and the tongue, no longer capable of words, lay—a lump of flesh, like the rest of him—dead inside.

.   .   .

Max didn't hear the other police cars arrive. The sirens wailed as they approached, blipped as the cars came to a stop, and went silent. The officers left their doors open when they exited. One team investigated Max's vehicle. Guns drawn and pointed, the others crept towards the two men by the road. His back to them, Max was still straddling the body of Lyle Govern but he had stopped the punching. At first they did not know which man, if either, was one of their own.

As they came closer, one of the officers recognized Max. Relieved, he holstered his gun, stood tall, and sighed. A hand in the air, he called out to the others. 'It's okay. It's Max Sorn. He's one of us. Everything's okay.' The officer stepped forward and touched Max on the shoulder. 'Max. Hey, Max. Everything okay?'

Unalarmed, Max turned and looked up. His one eye was glossy, the other swollen shut. His face was splotched with blood. He was holding a pocket knife like a pen. Lyle Govern's shirt was ripped open.

The officer stepped back, drew his gun, and trained it on the man he thought he knew. He spoke in a purposefully calm voice. 'Drop the knife. Step away from the body.'

Max grinned. He stood and turned, a foot on either side of Lyle Govern's body, let his arms hang at his sides, and looked at the officers. There were six of them. Each had a gun trained on him.

'I'm glad you all could make it but as you can see I have things under control.'

'Drop the knife, Officer Sorn. Step away from the body.'

Max looked at the knife in his hand and nodded. 'Oh, yes. I was just leaving a note.'

'Drop the knife. Now.'

Max held his hands out and tipped his head to the stars. 'Ah, men. Oh, men. What a beautiful night for vengeance.' He breathed deeply in, held it, and exhaled with purpose. 'He thought he could hide.' Max looked at the other officers the way a stage actor looks over his audience. He shook his head. 'But I knew I'd find him.'

Max flicked the knife in the air as though flipping a coin. He watched it spin and land, blade in the earth, at his feet.

Two officers were on him in an instant. They put him to his knees, brought his hands to his head. He did not resist. They cuffed him and took him away. Two others cordoned off the area. One on his radio. Another jotted notes in a book. They were all doing their best to maintain the integrity of the scene.

Later, during his investigation of the body, the Coroner took photos of the 'note' Max had left. Scratched into Lyle Govern's torso as though it were a tablet of stone was the message: 'DEVIL MAY CARE.'

THE BEST LIFE PERIOD

Clippings (17)

(taken from personal texts)

—The bird has landed.

—How covert of you.

—In another life I'd have made a great intel officer.

—How do I know the flight attendant thing isn't a cover?

—What, you don't trust me?

—For all I know you're Jane Bourne.

—Between Bourne or Bond I'd take Bond.

—How come?

—Cooler, more cultured, better lover I'm sure.

—I'm getting in the Saab. I'm turning the key.

—Careful. There might be a bomb.

—On the plus side I wouldn't feel a thing.

—Sure, but then who would pick me up?

—Hey, is it still illegal to text and drive?

—Nothing's illegal if you don't get caught.

—Hmn. Turns out I'm fairly dexterous with my left thumb.

—Sounds like the porn parody of My Left Foot.

—Opening scene: me in the kitchen thumb-painting Da Vinci style nudes on the floor. Flashforward: hospital room. Me sitting there in a wheelchair, Scotch in a mug with a handle I wrap my thumb around. You with your stilettos and a white coat unbuttoned to your sternum. I say, mouth all twisted, 'Fuck the rules.' You saunter over, climb on, and say, 'No. Fuck me.' The music comes in and we do our thing.

—A regular Oliver Stone.

—Maybe I'll go into film.

—Uhp . . . battery's dying.

—Seriously, though. I can't wait to see you.

~

I didn't know if my last text went through. It was the type of thing that after I'd sent it I wished I hadn't. Too close to sounding like a message sent from a man falling in love. Despite what he now knew.

.   .   .

My one-scene texted screenplay was a subtle attempt at letting her know I'd broken into the laptop she'd left behind. I was trying to let her know I'd seen finished product of her own film endeavours.

When I dropped her off I noticed the laptop and asked her, 'Don't you want to take that?' If she'd said something like, 'Nah, I barely use it,' I wouldn't have been enticed at all. I'd have left it there in the backseat, untouched. I'd never have known.

But that's not what she said. Instead she looked at me, raised a single brow, and went, 'No. I trust you.'

How could I not look? Who wouldn't?

This is what it all feels like now: it's like my old self is the protagonist in a psycho-thriller and my current self is watching, futilely telling my old self to turn and run when he sees the light emanating from beneath the door at the end of the hall, but there's no way my old self is not going to open that door. Any old self would. The same as any current self would say, 'Don't. Don't do it,' hands over his eyes, fingers cracked just enough to peak the moment the door's given a nudge.

Curiosity is far more powerful than fear.

.   .   .

There were signs all the time and I failed to see them, but here's something I've learned: danger (or any of its close relatives) never fully discloses itself until it's too late.

Vancouver International Airport: Vancouver, BC

I pulled off to the curb where the sign said Kiss 'n Ride and leaned against the Saab she said was mine while I was hers, jeans and hoodie on, the way she'd left me, like a moment hadn't passed though another ten days had gone by, hands pocketed, birkenstocked feet crossed, hood up. A relaxed, unshaven Ryan Gosling doing a sort of reinvented new-millennial James Dean. I was letting her know without saying anything that I had range.

I hadn't decided yet if I was simply going to come out with it and tell her I'd broken into the laptop and seen her little por-numentary on Danny Mann or if I was going to go for something more subtle and playful like, 'Hey, you know, I've never consid-ered a career on screen, but if you think you see something in me I'm game for giving it a go. My only request is that I see a script next time. I'm not very good at improv.' But then again I didn't know yet if she was filming me. I'd only seen the one installment. *Daniel: In the Lioness's Den (episode three).*

I raised a hand when I saw her and she walked straight for me, all neatly tucked into her navy uniform, full of purpose and confidence. A step or two away she smiled and in one fluid motion let go of the handle of the suitcase she was pulling, undid her scarf, drew it around my neck, took my face in her hands, and kissed me, eyes open.

Her eyes were always open.

#305 36 WATER STREET, TERMINUS BUILDING: VANCOUVER, BC

As the elevator doors began to slide shut in the underground parking garage of her loft she put a hand on my chest and shoved me against the mirrored elevator wall. She went to her knees, unzipped my jeans, told me to watch, and took me in her mouth. Her eyes never left mine. I couldn't speak.

The ride up was less than a minute. When the elevator came to a halt she stood, tucked me away, patted the front of my jeans, and wiped the corner of her mouth with a thumb. She stood beside me and gripped my hand. My heart thumped. My whole body thumped. We faced the mirrored doors and she glanced up at the camera in the corner of the ceiling I hadn't noticed until then. She was grinning. When the doors slid open there was a young couple waiting to get on. The man had a tight grip on his dog's collar. The golden lab looked at me and barked. The man told the dog to stop, not aggressively, and the dog obeyed. The woman had her hands on the little shoulders of her son who stood in front of her. The son was staring up at me. Like he knew me. Valerie stepped out and past them and I followed. We exchanged nods. The mother guided her son onto the elevator and the husband followed with the dog. As the doors slid shut I looked over my shoulder. The man's sunglasses hung from the neck of his shirt. He put an arm around the mother of his son and kissed the top of her head. She looked at him and smiled. The boy had his hand on the dog and the dog was nuzzling into him. They looked like they belonged in an ad for the perfect life and I had a flash of Max and Rayn and me as a boy. It was a picture of a time I often longed for and I thought, in moments like these, remembering life before loss, that I might be able to find something like it again in some vaguely familiar way with a woman like Valerie Argent in the role of the perfect woman I loved.

Despite myself, I'd fallen.

.	.	.

Upstairs she pushed me onto her bed and pointed a small silver remote at four spots in the room. She pretended it was a gun and made a playful little firing sound each time she pushed a button: *pshew, pshew, pshew, pshew.* Music came from speakers embedded in the ceiling—Coltrane this time—and the fan above the bed began to spin. She turned on the spot and moved her hips to the music. Everything in the room was slow.

She stepped out of her pants and pinky-slid her panties to the floor. With her back to me she unbuttoned her shirt and let it slide off her shoulders to expose the Silver Light tattoo needled cursively between her shoulder blades. She set her head in profile and looked at the floor behind her.

Turning toward me she leaned forward a little and opened her shirt enough to reveal the inside curve of her breasts. 'Did you miss me, Victor?'

I was sitting on the edge of the bed. I heard her say Victor but I didn't care. I figured it was part of the act. My stage name.

I nodded and went to stand.

She shook her head and stopped me with a foot on my shoulder. That perfect foot. The subtle weight of it. The grip of her toes.

When I reached up and touched the inside of her leg she bit her bottom lip and I traced the back of my hand down to her foot, which I held, and softly kissed the four-leaf-clover metatarsal tattoo.

I pushed my hands up her body, the heat and the hardness of her nipples against my palms. I gripped her waist again and felt the torsal muscles tighten and move as she worked herself against my mouth.

'Look at me, Victor.'

I did what she said.

In control of everything, it never took her long. After, she fell forward, rolled to her back, and draped a leg over me, her nose nuzzled into my neck, a hand on my chest. Soon her breathing deepened and I lay there, heart thumping, eyes half-shut like I'd been drugged.

She woke me by squeezing my nostrils shut. I struggled a bit and she let go. I sat up and rubbed my face, adjusted my eyes to the light. She was on the edge of the bed. Her hair was down and she was wearing black thick-rimmed glasses. She was dressed and I was not. Earlier she had woken me with her mouth, then climbed on and moved in a slow rhythm over the length of me until we both reached the end. Neither of us said a word and again we fell asleep.

The day had gone and the evening had come. She looked like a psychiatrist sitting there with her glasses on, examining me.

'So, Doc—what do you think?'

She sighed and fell into role. 'I'm sorry to have to tell you this.'

I put my hands together and leaned forward. 'What is it? Give it to me straight. I can take it.'

'It's an acute case of post-sex siesta.'

'Is it treatable?'

'Yes. But it's a vicious cycle, I'm afraid. The only treatment is more sex.'

She smiled and handed me a beer.

'Well, fuck me—and I mean that literally—here's to modern medicine.'

We clinked bottlenecks and drank. In moments like these I thought about taking charge: throw her down, hold her hands together above her head, blindfold her because I knew how much she liked to see, tease her until she ached for it. Take on the double role of director and leading man.

Grinning, she shook her head. 'I keep forgetting you're still a boy.'

I grinned. 'That's not very nice.'

'Oh, Victor. I hope by now you know none of this is about being nice.'

I nodded. 'Can I ask you something?'

'You just did.'

'Right. What's with Victor?'

'I usually dub the name in afterwards but since you're not exactly in the dark about things I thought I'd save myself a little work.'

'I'm not exactly in the light either.'

She looked at me and drank. 'The others haven't been as smart as you. I don't know which I prefer.'

Others. With an s.

I didn't ask for a number and she didn't tell me.

She crossed her arms. 'I think my members will like the twist of you knowing.'

Members. Again, I didn't ask and she didn't explain.

She grinned. 'Change is good.'

'Adapt or die.'

'Exactly.'

'Rayn used to say that having the ability to handle change is the only thing that separates misery from happiness.'

I knew what I was doing and she knew that I knew. Still, I thought about holding back and not giving her what she wanted. All I had to do was get dressed and leave. It was that simple. Ending something is always simple. All it requires is a conscious switch: cut the current to the light.

'Rayn was your mother.'

I nodded.

She held up a finger. Reaching for the silver remote she asked me to repeat what I'd said about Rayn. Making the fake gun sound she nodded and mouthed the word 'Action.'

I drank and fell into my role.

'Rayn used to say that having the ability to handle change is the only thing that separates misery from happiness.'

'Rayn?'

'My mother.'

She touched my arm.

'Tell me about her, Victor. I want to know everything. I want to know everything there is to know about you. Start at the beginning.'

I sighed and looked at the ceiling.

Now that I knew the game I knew what I had to do to make it last.

I talked for two hours. I told her about how perfect my childhood was, how I was an only child and why. I painted pictures of Christmas mornings and Halloweens, backyard treasure hunts and canoe trips down the Heron River. I told her about the paddle Stephen had cut down and customized for me when I was a boy. I went on tangents about Stephen and Serra. How they'd met. How they'd made their fortune young. How they'd left the city for a quieter life and opened a store they still ran called Down to Earth. How their only daughter, Rayn, fell in love with the river the town was built on and became one of the fastest paddlers in the country. I told her how Stephen had paraded her around on his shoulders one time after a race, saying, 'Hey everybody, this is my little girl, Rayn Down. Ain't she something? Ain't she something?' I told her the story of when I was four and won a race down the main street of the river town I grew up in as though I actually remembered it. I made it sound like I fell instantly in love with the effort it took and dreamed my whole life of one day making the Olympics. I gave her birthdays and summer vacations. Home-movie-like detail. I gave her a sepia-filtered version of my youth and she loved it, I could tell. She loved, as I would come to know, the character I was becoming.

.   .   .

Midnight. She was sleeping. I was not. I got out of bed and went downstairs to the window in the living room where I stood for a while and watched the city below. I felt for my phone and when I turned it on and looked there was an unopened email I had missed.

CLIPPINGS (18)

(taken from personal email)

Vector Sorn:
A simple reminder: assignment number one—recall, *Why: you tell us*—is due at the beginning of your September 2ND Cornerstone class.
Beyond this message—and this is not meant in any way to sound ominous but rather to highlight one of our main policies—we will not remind you. Of anything.
In anticipation and with curiosity,
The Faculty at Quest

~

It took me a while to write it. Although I knew what I wanted to say before I started I struggled with the wording, which in my young academic life I'd never experienced. Words and the diction I set them in had always come easily.

The experience filled me with doubt and at the same time left me satisfied. Writing—so the epiphany came—was like running. I would come to love and hate it with equal vigour.

'Do-Be-Do-Be-Do'

Assignment #1

Vector Sorn

I needed to escape. I wasn't being chased but I felt things closing in around me: people to be more precise—and ghosts.

Not that I'm Hamlet—not at all—but like him (and every other breather of air I suspect), I find myself in perpetual wonder. I'm in awe of why.

The word *why* in isolation, though, is not a complete question (similar to the way a person in isolation is not a complete person). It needs to be around other words to achieve real meaning.

What is meant, I take it, by the word's weighty forlornness as it comes unchaperoned in the role of this assignment's singular question is this: why *be* and why *do*. Existence and action. Why exist, why act? Sartre suggests that it's our actions which define why we exist: we are thrust into being and whatever we do becomes the reason.

Allow me to share a personal example.

I came to Quest with the intention of discovering myself (pretentious, I know) and the world around me (as advertised). I had a clear objective. I had reason and direction.

But then, so the story goes, I met a girl. Despite having made a promise to myself not to venture into any sort of romantic *do*, I found myself doing and being what my brain told me not to.

Enter the heart, which is metaphorical for what the poets have been trying to get at for centuries.

Not to mention the ungainly entrance of the other organ to which (and far be it from me to intervene) evolution and the propagation of the species have guaranteed an unrivalled level of attention.

So here's what I did.

I skipped the Meet & Greet. But not because I wanted to and not because the girl asked me to.

Let's go back a little. I met the girl on the plane I took out here, spent the night with her (although it turns out the word 'spent' did not carry the same level of meaning as it usually does in such context—I was drunk and recovering from a state-altering punch to the head (a story for another time)), and so, went on an assumption of what happened rather than an understanding (too often this type of *do* gets in the way of how we *be*), and waited ten days to hear from her again. Eventually she called and, so the saying goes, I answered. To her door I went a-running.

Why did I do that?

To get laid again (or, much to my ignorance, not again but for the first time)?

Probably.

But why, then, when the act had been enacted didn't I leave? Love?

Impossible. I'd read enough early Donne to know better, and having some familiarity with Romeo's lingual persuasions I knew that a man's precipitate use of the L-word had far more to do with lust and locomotion than it did trust and devotion.

(Pardon the rhyme.)

So no, I didn't do it for love.

The night ended and the following day she was gone. Instead of heading directly for Quest I went out and got a tattoo, the design of which came from what the girl herself had playfully finger-drawn across my back the night before. I did this not because I wanted to, and not because she had suggested it.

Why then? Why did I do it?

When I saw her again (which was yesterday, to note—mere hours ago, actually) after yet another ten days had gone by, I neither told her about nor made a point of showing her the tattoo. I'm sure she saw it but she made no mention of it.

Another question: why did I break into the laptop she left in a locked case on the backseat of the Saab she said was mine while I was hers when I knew it was a test? I knew it.

'Don't you want to take that?' I'd said.

I'd noticed the case in the rearview mirror when I dropped her off at the airport. She glanced over her shoulder.

'No.' She raised an eyebrow at me. 'I trust you.'

Even more perplexing: why did I tell her about breaking into the laptop even after I'd managed to resecure the lock on the case such that I was sure she wouldn't be able to detect the breach of privacy? Why didn't I ask her more about what I'd found? Why didn't she ask me? Why did I stay with her even after I knew what I knew?

As simple and inconclusive as it sounds, here's what I've come to so far: I don't know why we do what we do. But we do.

Quest University: Squamish, BC

I'd mistaken Karl Knotold for someone only a few years my senior the night I met him at Shebeen. How drastically different someone can seem (or actually be) given where you see him and who you see him with.

I recognized him from the Clark Kent glasses and the way he moved his hands when he spoke. He looked older. It wasn't his face or the way he dressed that added the years but rather the way the group of students were gathered around him, all raptly listening. An image of Socrates and his disciples minus the sandals and robes.

'Mr. Sorn.'

I nodded. 'Dr. Karl.'

I thought maybe he'd stumble a little—realizing his secret identity had been discovered, however inadvertently, by this library-card-toting neophyte—but he reacted to my presence and my calling him Dr. Karl in no particular way. He stood and offered me his hand, which I shook, and gestured for me to sit among his listeners.

'So there I am,' he continued, 'walking innocently along, inside my head trying to work through a problematic ending for a story I was writing, the sun going down, the temperature dropping just enough to be pleasant, blissfully alone on a quiet trail in the middle of the woods, ruminating, when all of a sudden, there she is, two maybe three strides in front of me, this wild, lithe-looking cat, staring me down. So what do I do? What are my options here?'

He looked around but no one spoke.

'Run? There's no way. Play dead? A lot of good that would do should she decide to pad over for a pre-prandial sniff and nibble.'

Quiet, quickly dissipating laughter.

'Scream? What if that excited her? Enlivened the blood. No, I could do none of these things. So there I was. Stuck. Nowhere to turn, nothing to do. You always, always have a choice, say the pundits of free will. Well, not me. Not this time. I was truly and utterly optionless.

'And that's when it came to me. There is no ending—not in the traditional sense—and that's when I knew I had something.'

He looked at me, but for no longer than he looked at any of the others.

The first time I'd heard the story I believed it. Why wouldn't I? Now that I'd heard a slightly different version in a very different context I was skeptical of the details and the actual truth of it, but far surer I understood the point.

A discussion ensued among three of his disciples who had been listening.

D_1: 'So what happened?'

D_2 looks at D_1.

D_2: 'It doesn't matter what happened.'

D_1: 'Even if it doesn't matter, something must have happened.'

D_2: 'That's not the point.'

D_1: 'Maybe not, but I still want to know.'

D_2: 'Listen. The end is apparent. It doesn't need to be revealed.'

D_3: 'No, no. That's not it at all. The point is we've been conditioned to expect endings and when we don't get what we expect we're left wanting and waiting.'

D_2: 'Like in Godot.'

D_3: 'Exactly.'

D_2: 'So narrative is a sort of agent which taps our expectations—'

D_3: 'Sure.'

D_2: '—and, regardless of the content, leaves us dissatisfied unless it's presented in a recognizable way.'

D_3: 'Yes. There needs to be familiarity.'

D_2: 'But the point here is that such familiarity is artificial.'

D_3: 'Yes. Everything about a narrative is a lie.'

D_2: 'The beginning of a story isn't really the beginning.'

D_3: 'The end isn't the end.'

D_2: 'The narrator isn't really the voice of the story.'

D_3: 'There's so much more to what happens than what happens.'

D_2: 'And so, really, there is no truth to be found in the way a story is told.'

D_3: 'Right. Form is a construct and constructs are lies.'

D_2: 'What's the point then?'

D_3: 'I thought we had it.'

D_2: 'We did. I don't know what happened. It's gone.'

D_1: 'Listen. What you two are saying doesn't make any sense. A life has a beginning and an end. What happens happens and that's it. What's said is said. What's done is done. Life is familiar, as you say, and there is nothing artificial about life. Certainly there is truth to be found in the way a life is lived.'

D_2: 'Maybe. But life isn't a story.'

D_3: 'We're so surrounded by stories that we confuse them for life.'

D_2: 'And when we don't get what we expect—'

D_3: 'Like an ending.'

D_2: '—we're left wanting.'

D_3: 'And waiting.'

D_2: 'Because we don't recognize the situation.'

D_3: 'And it leaves us feeling uneasy.'

D_2: 'Thesis: that which we do not recognize makes us uncomfortable and so prompts us to wonder.'

D_3: 'Antithesis: that which we recognize leaves us satisfied and so we're less likely to question.'

D_2: 'Synthesis: discomfort leads to discovery.'

D_2 and D_3 reclined in their chairs, satisfied. D_1 wasn't smiling. He had his forearms on his knees. He shook his head and looked at Karl Knotold.

D_1: 'Okay. But I still want to know. What happened?'

After the congregation of students dissipated I remained. I wasn't sure between the two of us who had the upper hand or if such a notion carried any weight or meaning in a place like Quest. He stood and motioned for me to walk with him. I did and we headed outside. He slapped me on the back where the tattoo had been freshly needled—like he knew somehow—and I tensed a little at the discomfort.

'It certainly is one of the truly beautiful places on this earth, wouldn't you say?'

He was standing—hands on his hips, nose in the air—like an ancient explorer in contemplation of his great discovery.

I nodded.

'There isn't a single place I can think of I would rather be.'

I nodded again.

'I'm sure you recognized my little anecdote back there. Just so we're clear, I'm not a minstrel. I don't go around busking the same story to crowds of curious listeners for kicks or for money.'

'I didn't think you did.'

'Good.'

'So you're a professor.'

'Yes. Well, a tutor. Students don't call professors Professor here. Or Doctor. Or Mr. or Mrs. They refer to them as tutors and use first names. It's part of the pedagogical philosophy, which means—'

'I know what it means.'

He looked at me. 'Of course you do.'

'I was surprised you weren't more surprised to see me.'

'I had a look at the list of first-years when I came home last week. Yours is a name not easily missed.'

'Neither is yours.'

'The Knotold part is made up. But I suppose that's obvious.'

I nodded.

'My real name—as I'm known here—is Karl Kent.'

'Really.'

'The glasses are on purpose.'

'Does Valerie know you have more than one identity?'

'Let me tell you something, Vector, and I'm sure you've already figured this out for yourself. Miss Argent knows everything.'

Students walked by in both directions. Occasionally one would nod or say hello and Tutor Karl would return the gesture.

Karl Knotold made a show of breathing deeply in and exhaling the mountain air.

'Listen, Vector, I'm not in the business of giving advice—God knows I could use some direction myself . . . you don't happen to know anyone do you?—but I will say this: be careful.'

Direct and clear. Again, fair warning.

'When you say *you don't happen to know anyone* do you mean a psychiatrist sort of anyone?'

'I was joking. But you're obviously going somewhere. So sure.'

'Do you remember what I told you about my father?'

He grinned, but not evilly. 'Not exactly the kind of information most people classify as forgettable, Mr. Sorn.'

'Well. The powers that be believed it was in my best interest in the wake of what happened to see someone professionally. At my age I couldn't really refuse. So I spent three years sitting in a wooden office every Sunday morning from nine to ten stretched out on a couch trying to stave off sleep by giving the good doctor enough material to work with so that he might feel as though he were effecting some real psychocatharsis on my behalf.'

'Like church.'

'Yes. Of which he was the self-appointed saviour.'

'You sound unimpressed.'

'Let's just say Dr. Carl—the psychiatrist sort of anyone I happen to know, whom I would recommend to no one—is no messiah. To put it plainly, he's a cranium-scratching simian. At best. Not to offend our evolutionary brethren.'

'Dr. Carl, you say.'

'Yes.'

'Quite the coincidence.'

'The original Dr. Carl would call it synchronicity.'

'Yes, he would—is that something you believe in?'

I shook my head. 'I believe in very little.'

Tutor Karl started away and I went with him.

'I'm curious. How did you know to call me Dr. Karl?'

'Valerie left me a postmodern note on Twitter the morning after the night at Shebeen.'

'Of course she did.'

'I checked her followers. You were the first one. @Dr_Karl.'

He nodded.

'I woke to find her gone and when I checked my phone I discovered a thirty-minute row between her and Danny Mann. Anyway, your secret identity is safe with me.'

He grinned and knuckled his Clark Kent glasses up the bridge of his nose.

I'm leading a double life. Through the week I'm a Quest student and the number one junior metric miler in the country on the cusp of becoming the number one senior metric miler in the country, which means this: I wake up and run, I eat, I read, I go to class, I discuss what I've read in class, I eat, I discuss what I discussed in class while I eat, I read some more, I run again, I eat and think about what I'm going to read next, I read what I planned to read next, I work on assignments, I sleep for seven or eight hours (if I can), I wake up, and I repeat. I have no time for anything else, which I'm okay with. It's the life I mapped out. It's why I left Heron River. It's why I'm here.

But every single time Valerie Argent calls (every seven to ten days, depending on her flight schedule—I've been able to figure out no real pattern), I answer. Without hesitation. I hop in the Saab she says is mine while I'm hers and I drive the hour south to the city. The route to Terminus Building (the irony in the name is not lost on me) has become second nature. The closer I get the quicker my heart goes. Every time is like the first time, only better. As I park in the underground garage and ride the elevator to the third floor I can barely contain myself. And she knows it. The door is left open and there's always a trail of some kind to where she is, waiting. Sometimes it's her clothes, casually but purposefully dropped, a trail up the stairs. Sometimes it's individually wrapped pieces of candy and when I find her she's wearing stilettos and a witch's hat and nothing else. 'Trick or treat,' she says and strokes the shaft of the broom she's pretending to ride. Sometimes it's a yellow brick road of sticky-notes, each with a single word making up a sentence telling me what she wants me to do. One time the notes led to the table in the kitchen where she lay like a naked Snow White in the glass case, a pillow under her head, a swirl of white icing on each nipple, one on her belly button, and the words on the notes went together like this: Wake me up, Victor. Please.

So, there are two of me: Quest student and middle distance runner, Vector Sorn, and Silver Light sex and story man, Victor, no surname required. Again, I'm okay with this. I certainly have my hand in the creation of it. I'm not innocent. Nor am I a victim of circumstance. It should be noted, in fact, that there is no shortage of effort on my part to keep Victor alive. It does indeed take some doing. The hour-long trips between Squamish and Vancouver go by in a flash while I mine Vector's life for the post-coital stories Victor tells. Eventually I will run out of stories, as we all do. I know this, and when it happens, Victor will cease to be. Without saying so she has made that fact clear. The sad truth of it, though, is nothing can really *be* without the inevitable end lingering in the untouchable but looming distance. If, like Victor, stories are the things that keep us going, it is the inevitable end— whether we're conscious of it as a driving force or not—that compels us to unearth the very stories that sustain us.

CLIPPINGS (19)

(taken from "Sorn Rounds Out Deep Field in Inaugural Hayward Fall Classic," runnerspace.com)

"Still only eighteen (which is difficult for this writer to believe), after a month off, and training now without a coach, Vector Sorn will make his debut appearance as a senior competitor at the inaugural Hayward Fall Classic. Talk about your high-stakes low-stakes race. The O-Ducks will host the one day invitational with the mile, as always, slotted as the premier event. As it stands, the lineup is an impressive one. Of the twelve on the ticket, the slowest PB (PR) is held by Sorn himself at 3:58.80 (the exact time it took Roger Bannister to edge out John Landy in the Mile of the Century, contested some sixty years ago at the 1954 Empire Games in Vancouver, the very place Vector Sorn now resides [sic]). Having run an effortless, unpushed 3:36 and change (for the metric version, it should be noted—one of six age-group world records he now holds) this past July to win the Canadian Junior National Championships for an unprecedented fifth consecutive time, the middle-distance phenom is projected to run in the low to mid 3:50s, despite his time off, which should put him in contention for the win. Look out, Eugene. Here comes Canada. Stop Vec!"

~

After the Canadian Championships I always take a month off which means August is a month of doing nothing. A month of long, slow, inebriating days. Time for my body to recover from eleven months of hard pounding. I can actually feel the soreness leave my legs like a soul being freed. Like some god of good feeling pulling the hurt from me the way a fisherman pulls his net from the sea: deep, invisible, and nearly forgotten until it comes to the surface and emerges full of the bounty only patience can provide. I relish those August days and yet I abhor the inertia of them. Every day I don't run my body aches for the return. There is no treatment for such a twisted addiction except the drug of running itself which fuels it.

And so, when September comes I have to be careful not to overdo it. It's what all the literature says. It's what Baron said, even though he took it too far. He kept me on a strict, to-the-kilometre militaristic regime from the time I woke to the time I hit the sack. I had to log every minute, calculate the average per-click pace of every run, record my pre-run, during-run, and post-run heart rates to aid in his determination of my recovery rate so that he could "program accordingly". I had to eat at precise times throughout the day and what I ate was prescribed to the calorie and designed with an exact 50-30-20 carb-to-protein-to-fat ratio in mind. I was young. I was winning. I bought in.

I have years of notebooks full of numbers relating to how I lived according to what I ran as Baron saw fit. They're in a box somewhere that I'll never open. Some day I'll burn them. When I'm done all this and I want the inebriating experience of a ritualized razing of Baron from my past.

When I came out west I decided not to keep track of anything. For two months all I'd worry about was volume. Somewhere around ten to twelve hours a week, give or take an hour or two. I promised myself not to measure a thing for two full months. I wouldn't even look at a track let alone run on one. I wouldn't wear a watch or even cursorily check the time before I stepped out the door or when I came back. When I felt like pushing I'd push. When I felt like taking it easy I'd take it easy. If I came to a street that looked a hundred metres long I might imagine it were the closing hundred of the Olympic final and I'd kick the length of it with every ounce of speed I could muster. But only if I felt like it. The only criterion I would set for myself for two full months was to do what I wanted when I wanted do it.

There are many theories on rest. In training jargon the term 'interval' actually means 'rest'. It is as important as its opposite in the world of athletics and high performance. When and for how long. What type

and why. Good programs revolve around it. The most significant vari-
able, though, is always the body (not to mention the mind) the program
is being delivered to and through. As for coaches, Bannister never had one
for the longest time. Landy trained himself. Seb Coe had his father who
relied on his knowledge and experience as an engineer to design his son's
regimen. Not exactly a traditional approach, but it seemed to work out
okay. Pre had Bowerman but they fought like dogs and in the end, if the
truth be known, Pre likely did what he wanted.

Not to compare myself to the greats, but my plan wasn't exactly
orthodox either. I had no coach and I ran what I wanted to run. I had
my years of experience with Baron to go on (socially insouciant primate
asshole that he was, he did know what he was doing on the track). I had
my own understanding of all the literature on running as a competitive
endeavour. I'd studied all the great runners. I had my ideas and I
believed they were sound. I didn't need (or want as VA would have it)
anyone. I would be fine on my own. I was sure.

The Hayward Fall Classic was to be my crossing-the-threshold race.
The first test of my coachless approach. All the Big-10 helmsmen who
had offered me the world to attend their schools would be there watching
from the infield. Tall, stalwart men with their arms crossed, sunglasses
concealing their critical glare. I wanted to show them I didn't need a coach
to push me. I wanted to show everyone I knew what I was doing.

How easy it is to convince ourselves that we know what we're doing.

To note, that '3:36 and change' the runnerspace.com writer mentioned was anything but 'unpushed.' Easy for spectators and sports writers to describe an athlete's effort as 'effortless' when all they have to do is
watch.

And just so it's clear, I put no stock in projection.

#305 36 Water Street, Terminus Building: Vancouver, BC

The sex was finished. Saying it like that makes it sound like a meal or a book or a chore of some kind. It was none of these things. The level of pleasure was beyond my ability to comprehend. In fact I didn't even attempt to comprehend it. It occurred to me that thought might ruin it or at least compromise it in some way. So I didn't think. I just did, as the god of victory commands.

My singular disappointment-slash-frustration at the time was that I couldn't locate one single instalment of Silver Light starring Victor online. In fact, I could find no episodes at all. I spent entire nights searching different configurations of Valerie Argent's name, of my name, of what I took as code words I'd heard her use. One night I had a eureka moment. The tattoo. The way she slid her shirt from her shoulders, turned her head in profile, and paused looking at the floor to reveal the two needled words on her perfect skin. She was posing for the title screen. I was sure of it. But when I googled 'Silver Light' I still found nothing. The only thing I ever found that was related in any way was her employee status at Air Canada and the scrolls and scrolls of tweets under the handle @vanval which often mentioned me (but never by name). I never came across anything resembling or remotely connected to her entrepreneurial film endeavours. There weren't even any pictures of her online. Not anywhere. Her profile picture was an airplane. She was an internet phantom. No YouTube videos (save the Sorn vs. Mann bout, but even then her contribution was only a ten-second offscreen soundbite). No Instagram. No Pinterest. No bit torrents. No subinternet sites. Not a blessed or unblessed thing. Whatever it was she was producing and sending her 'membership,' as it were, was impossible to find. An -ography of ghostfilm. Wshhhh. Into thin internet air.

Time now for the interview segment. The talking bit. The character development and revelation. I wondered when she pieced it all together if she made what I said look like a confessional. I could see that. It felt like it sometimes. Appeal to the believers among her members. Or maybe she edited the footage down into a montage of soundbites and found background sepia-filtered images (still and filmic) of some boy who was believably me so that whatever it was I happened to be talking about might take on a more genuine feel. Pictures always enhance the believability of what's being said. The 'news,' as it's charmingly (however misleadingly) still known, survives as it does as a mass-audience-feeding genre on the very true— however old-fashioned and, in today's context, meiotic—notion that a picture is worth a thousand words. Long ago, the pictures that accompanied the news were actually connected to the source of the event being reported on but it didn't take long for the newsmakers to realize that almost any old picture would do. Find an obscure or forgotten-about National Geographic shot of a blizzard in the far uninhabited north to help illustrate what the meteorologists were predicting as 'The Storm of the Century' and the viewers would get an instant and far better sense of what it was they should be preparing for. Locate a Hollywood-produced backdrop of a post-apocalyptic earth for the armeggedon campaigners to show just what the end of the world will look like and the campaigners are far more likely to attract a fresh flock of reborn Iambic followers: 'brothers and sisters and children of our heavenly righteous father, accept Jesus into your life before it's too late and pray he takes you heavenward with him while the millions [sic] of pleading heathens die a slow and satan-fated death walking aimlessly over the scorched and everlasting terra firma hell that this earth shall surely, as God as my witness, become' (see any number of the sweeping cinematographic scenes of a lifeless, ash-ridden, smoking coastal USA from the film version of Cormac McCarthy's *The Road*).

I digress.

I often felt like talking this way when the sex was finished. Especially when I'd just come from one of my Fate & Virtue classes at Quest. The things we'd get into in a session. Here's an example: one time the tutor brought a twenty-six sided Scattergories die and set the parameter of sticking to figures whose names began with whatever letter came up. We all agreed and she rolled an S. Beginning with Socrates we drew a connect-the-ideas circle through Spinoza, Schopenhauer, Sartre, Satan, Santa Claus, the biblical Sarah, the Alaskan political Sarah, the Canadian singer-songwriter Sarah and all the symbolic resonances *within* and *of* her "River" cover, the Canadian filmmaker Sarah and her award-winning genre-bending autobiodocudrama *The Stories We Tell*, all the way back to Socrates.

Three hours went by in a flash.

Again, I digress.

To the interview then. The talking bit. An example of Victor developing. Victor revealing. Victor creating pathos. Vector making Victor a character the members would be interested in.

The DIRECTOR fires her silver remote—*pshew*—and music comes softly from the ceiling.[1] VICTOR recognizes the song: Amelia Curran's 'The Mistress'.

The DIRECTOR sits in a chair by the bed in a pair of jeans and a t-shirt. On the front of the t-shirt there's this:

Fartlek:

it's a running thing —

On the back, there's this:

— you wouldn't understand

VICTOR believes as long as she's wearing one of his t-shirts he's fine. It's an objective link between them. It means she's still interested. It means he's safe.

The DIRECTOR snaps her fingers in front of her face three times and does an exaggerated wave.

DIRECTOR

Is anybody home?

Amelia Curran sings this exact line at precisely the same moment the DIRECTOR says it.

VICTOR

Sorry.

---

[1] I use the screenplay format here to help replicate and make real the episodic nature of the post-coital chats VA and I always had. Since I have no access to the actual recordings, I am, it should be noted, relying strictly on memory, which I have unlimited access to, and which, in my case (not to brag), can be, and usually is, highly reliable.

> DIRECTOR
>
> What were you so deep in thought
> about?

> VICTOR
>
> I've got this thing.

The DIRECTOR leans forward.

> DIRECTOR
>
> Care to be more specific?

> VICTOR
>
> They invited me to a race at Hayward
> Field. In Eugene, Oregon.

> DIRECTOR
>
> I knew you were good, but *invited*.
> Well.

VICTOR shrugs.

> DIRECTOR
>
> Hayward Field. Isn't that where, oh,
> what's his name?

> VICTOR
>
> Prefontaine.

> DIRECTOR
>
> That's it. He was like a rock star.

> VICTOR
>
> He was.

> DIRECTOR
>
> Like you.

                         VICTOR
            I don't know about that.

                        DIRECTOR
            Don't kid yourself. People know who
            you are.

                         VICTOR
            Track people maybe. As far as circles
            go they don't get much smaller.

                        DIRECTOR
            Your circle extends farther than you
            think.

VICTOR looks around the room wondering where the hidden
cameras are.

                         VICTOR
            Yeah, but they don't really know me.

                        DIRECTOR
            They want to.

The DIRECTOR looks at a notebook in her lap, flips a page.

                        DIRECTOR
            Membership has gone from 50,000 in
            the first two years to more than
            250,000 since Victor's first episode. In
            less than two months.

                         VICTOR
            You must advertise well.

DIRECTOR
I don't advertise. More than 200,000
submissions in six weeks. At this rate
we'll hit a million by the final show.
Imagine. A million. That used to mean
something.

VICTOR ignores the phrase 'final show.' He shrugs.

VICTOR
So. What's the story today?

The DIRECTOR glances at the backpack on the floor by the bed.

DIRECTOR
Did you bring it?

VICTOR nods.

DIRECTOR
Why don't you read something from
it, let the story go from there.

VICTOR shakes his head.

VICTOR
They don't know enough about her yet.

The 'her' is Rayn. The 'it' is Rayn's journal. Off-camera he's
explained about how he came to have the journal and how he
has yet to read any of what it contained.

DIRECTOR
I agree. Closer to the end then. Maybe
for the final show.

Again, VICTOR pretends he doesn't hear the phrase 'final show.' He reaches for the bag and pulls out another journal.

> VICTOR
> I brought this one. I thought you might be interested.

> DIRECTOR
> Whose is it? His?

By 'his' she means VICTOR's father, Max. The 'murderer' as VICTOR described him that night at Shebeen.

> VICTOR
> Max isn't the journal-keeping type. It's mine.

> DIRECTOR
> Yours.

She shakes her head.

> DIRECTOR
> You keep getting better, Victor. Maybe when all this is finished I'll keep you on as story editor or character developer or something. Think you could handle that?

He is absolutely sure that he could not.

He nods.

> VICTOR
> Maybe. But I thought you liked to work alone.

This is VICTOR probing.

DIRECTOR

I never said that.

VICTOR

So there's a silent partner somewhere. Behind the scenes.

DIRECTOR

I never said that either.

VICTOR

There must be. A Zuckerberg type handling the computer end. Keeping it all under lock and key somewhere.

The DIRECTOR grins.

DIRECTOR

You've gone looking.

VICTOR

I'm no expert. But it's like hunting ghosts looking for what you send your 'members', as you call them.

The DIRECTOR looks at the tattoo on her foot. She points her French manicured toes—replete with curlicued Vs on each little digit's nail—and wiggles them.

DIRECTOR

You are intuitive, Victor.

He waits for her to explain.

DIRECTOR

It just so happens the software we use is called Ghost.

VICTOR

We?

DIRECTOR

I meant it royally.

VICTOR

Right.

DIRECTOR

Ghost is going to revolutionize online
intellectual property.

VICTOR

No doubt.

DIRECTOR

Silver Light is its pilot. Members who
are given access to an episode can't
rewind, fast-forward, pause, record,
save, or manipulate the file in any way.
If they try to use their phones or some
other device to record an episode—
video or audio—all they get as a result
is a scrambled screen or a garbled mess.
An episode exists online for the thirty
or forty minutes of its lifespan and then
it's gone. It vanishes. Wshh. Into thin
internet air. Regardless of any user's
abilities—even the hackerist of hack-
ers—the files are untraceable, undownloadable, uncopyable, unsaveable.

VICTOR

Impressive.

DIRECTOR

Yes.

VICTOR grins.

VICTOR

You'll have to show me how it works some time.

The DIRECTOR shakes her head.

DIRECTOR

I don't think so. I come from the Woody Allen school of film. You only get to know what I say you need to know.

VICTOR salutes her.

VICTOR

You're the boss.

DIRECTOR

Yes. I am. So we understand one another.

VICTOR isn't sure they do. But what can he say?

VICTOR

We do.

DIRECTOR

Good. So here's what you need to know today. Put the journal back in your bag and we'll start from you reaching for it. Say something like, 'I've kept this journal since the day Rayn died,' and then pull it out and hold it up. I'll

edit in a voice-over that reminds the
audience who Rayn is. It'll add a layer
of interest that you call her by her first
name. Read a bit from the journal and
then fall into a story from there. Maybe
something about you running. A prelude to the race at Hayward Field. I'll
get some footage of you on the track
and merge it in. It'll be great.

VICTOR returns the journal to his bag and awaits further
direction.

The DIRECTOR fires her silver remote—*pshew*—and the music
fades out as Joe Keefe from Family of the Year sings about how
he doesn't 'want to be a big man, just wants to fight like everyone else' and the little red record button goes on somewhere out
of sight and the DIRECTOR mouths the word *action* and VIC-
TOR falls into role, which is little more (or less) than a slight
exaggeration of his true self.

VICTOR leans over and pulls the backpack onto the bed, opens
it, looks at the DIRECTOR, and retrieves the journal.

                    VICTOR
          I've kept this journal since the day
          Rayn died . . .

He holds the journal up, opens it, flips to a page he has marked,
and begins to read.

                    VICTOR
          National   Youth   Championships,
          Varsity Stadium, Toronto. We were at
          the start, the twelve of us. We looked
          like we'd been punched from a mould

on a factory line. Tall, lanky ectomorphs. Springy. Sinewy. Like gazelles.
One guy was short. Another, overmuscular for his age and looked more like a
sprinter. One had a beard already. For
the most part, though, we were physically the same. We'd been engineered
to do this. Not by choice or by happenstance but by evolution. Every anatomically equipped human being can run—
opposite arm, opposite leg, one foot
after the next—but we were among the
few whose muscles fire at a greater rate
over time, whose hearts pump more
blood more efficiently, whose bodies
can withstand more pain because of a
brain more willing to push. We were
the rats in some god's science lab.

Hayward Field: Eugene, Oregon

It was difficult not to get caught up in the history of the place. The tradition. The energy. The stories that had been written there. Like Fenway or The Forum or Madison Square Garden. Being there quickened your heart and made your body want to run.

For athletes the track opened an hour before the meet was scheduled to begin. I spent most of that hour walking around in quiet awe. I pictured Prefontaine circa 1974 pounding out the laps in his first race back from the hiatus he took after Munich. I played out the season-beginning Bowerman speech in Donald Sutherland's voice from the movie *Without Limits* I committed to memory when I was fifteen: 'Men of Oregon, I invite you to become students of your events. Running, one might say, is basically an absurd pastime upon which to be exhausting ourselves. But if you can find meaning in the kind of running you have to do to stay on this team, chances are you will be able to find meaning in another absurd pastime: life.' I saw the ever-smiling late 90s Gebressalassie kicking down the finishing straight, crossing the line with his hands above his head, never in a solely celebratory way, I imagined, but in large part as a submission to the story he always seemed to know was greater than him. I could see the supernatural-seeming strides of the 1980s Seb Coe ushering his body around the oval in performances otherwise reserved for gods, driven, it seemed, by an effortless, unrelenting engine. I thought of Alan Webb, the eighteen-year-old phenom who set an age-group world record here in 2001 with the improbable mark of 3:53.53. The symmetricist in me wanted to let the palindromic beauty of that performance stand forever but the competitor in me, far fiercer than the asthenicist when it came to tearing up the track, wanted to wipe it unapologetically from the record books. The potential story of the feat attracted me as much as the feat itself. As I've mentioned, I—sorry, *Victor*—was in great need of stories.

.   .   .

'It's him. It's fucking him. I told you it was him.'

'Ohmygod. It is.'

'Victor. Hey, Victor.'

'We fucking love you, Victor.'

'We. Fucking. Love you.'

I was on the third lap of my warmup. Spectators had begun to fill the stands. The two girls shouting were leaning against the rail that separated the stands from the track. I turned and smiled.

'Ohmygod he smiled at us. Did you see that?'

'I did. He fucking smiled at us.'

'I can't believe it. I can't believe he's real. Pinch me. Fucking pinch me.'

Entering the bend that would take me to the far side of the track, I could still hear them. For reasons that belong solely to ego and contradict all impulses toward reason, I looked over my shoulder as I jogged away and waved.

'Ohmygod did you see that?'

'He waved. He fucking *waved*. At *us*.'

I spent ten minutes on the far straight doing running drills and strides. Occasionally I'd look across the infield to the stands to see if they were still there. Whenever I stopped to look, hands on my hips, I'd see them grab the rail and point.

Minutes before the meet was scheduled to start, the announcer came over the loudspeaker and started in on his welcome speech. He asked all spectators to remain seated and referred them to their programs, pointing out the various stages the athletes would take in the field, highlighting certain events. As the announcer continued to speak I jogged over to the bleachers which were now to capacity. I found someone with a clipboard wearing an O-Ducks shirt who looked like an official. I asked him for a pen and a piece of paper which he gave me. I jotted a note

that read, 'Meet me at the East 19TH Street Café after the race,'
folded it in half twice, and asked the official if he wouldn't mind
delivering it to those two girls in the stands. I pointed in their
direction. Beaming, clutching each other, they waved again and
so did I. The official said of course he'd deliver it, of course, no
problem, no trouble at all, but before he did he was wondering if
it would be too much to ask for an autograph. I looked at him and
thought he was joking, but then I remembered where I was and
that people who knew running were more than likely to know
me and probably considered my scribbled name something worth
asking for. I took the pen again and he held the program open on
the clipboard to the page dedicated to the mile. There were two
other signatures there already that I couldn't make out. I thought
of Max and Rayn and what they used to write when strangers
asked them for their autographs. I thought about the first time I'd
been asked. Fame by association. I was ten and instead of my own
name I'd written Superman. My first secret identity. I smiled and
considered scribbling the hero's moniker for old time's sake. I
noticed my name at the bottom of the performance list. Next to
it was my seed time: 3:58.80. I thought about writing R. Bannister
across the bottom of the page but I wasn't sure the official would
appreciate it. If ever in my short life I'd taken refuge in anonymi-
ty, that was clearly over now.

I wondered as I jogged across the infield whether the two
girls in the stands had actually called me Victor. Maybe they'd
said Vector and I misheard them. I was so used to Valerie calling me Victor. Maybe they were track groupies. It wasn't
unheard of. Prefontaine had droves of female followers. And
male. They wore t-shirts: *Stop Pre!* Maybe running as a spec-
tator sport was making a comeback. Fashion and music were
always giving nods to the past. Why not athletics? Maybe it
was our time again.

The gun went off and we tore through the first three hundred metres like we were kids in a field racing to a tree, undaunted and unaware of the impending pain. There was no pressure,
no purse to be won. We'd all been given a nominal appearance

fee and that was it. There was no point in running tactically. It was a hard workout early in the season in front of a crowd that wanted us to run fast. They didn't care who won. We didn't care either. None of us did. We were loose and unpressured, cajoling even as they lined us up and called out our names, each of us decorated with various national and international successes. As the announcer said our names each man raised a hand and smiled and we put our arms about one another's shoulders for the photo op before the gun: a fraternity whose members knew something of each other no one beyond their shared circle of pain possibly could. We had nothing to lose—not a single thing to prove—which is exactly how we ran.

I've often wished the high stakes races unfolded this way. I've tried more than once to set such a tone at the big meets and I've been called things for it by the media and other runners: arrogant, suicidal, flippant, selfish. So be it. I can't change what people think of me, and I don't care. Not really. But just imagine for a moment something like the Olympic final being contested by twelve men at their absolute peak who run from the gun like they had nothing to lose, like every stride was their first and their very last. Unadulterated effort, untinged by tactics and politics and individual dreams of Olympic gold. Imagine the paradoxical beauty of a race that has to, by definition, be won by an individual but is run by twelve who care only about pushing every single moment as hard as their minds and bodies will let them, who collectively do not care, not in the slightest—and not because of indifference but because of their utter devotion to making the thing which is bigger than they are, of which they are each a single but collective and vital part, as good and as true and as beautiful a thing as they can—which of them crosses the line first. Imagine.

At the end of the first lap the clock read :53. On pace to take down the world record which surely none of us was in shape to do. The crowd stood and ushered us on with a roar. It might as well have been forty, fifty, sixty years ago, harkening back to the glory days of distance running. It might as well have *been* the Olympic Games. Flags of all nations undulating in the wind. The eternal torch burning. The rings in all their symbolic unity emblazoned around the field. The hearts and minds of those bearing witness filled with hope and uncontainable excitement, willing the athletes on to greatness.

As we crossed the line and saw the time the three of us out front glanced at one another, eyes wide, as though to say, 'We keep this up, it'll be our death.'

On we went, around the first bend, down the back straight, around the second bend, and home again. Full of running. Hearts thumping, muscles beginning to burn, not yet at the point of begging the heart to send more blood but letting the mind know, like soldiers at the front, reserves would soon be needed.

At the line again and the clock read 1:51. Five seconds slower on the second quarter but still on pace at the half for the world mark. I felt the tension rise in my face and I had to force myself to relax. Keep the shoulders low. Maintain cadence. Keep the rhythm. Clear the head. Fend off the negative.

Third lap. The far reaches of hell for any miler. Alone together and too far from home to return, too close to the end to concede.

Then came the pain. An onslaught of it. Indescribable. Body-wide. Impossible to defend against. A matter of survival. The morphine of giving in—of stepping off the track and dropping to the cool grass, of lying back and sinking into the earth, eyes half-open and skyward, arms flopped out to the side, chest heaving but slowing with every desperate breath of soothing sucked-in air, inebriated by absolute inertia, the deep sweeping pleasure of moving not one single muscle—is right there, always.

Above the sound of the bell tolling, an official called out the elapsed time—2:52, 2:53, 2:54—as the twelve of us, packed and pushing one another on, approached and passed the line for the penultimate time. Ten seconds slower than our opening effort but it felt even slower. The stands were filled with arms overhead and open mouths screaming. I could make out none of the individual calls the way I used to think I could hear Rayn, singled out and willing me on, and although I knew it to be close and thunderous the noise of the crowd, as ever at this point in a race, sounded distant, like I was under water and looking up, eyes wide open, desperate but unable to breach the surface.

I was out front as we entered the final push but not by much and everything in my body was pulling me down. The month off and six weeks of long easy running was upon me and there was nothing I could do. Every stride felt exponentially slower. When I went to drive my knees it felt like they were being knocked down by a circus strongman's bell-ringing hammer. *Swing, thwump. Swing, thwump.* The sound of spikes smacking and ripping at the track behind me summoned the last drip of adrenaline. I was filled with the rush of it.

On we went again—one final lap—through the bend and down the back straight. At the top of the homestretch someone recorded our 1500m splits. I went through in 3:38 and change. Only two seconds slower than my effort three months prior at Nationals when I was apparently at my peak—whatever that says—and still with a hundred and nine metres to go.

Two others had pulled up alongside me and so there were three of us now in front. Shoulder to shoulder. Stride for stride. Like we'd planned it. Like someone had choreographed the final hundred metres and we were the dancers dancing it out. Well beyond the point of running with purpose and poise and measured, thought-about rhythm, our bodies were at their ends. Nothing drawing us forward but the magnetic pull of the relief and elation that lay like a terra firma heaven one single step beyond the finish.

As we fell across the line, the crowd again on its feet and roaring, it was in absolute unison. We stopped the clock at 3:53:53. Three torsos bent at exactly the same angle at exactly the same place at exactly the same moment. To the hundreth. To the thousandth. The odds were like those that put any of us on this earth in the first place. But it happened just the same.

It was fitting. No clear winner in a race that meant nothing to the individual.

In the end, no one in the field ran slower than 3:55.53. The fastest collective mile in history. Twelve men within two seconds of one another. Held together by shared experience, by indescribable fraternal pain, by inarticulateable understanding.

We jogged a victory lap together, side by each, and waved to the crowd. In front of the stands we turned and draped our arms about one another's shoulders again, as we had before we'd started—our nations' emblems like flags on our chests—and held for the flashes of the photos that would, despite their digital resolution, resemble the wartime images of boys who'd come home.

Above the dying noise of the crowd I heard my name.

I scanned the crowd for the voices and located my two groupies amidst the throng. They saw that I'd seen them and they waved. Despite myself, I smiled and waved in return. What else could I do? What else would any man do?

East 19th Street Café: Eugene, Oregon

I wore a rust-coloured long-sleeve running shirt with a white Nike swoosh on the left chest and on the back, spanning the shoulder blades, were the words 'What God left out,' an em-dash and Bowerman's name below the quotation. It was autumn in Oregon and I liked to dress, when I could, for the occasion.

I had said five on the note. It was now seven. There had been duties (interviews, more photo ops, autographs) I hadn't expected following the race. ESPN did a bit they said would run as a headliner the next day. They dubbed us 'The Twelve Apostles' but I was certain no one involved in the segment could tell us what we were supposed to be the disciples of.

When I walked into the pub I spotted my two fans across the room in a booth facing the door. They grabbed each other's arms as I walked toward them. I staved off a grin. I hadn't much experience as a celebrity. To say the least.

I sat and looked at a menu, made a show of flipping through it. 'What's good?'

They touched foreheads and whispered something I couldn't make out.

A waiter came by, a pencil behind his ear, arms crossed. 'So—you're the one.'

He was about my age. The look on his face was a mixture of deference and disdain.

'*What can I get you*, I keep asking. *Nothing, thanks. We're waiting for someone.* For two hours. At least six guys have sat down and tried their luck.' He stared at me. 'I thought Jesus himself must be on his way.'

'Well, I couldn't tell you for sure but my gut says no.'

'So what are you then, some kind of actor? Singer? My interest is piqued.'

'A miler.'

'A miler.'

I nodded.

'Like a runner.'

I nodded again.

The waiter turned and called out to the bar.

'Guy's a runner for Christ's sake.' He laughed but not insult-ingly. 'You believe that?' He looked at me again, took the pencil from behind his ear. 'If that's all it takes I'm going to start jogging between tables.' Grinning, he looked at the girls. 'Now, ladies. At long last. What's your pleasure?'

They were staring at me. One of them answered. 'Him.'

The waiter did a little bow. 'Forgive me for doubting. You are Jesus.' He made the sign of the cross. 'You must be thirsty. Heaven's a long way from here.'

I grinned. I liked him. 'I'll have a beer. Whatever's cold.' I toggled a finger between the two across the table. 'Can I get you two something?'

They spoke in unison. 'You.'

The waiter spun to the bar and held three fingers in the air.

'Three Hammers. On the double. Christ is in the house and he's here to heal.'

In no time the waiter returned with the pints and set them on coasters. 'Enjoy.' With both hands on the table he bent down and looked right at me. 'And I mean that on behalf of every man on earth who's ever dared to dream.'

He stood and I watched him go.

Across the table my two fans were holding their pints in the air. I took mine up and clinked each of their glasses. We drank and one of them—which confirmed what I'd known in my gut, that they were indeed members of Valerie's flock—said this: 'To the Victor go the spoils.'

.   .   .

An hour went by in a snap and so far my two groupies—Jersey and Montana, I learned—had done most of the talking:

'What's she really like, the woman with the Silver Light tattoo?'

They made her sound like a character from a Stieg Larsson novel, which she could have been to them I guess.

'Is she smart?'

'I bet she is.'

'She seems smart.'

'Wicked smart.'

'Smart and wicked.'

'You're in love with her. We can tell.'

'I bet you are.'

'She makes it seem that way.'

'I mean, how could you not be?'

'God, if I were into women I would be, too.'

'We're dying to know what she looks like.'

'I bet she's beautiful.'

'She must be.'

'No one has a body like that without a face to match.'

'She's perfect.'

'She really is.'

'Absolutely.'

'So this is probably a stupid question, but do you ever see other people?'

'We know she does, which upset us at first, but do you?'

'I bet you don't.'

'Who would if you had her.'

'Plus—you love her.'

'He does.'

'He really does.'

'But you know, people in love have open relationships all the time.'

'You're right. They do.'

'You should think about it, Victor.'

'Really. You should.'

They looked at each other, then back to me. 'God, what we wouldn't do to you.'

'Seriously.'

'You'd think you were a fucking porn star.'

They both laughed.

'Shit, he *is* a porn star.'

'For women, though.'

'Which makes it not porn.'

'Exactly.'

They both leaned in.

'Listen. We have to know. Were you really a virgin before you met her?'

'Or was that just for the show?'

'You couldn't have been.'

'God, if you were you couldn't tell.'

'You don't say much, do you.'

'What would it take to get you to talk to us the way you talk to her?'

'We'd do anything.'

'Seriously.'

'Anything.'

'You could film it.'

'Take it back to her like a little homework project.'

'She could use it in an episode about your race today.'

'Call it something like Victor Goes the Distance in Oregon.'

'Think about it. Really.'

'Really.'

They both leaned back in unison and sighed.

'We're going to go freshen up, 'kay?'

One pointed. 'Don't go anywhere.'

They smiled and left.

I was beside myself.

As though on cue my phone hummed an inch across the table.

I picked it up and looked.

—I saw you run. You were amazing. I had no idea. Really.

For a moment I thought she must have come to Eugene without telling me. A stopover. Or maybe she cashed in some of her frequent flyer miles and flew down here off duty. Maybe she had another car in another building in another city where she

owned another condo that was the site of another stream of Silver
Light starring some other man-boy virgin she picked up in the
grocery store or the gym or the library. How would I ever know?
Everything she did she did in secret. Which is exactly what my
two fans meant when they said she saw other people. Maybe it
was some sort of competition.

I read her text again and pictured her in the stands at
Hayward Field, sitting there incognito behind her silver sunglasses taking mental notes on how she might use the experience in
an episode, using her phone to capture raw, novice-seeming
footage she could splice in during post-production to get that
sentimental home-video feel.

I did a quick scan of the bar. Maybe she'd followed me here.
Maybe she was watching right now. Espionage another one of
her myriad skills.

I read the text again and responded.

—You had no idea? That hurts.

—Tell me where. I'll kiss it better.

—Don't tease.

—But I'm so good at it.

—Yes. I know.

—Tell me where you are.

That was her tone. Right there. *Tell me where you are.*

—The hotel. I'm beat.

It was the first time I'd lied to her.

—Better get your rest. You'll need it.

—There you go again.

—You love it.

—It doesn't seem fair somehow.

—What doesn't?

—Nothing. Nevermind.

—You sound bored.

—A little.

—Up for a dare?

I looked up. Jersey and Montana were at the bar collecting
another round.

—Shit. The pizza guy's at the door.

Another lie.

—Ignore him.

—I'm starving. I haven't eaten since before the race. Hours ago.

—Well. A man needs his strength.

—He does.

—I should go anyway. The bird awaits.

—Where to tonight?

—Montreal.

—Tu me manques.

—Cute. I'll text you when I get back.

She was always in control. Even when the effort felt collaborative, all she had to do was lift a thumb and I was reminded instantly of where I stood: on the dancing end of the strings. Jig, little man, jig.

I set my phone on the table and watched it like a dead thing, willing it back to life.

'We're ba-ack.'

I looked up and took the pint Montana offered me. I noticed her French manicure. The design was exactly like Valerie's: two thin icing-like curlicues making a V from the cuticle to the cummerbund of white at the straight and perfectly sculpted tip. I glanced at Jersey's hands and saw her nails were the same. They both wore silver bracelets, too. They may have been fans of Victor but there was no doubt who they worshipped.

'Miss us?'

'Of course I did.'

What redblooded man wouldn't? Montana Blonde. Jersey Brunette. The very best the sweet and free US of A had to offer. They looked like they spent summer mornings contorted on benches and locked into machines, ass-flexing and ab-sculpting, twisting and tightening their taut little bodies into airbrushed quality shape only to let themselves come completely undone post meridian, sipping pink drinks through the lazy afternoon hours, floating on inflatables in crystal-blue pools, sunkissed all afternoon, eyes closed behind oversized fuck-off-and-don't-even-think-about-it Oakley's, dangling their fingers in the cool blue water. The kind of languor that inebriates. Unforgettable. Until they weren't.

'We saw you texting.'

'Was it her?'

'Did you tell her about us?'

'What did she say?'

'Lemme see.'

Montana grabbed my phone before I could stop her. Jersey huddled in and finger-scrolled through the texts.

I leaned forward and made a lame attempt at reclaiming the phone.

Jersey swatted my hand. I relented.

I drank and watched their eyes scan the textlogue. What could I do?

Montana looked up. 'You lied.'

I nodded.

'Victor would never lie to her.'

She said it like Victor wasn't in the room.

'Well. I did.'

'Why didn't you tell her about us?'

I shrugged. 'What should I have said? Hey, guess what, I ran into these two superhot girls who happen to be members, not to mention big big fans—I mean borderline fucking fanatical big— and they were wondering if they could do a guest spot on the show. On *me* to be exact. What do you think?'

'Sure, why not?'

'And what do you think she would say?'

'I don't know—let's find out.'

Montana started thumbing a message.

Unhurried but forceful enough to let her know I was serious, I pinned her arm to the table and liberated my phone from her hand. 'I don't think so.'

She held her arm where my hand had been and grinned. 'So you want to play boss.'

'I don't know that I want to play anything.'

'Sure you do,' said Jersey. 'Or you wouldn't still be here.'

'And you wouldn't have lied.'

I sighed, put my hands in the air, and laced my fingers behind my head. 'You got me.'

'Not yet.'

I heard the light slap of dropped sandals on the floor. They both edged forward on the bench and I felt their toes climb the inside of my legs.

I reached under the table and grabbed their ankles. They both gasped a little and grinned.

Montana, encouraging: 'That's it.'

Jersey, submissive: 'Tell us what to do, Victor.'

They had me, the way two women like this would have any man.

I let go and put my hands palms-down on the table. 'What I want you to do is tell me what you know.'

They looked at each other, then at me.

'What do you mean, what we know?'

'What we know about what?'

'Me, for one. I want to know what you know about me. Or what you think you know. And I want to know everything you know about Silver Light. That's the name of it, isn't it. The 'show' as you call it. I want to know where you heard about it, how you became members, how much you pay, who you pay, when the show airs, where it airs, how I get on the list. Everything. I want to know everything.' I drank and looked at them both.

Looking at each other they shrugged.

They took turns speaking. In effect, as they had been doing all along, they spoke as one.

'Okay. Well. We know about your childhood.'

'How perfect it was.'

'How you had no brothers or sisters.'

'And why.'

'There's an episode called Born to Run that shows you falling in love with running the way Rayn fell in love with paddling.'

I winced when I heard Rayn's name but I didn't say anything. I didn't stop them.

'This all comes after, you know, the sex.'

'But it's the way she puts it all together.'

'It's so good.'

'So good.'

'Anyway, in Born to Run there are a string of home videos of you as a four-, six-, eight-, ten-, and twelve-year-old in various running outfits charging down the main street and around dirt tracks and across fields to distant trees.'

'You were so cute.'

'Springsteen pounds out the title song in the background while the camera flips back and forth between you as a boy, running, and Rayn as a girl, paddling.'

'It ends with you as a teenager on the track winning your first big race and Rayn on her fourteenth birthday winning the town's annual river race and beating her dad—'

'Stephen.'

'—right, Stephen, who parades her around afterwards on his shoulders.'

'Let's see. What else?'

'We know about your coach and how Rayn didn't like him.'

'We know about Dr. Carl and how you didn't like him.'

'We know about Max.'

'We know the story of how he and Rayn met at the zoo.'

'The way you tell it. It's so good.'

'She doesn't change a word of what you say.'

'It's your voice the whole time.'

'With pictures of Max and Rayn in the ads they did.'

'And Max at the Olympics.'

'It's our favourite episode.'

'Accidental Love.'

'It starts out with shots of you and her.'

'They all do.'

'In this one she leads you by the hand upstairs.'

'You slow dance by the bed.'

'And start to kiss.'

'She undresses you.'

'And you her.'

'The dance continues, naked.'

'But not gross naked.'

'Hot naked.'

'So hot.'

'Closeups of your hands exploring each other's bodies.'

'She puts a finger in your chest and gives a little push.'

'You pull her down with you onto the bed.'

'All those silver pillows and silver sheets.'

'It's like we can feel the silk on our skin as we watch.'

'For a moment, before anything begins, she twists her hair into a ponytail with one hand and lifts it.'

'And we see the tattoo.'

'Her trademark title shot: Silver Light.'

'The screen fades out. When it fades in you're already in the middle of it.'

'The angle switches and we see you looking up at her from the side.'

'Your hands on her waist.'

'The way you hold her.'

'You fucking adore her.'

'You do.'

'It can't be acting.'

'If it is don't tell us.'

'God no. We don't want to know.'

'Anyway, U2's One begins to play and the duration of the scene is cut down to fit the length of the song.'

'The way you look at her.'

'So intense.'

'Only when she comes do you close your eyes.'

'You can see her getting close by the way she moves.'

'And the look on your face.'

'You can hear her behind the music.'

'Calling on God.'

'But we never hear you.'

'Never.'

'It's like it's all about her.'

'The whole act—start to finish—it's like she's creating a work of art or something.'

'The first time we saw it we thought it was fake for sure.'

'But the look on your face.'

'And the way her whole body goes off.'

'It's real.'

'Abso-fucking-lutely.'

'And there's not a single woman watching who wouldn't do anything—anything—to feel what she feels.'

'Then you kiss her as she comes down and the song ends and you touch her face.'

'But we never see her face.'

'Ever.'

'You touch her and look at her the same way every single time.'

'Which makes the whole thing even better.'

'So intense.'

'So perfect.'

'And real.'

'So fucking real.'

'Then the screen goes black and she cuts to the story about Max and Rayn.'

'Similar to the two-storylines in Born to Run, she balances the one of how you two met on the plane with the one you tell about Max and Rayn at the zoo.'

'It ends with a cliffhanger.'

'Like something bad's going to happen.'

'But don't tell us.'

'We don't want to know.'

'We want to see it.'

'We want to hear you tell the story.'

They stop, check with one another, and return their attention to me.

'So that's it.'

'That's what we know.'

Jersey shook her head. 'I can't believe you've never seen your own episodes.'

'We just assumed you were like a partner or something.'

'You're so different from the others.'

They waited.

I sighed. 'Well. I'm not. A partner that is. And I'm not so sure I'm so different.'

'Trust us.'

'You are.'

I looked away, like I was hitting a reset button, then leaned forward on the table.

'I have to know. When you say *others* how many do you mean?'

Their eyes went to the ceiling.

They whispered a number to each other and nodded.

'Six.'

'That we know of.'

I nodded. Like I agreed or something.

'Five in the first two years.'

'Which isn't a lot, really. When you think about it.'

'And the other one she has in Montreal right now.'

'She calls him Wolf.'

'We hate him.'

I leaned back and drew a hand down my face. 'What do you mean *now*.'

The unstoppable reel of Valerie Argent doing to some guy she called Wolf what she did to me came streaming into my head and I couldn't get it out. His hands on her body, fingers tracing her tattoos. His mouth on her skin. Him, inside her. Her, calling on God.

My eyes widened and I held them both by the wrist. 'I have to see it.'

Jersey shook her head. 'You don't want to see it, Victor.'

Then Montana said exactly what I wanted to hear. 'Maybe he needs to.'

I nodded. Fuck Valerie Argent and her *want*. Fuck her.

'I do. You're exactly right. I *need* to see it.' I finished my pint in one go and wiped my mouth with my sleeve. 'Shall we?'

I'd never asked that question in my life and saying it made me feel like someone else.

They bit their bottom lips—my two surrogate Silvers—and escorted me from the table to the door.

'Hey, Jesus.'

I turned and looked.

It was the bartender. He put a hand like a megaphone to the side of his mouth. Referring to the group of men sitting on the stools in front of him at the bar, he said, 'You've made believers of us all.'

I raised my right hand and pretended to bless the place. They all laughed and one of them said, 'Come again,' which made them laugh even more. I was playing a part. At least now I knew it.

UNDER WATER & LOOKING UP, EYES WIDE OPEN

Despite the body and what it can do, were we without language and reason and the intellectual drive to go after answers to problems like *why we do what we do* and notions of truth and the thing we call the heart, how terrible and barren our time here on earth would be.

After Rayn, Max lost all reason. He assumed a language of defeat. His heart—at one time as full of fire and light as any man's—went cold and dark. And the truth haunted him, I'm sure, until the very end.

It's the only answer I have.

CLIPPINGS (20)

(taken from "Two–time Olympic Silver-medallist Found Dead," quotidienquidnunc.com)

"Ward of St. Joe's Mental Health Ward for five years, Maxamillian [sic] Sorn, who swam for Canada and won her two silver medals at the Soul [sic] and Barcelona Summer Olympic Games, was found dead yesterday after his body washed up on the Toronto shores of Lake Ontario. He is survived by an estranged son, Victor [sic] Sorn, who is himself already being touted as a gold medal favourite for the next Olympic Games. Authorities maintain there was nothing suspicious about Sorn Sr.'s death. To note, no person, not even an Olympic-level swimmer like Sorn, could last more than, say, fifteen minutes in the frigid February waters of Lake Ontario in which he perished in [sic]."

~

When I got to the hospital they told me he'd been doing much better. To the point where they thought he might actually be coming out of the walking stupor he was in. That's not what they called it. 'Walking stupor' was my phrase. They had innocuous sounding medical descriptions like 'altered mental state' or 'temporary transgressive cerebral confusion.' Euphemisms for 'out of his fucking head,' if you ask me. But whatever. They're the professionals. They're the experts. They should know. They said things like, 'He was on his way back to us,' and 'There was real progress being made,' and 'If only the life-purpose forming before him had been clearer that day.' Who was 'us,' I wanted to know. And what was 'progress'? And 'life-purpose'? Please. As soon as

they opened their mouths they reminded me of a band of Dr. Carls. It
was all I could do to listen to them for the ten minutes I was there without
telling them how explosively bursting with excrement I thought they all
were. Instead I sighed a number of times on cue—which could have been
interpreted any number of ways—shrugged, and said, 'Well, we do what
we do, don't we.'

They said they'd tried contacting me a number of times to keep me
updated on his steps forward—'forward,' fuck them—but I was never
home when they called. The woman they talked to ensured them she
would pass the message on. But we never heard from you, they said. You
never came. I told them I'd been out west since the end of August for
school and there was really no way I could've come home with any kind
of regularity. Knowing my story and the rumours around the amount of
money I'd inherited when Rayn died, they looked at me and tried not to
judge, but it was easy to see the disparagement in their eyes. A child who
abandons his sick father and leaves him with no hope or connection to the
outside world. What kind of son was I?

Fuck them. What did they know.

I folded my arms and asked how a man like my father was able to
get out, how it was possible that a man in his condition, a man who had
done what he had done, was allowed to roam the city streets in the middle
of winter unattended.

Like we said, they told me, he was showing signs of great improvement. On our recommendation, the courts allowed for one chaperoned day
pass a week. He'd been doing very well. The first pass was a week before
Christmas. He wanted to go to the University to watch the varsity swim
team practice. We arranged it with the coach. They were excited to have
'the' Max Sorn, decorated Canadian Olympian, on deck. Your father
continued to be very well respected you know. Despite the inglorious incident that put him with us, the swimming world still held him in high
regard. The next week he wanted to go the Y. He bought a pair of gog-
gles, a suit, and a string of tickets. He spent two hours in the pool, once
a week. Then twice a week. By the eighth week he was in the pool every
other day. Like we said, he was doing very well. He requested an
unchaperoned day pass and based on what we'd seen there was no reason
not to recommend to the courts he be given one. On February 18th, he
struck out on his own with money in his pocket, a Michigan State sports

bag, and a Go Canada Go toque on. We reminded him of his curfew when he left. He threw the bag over his shoulder and waved. He joked about picking up pizza for dinner on the way home. We were certain he was on the rehabilitative track to making an exit from controlled care.

He was a convicted murderer, I said.

Who had experienced a severe yet temporarily altered state which caused him to act as he did at the time of the incident, and so, as the courts decreed in trial, you might remember, was remanded to us for rehabilitative treatment.

For life, if I'm not mistaken. With no possibility for whatever you people call parole. I do believe that was a fairly clear stipulation.

Things change, Mr. Sorn. Like we said, we tried to contact you.

Listen, do you really believe the kind of 'altered state' or whatever the fuck you want to call the thing my father suffered from was curable? You honestly think a man can recover from that sort of thing?

Every mental condition is treatable and eventually manageable through careful observation, honest discussion, and, in some cases, the administering of appropriate and controlled medication. Your father had the best of all three. To note, according to the autopsy report, his meds were indeed in his system when he passed away.

He drowned. In the frigid waters of Lake Ontario. There was no passing (I used finger quotations around 'passing') involved. And though he may have been trying to get away, the waves pushed him back in. The water won. Let's be precise and not euphemistic. He drowned. One of the most horrific deaths available to us as a species, I'm sure you would agree.

Yes, Mr. Sorn.

Thank you.

To be clear on a point you made earlier, it is true that no one can ever truly 'recover' (they used finger quotations around 'recover,' mocking me no doubt), as you say, from the sort of loss your father experienced. I think you should know that. Unfortunately, loss is not curable.

That's the first thing you've said that makes any sense to me at all.

Again, Mr. Sorn, we are sorry.

I signed the papers they set out in front of me and left.

When I talked to the police they couldn't tell me much more. His death would be filed under 'accidental drowning.' There was no evidence of suicide. No note. No stone tethered to an ankle. No narcotics or alcohol in his system. No drugs at all save the caffeine from what I can assume was his last coffee and the meds they had him on, the ones aiding him in his apparently imminent, erumpent recovery. When they found him washed up on shore he was blue. Out for an invigorating swim, it appeared, in the middle of February. Nothing peculiar here, I suppose, save the image of a half-naked goggled man in a Speedo backstroking through the roiling grey waves of a winter great lake, eyes wide open, looking up.

#305 36 WATER STREET, TERMINUS BUILDING: VANCOUVER, BC

I was looking away from her. 'I know about Wolf.'

'Really.'

I nodded.

'How long have you known?'

'A few months. Since Hayward Field.'

'That long.'

I nodded again.

She folded her arms. 'Why are you telling me now?'

'I don't know. Why does a man ever tell the woman he's sleeping with anything?' I wanted to say *the woman he loves*.

'Guilt. Fear. Hope. Because he wants something in return.'

I stood and went to the living room window and looked down on the glazed street below. Cars splashed by. Bodies with umbrella-heads floated behind a filter of rain down the sidewalks. Like ghosts. Beyond the buildings of Gastown the sun, which was buried beneath the sky's layers of grey, was giving in. The city was rain on rain quiet and moved like a dream.

The sex was finished. We were in transition.

I had jeans on but no shirt. I stretched my arms out to the side, reaching with both hands as far away from my body as possible, making a cross of myself.

Valerie was on the couch, feet tucked under, my burnt orange 'Kick or Be Kicked' shirt on and nothing else.

'Is it never not not rainless in this place?'

'Triple negative. Clever.'

'Quadruple actually. A never, two nots, and a less.'

'I don't think lessing something counts.'

'Guiltless. Fearless. Hopeless. Because-he-wants-something-in-return-less.'

'Opposites. Not negatives.'

'Hopeless. No hope. I'd say they're the same thing.'

'What you hear first matters. *Hope* or *no*.'

I turned to her and pocketed my hands. 'The sun is giving in.'

My intention that day as I drove up to her building had been to tell her about Max and then leave. But I didn't. I stayed. As usual. I really have no idea why I chose that moment to tell her that I knew about Wolf. So much for intentions.

She moved her feet from under her and made a spot for me between her knees. She put her hands out: a silent invitation. I sat and we both spoke looking out the window.

'Are *you*?' she said.

'Am I what?'

'Giving in.'

I held her knees, her thighs like armrests. 'I don't know what I'm doing.'

She set her face against mine. 'Most would disagree.'

I took one of her hands and kissed the palm.

She said, 'It's over, you know.'

My stomach dropped and my heart went.

'He howled his last howl a month ago.'

I nodded, relieved. 'Too soon for jokes I think.'

'Sorry.'

'No, you're not.'

She crossed her ankles and cinched me in.

I said, 'There's something else you should know about me.'

Grinning, she whispered in my ear. 'I thought I knew everything there was to know, Victor.'

I shook my head. 'I don't think you know this.'

'Try me.'

'Okay . . . I'm a member.'

I felt her pull away.

'I've been one since Hayward Field.'

She sat up a little.

'I've seen every episode—his and mine—since October.'

She pushed me away. Holding me at arms' length she climbed out from behind me, stood, walked toward the kitchen, and turned, arms folded.

'How?'

'Does it matter?'

She shook her head. 'There's no way.'

I shrugged.

'Even if you found someone to nudge you, your submission would have been rejected outright.'[2]

'I submitted as Rayn.'

'Impossible. There's a built-in check for that sort of thing. The IP address you send your submission from has to match the information in the submission itself.'

'It did. All my money comes from Rayn's accounts. The laptop I use is hers.'

'I don't believe you.'

'I can show you.'

'I mean I don't believe you're a member.'

'I can tell you the names of the last eight episodes. How else could I do that?'

---

[2] Let me explain. A submission is an application to become a 'member' of Silver Light and the only way to acquire the opportunity to make a submission is to get nudged. Each member can nudge only three times which puts a strict control on the number of submissions. VA is all about control, which is obvious by now, I'm sure. Although it would have meant more money, she didn't want the thing going viral. It wasn't strictly about the money. As for my submission, it didn't take much to convince Montana and Jersey to nudge me. I got them both to do it, in case I didn't get in with the first. The submission itself is comprised of six simple questions given one question at a time. Once you hit enter on an answer you can't go back. If at any time you provide false or incorrect information your submission is rejected. You're warned of this from the outset. The truth of every answer is checked somehow against governmental databases and the like. The inventor of Ghost (the software platform), it goes without saying, is good. There are two ways to be rejected even if all the information you provide is correct: a) if you are under 18 at the time of the submission, and b) if you are a man. My submission, as VA pointed out, should have been rejected outright.

'Your little fans in Eugene keep you updated, no doubt. You may have even gone down there once or twice for a reunion and a private screening while I was in Montreal with Wolf. There's no stopping non-members from watching a broadcast on a member's screen. It's the one thing we can't control.'

'You got me. In fact, we rented out the local library and projected episodes on the big screen. Tickets went for twenty bucks a pop. I signed autographs after the show. Thick black Sharpied Victors across heaving cleavage. One night I had three marriage proposals and six offers of lifelong, no-strings-attached sex. All in all a smashing success.'

'You're joking, but you should know, in case you've given yourself any ideas, as soon as a member tries to project an episode beyond her own screen, she's booted out for good and the episode shuts down.'

She reached into the belly of the kitchen island and pulled out a bottle of red.

I stood from the couch and pocketed my hands. 'It didn't mean anything you know. I haven't been down there since.'

'Everything means something, Victor. There's no avoiding it.'

'I was using them.'

'That's not very Victor like.'

'They knew going in. Consensual—not to mention mutual—exploitation.'

She smiled. 'My, my. The monster I've created.'

'Wasn't Victor the creator?'

'Sure, but really, who's the mad scientist here?'

'Fair enough.'

'And the monster learned about himself from those who watched him.'

She twisted the screw down in, set the groove on the lip, levered the handle, and popped the cork.

'Someone once told me you knew everything. Hyperbole, I figured, to make a point. But I'm beginning to think he was being literal.'

'You're curious how I came to know about Jersey and Montana.'

'I am.'

'They blogged about meeting Victor.'

She put her finger-quotations around the word "meeting".

'The public online activity of every member is sent through a filter. As soon as any content relates to SL I'm notified.'

'Do members know that?'

'No.'

'Isn't that a breach of privacy? It's a breach of something.'

'In addition to being a computer genius, the ghost behind Ghost has a law degree. He knows exactly what he is legally allowed and not allowed to do.'

'He.'

'Yes.'

'So there is an Oz.'

'You know there is, Victor. Don't pretend.'

'And you get away with Big Sistering your members because of the little box they check that acts as a surrogate signature of agreement attached to a document no one ever reads.'

'Exactly. Everyone checks the little box.'

The wine glugged as she poured. Finished, she stepped out from behind the island and leaned against it, my burnt-orange shirt like a minidress on her perfect body. 'Kick or be kicked,' I read again and watched her extend a hand like a Siren, cradling the belly of the glass for me to take.

'I have a theory about who your ghost is.'

'I'm sure you do.'

'More than a theory actually.'

'I don't doubt it. You've managed much more than I thought possible already.'

We clinked glasses and drank.

'You're not angry then.'

'About what, your little fans? How could I be? We're not exactly in a traditional relationship here.'

'I meant about me being a member.'

She shook her head. 'That wasn't anger. It was shock. For a moment you had the upper hand.'

'For a moment.'

'Yes. Now that I know the cards you were holding, the advantage returns to me. Knowing is everything.'

'I agree and so there's something I want to know—what it is *you* stand to lose?'

The way her eyes and her mouth went, she looked, for the moment, unarmed. It was the first time I sensed from her something close to a desire to unburden her heart.

'Control.'

She pointed the silver remote at the ceiling and made the sound of the gun. The Decemberists came in singing 'Weighty Ghost'.

I poured more wine and drank. 'It's killing me. I've got to know. Why Wolf?'

'He had an inability—more like an unwillingness—to savour anything. And it's not often you meet a virgin with grey hair.'

'I don't get what you saw in him.'

She shrugged. 'I thought he was interesting. As a character.'

'Interesting.'

'Yes. Interesting.'

'And you thought it would be, what—interesting?—to pit us against each other. In some sort of sex-off. Let's see who makes Miss Argent come harder, bonus points to the one who recounts the better post-coital tale of woe.'

'You should know—it wasn't even close.'

'What about Danny Mann?'

'He was physically perfect and intellectually bereft. I thought I could help him. I was wrong. But again, the dichotomy of extremes was interesting. Who knew he'd fall so hard.'

'And me?'

'I don't think you've fallen. Not really. And I don't think you will. You're too smart.'

'No, I meant why did you pick me? What made me interesting?'

She took a mouthful and held it before swallowing, tilted her head and looked at me with narrowed eyes. 'The element of surprise. You continue to surprise me. There's no way Wolf or Danny could have watched me with anyone else. There's no way

any man could. Or woman, for that matter. I mean, really. I
don't even think I could watch your little rendezvous with Betty
and Veronica.'

'I have a copy if you want.'

'See, that's part of it, too. A coolness you're not fully
aware of.'

I shrugged.

She poured herself another glass. 'How *did* you stand it?'

'How did I stand what?'

'Watching me with him.'

'I don't know. I couldn't not.'

'That's it, too. The way you fixate. It's like a mania.'

'So I'm a maniac.'

'Take it as a compliment. From one to another.'

I checked my watch. 'Listen. I don't think I can do storytime
today. I've got to run.'

'You're one of the few who can say that and actually mean it.'

I nodded. 'I have to head home for a few days.'

She drank. 'Yes. I heard. I'm sorry.'

Of course she'd heard. If she knew about what happened in
Eugene, she'd certainly know about Max.

'Don't be. He was gone long ago. Dying was a detail.'

'Still.'

'Still what?'

'Nothing.'

I checked my watch again.

'You've got to go.'

'I do.'

The way I said it sounded far too much like a vow.

She slipped my shirt over her head and held it out for me to
take. 'Love me and leave me. I see how it is.'

I wanted to tell her that I did love her, actually, despite myself,
and that I'd never leave her if she'd let me not, and that's exactly
how it was, if she wanted to know the truth. But I knew if I said
anything like that she'd stand there—her perfection the only evidence any theist would need to convert the unbelieving—smile,

and say something like, 'Oh, Victor, don't reduce what we have here to love.' Which would kill me.

So I said this: 'I don't want to leave.'

'Then don't.'

Everything was always that simple for her.

Here was another chance for me to take control. Throw her up against the wall, pin her there, one hand like a cuff on both wrists.

Instead I took the shirt she held out, pulled it over my head, and said I had to go.

'Obligation,' she said. 'There's the real monster.'

My mind went back to Fate and Virtue class.

'Kant calls it Will and Duty.'

'Sounds like a bad sitcom.'

She stood there, grinning, invulnerably naked and perfect. Sure of everything. A human embodiment of the Keatsian beauty and truth. A poet herself, and if I didn't believe in luck or some version of God, I should have. There was no other way to explain her.

I left without touching her: my attempt at a different kind of control.

When I got to the door she said my real name and I turned.

'You owe me a story, Vector Sorn.' Setting her back to me she twisted her hair into a ponytail and lifted it. 'I'll be waiting.'

STEPHEN & SERRA'S: HERON RIVER, ON

I flew home, caught a train north from Toronto, took a transfer on a bus which let me off in town, and walked the five minutes home. I didn't knock and Serra didn't come running when the back door creaked open and snapped shut behind me. I heard the radio in the kitchen. The Sunday Edition. I smelled baking bread. Through the archway into the living room I knew I would find her in the armchair by the woodstove, needles clacking away in her hands, automatic in their movements and rhythmical. Ceaseless. Like a clock. The winter weekend ritual for as long as I could remember.

I hadn't called much since leaving, something I realized in the moment. She deserved no hurt and if I was in any way the cause of such a thing I deserved the guilt I felt. Though I would never know because she would never say and none of her actions would ever allude to any feelings but love and quiet relief upon seeing me.

When I stepped sockfooted into the living room the rocking stopped and the needles went quiet. Unhurried, she set the needles and the sleeveless sweater on the pile of wool beside her, stood, and stepped towards me, hands out to receive me, head tilted, blue-grey eyes full of age and light and forgiveness, mouth drawn tight in a semi-grin as if guarding against a deep and hidden sadness. She hugged me and I hugged her back.

She pulled away and patted my stomach.

'You're too thin.'

I smiled. 'It's the running.'

She walked to the kitchen, pulling her grey hair up, fixing it with an elastic. 'I'm sure it's not the running.'

She put the kettle on the stove and opened the oven to check the bread, took a plate of meat and a block of cheese from the fridge and set them on the table.

I leaned against the archway, arms folded, and watched her. 'I'm the same as I was.'

The cutlery drawer clanged shut and as she set the knife and fork beside the plate in the place at the table I'd always sat I thought how strange it was that the sight and sound of things so ordinary as a knife and a fork could carry with them such strong feelings of being home.

She pulled her oven mitts on, slid the bread, golden and fully risen, from the oven, and set the pan on a cutting board for the loaf to cool. She stacked the oven mitts on the counter and looked at me. 'How could you ever be the same? How could anyone?'

She sat with me while I ate and we drank a pot of tea, talking about books and music the way we'd always done. She didn't tell me she was sorry about Max—she didn't have to—and we never once mentioned Rayn though she was present in nearly everything we said. An hour went by like a minute and when she saw me check my watch she told me he'd be out there for *a good while more* if I wanted to go see him. One of her rural generation's phrases about time (no need to be too specific): a good while more, not too long, as the sun comes up, when the moon is full, in the spring when the ice melts, come winter and the loss of light.

'I think I will.'

'He'll be glad to see you.'

I shoved the chair back and stood. She sipped her tea and smiled.

'Same spot?'

'Never changes.'

'Key?'

'Should be in it.'

I nodded and without meaning to I looked at the cupboard above the fridge where he'd always kept a bottle. I looked at my feet and checked my watch again. 'It's some cold. I'm not used to it anymore. A few months away and I'm soft already.'

She grinned. 'He takes the heater with him.'

An unspoken understanding not to get too 'warm' passed between us.

'Back for supper then.'

She nodded.

When I got half way to the drive-shed I turned and saw her in the doorway. She put a hand in the air, turned her head, and fell back into the house. A gesture which had always meant, I'll be right here and I'll remain right here for as long as I'm needed, for as long as I have a say in the matter. There was little else that made me feel so untroubled and safe, so quietly without worry and discontent.

The key was where she said it was and the snowmobile started on the first pull. The helmet I took from the shelf smelled of him and again I felt like I was home. I took the path through the cedars to the river and anticipated every rise and fall in the ground beneath the snow. Out to the river's mouth where the water ran into the lake and west a single mile.

The hut was no bigger than a garden shed, a relic from years ago. I cut the engine, disembarked, removed the helmet, and crunched my way through the snow. The door nudged open as I reached for the handle. I ducked my way in and sat beside him. Everything, like the house, was as I remembered it. The smell of minnows and burning cedar. The little woodstove and the pipe leading out. The old foam cushion on the bench, stained in spots and strangely comfortable. The net in the corner at the ready. The bucket of bait between his Wellington-booted feet. His plaid shirt rolled to the elbows. His sinewy forearms. The suspenders of his bibbed snowpants. The little radio tuned to the CBC on the shelf above my head, the volume barely above zero. A framed picture of Rayn in her canoe on the Heron. One of a younger me on a track somewhere, hands on my hips, squinting in the sun. An old one of Serra standing in front of Down to Earth the day they opened, 1968. Beyond the snap of the wood in the stove and the low chatter of the radio, only the quiet of an empty earth.

'Any luck?'

He pursed his lips, gave a nod. 'A little.'

I reached under the bench and felt the weight of the flat container before I moved it. I slid it out, looked down, and saw two trout laid out within it, one beside the other. Like siblings. I nodded and shoved them back under.

'Nice fish.'

He sat upright and stretched his back. 'They'll eat well.'

Like a magician he produced the bottle from nowhere and handed it to me without looking. I was fifteen the first time he did this. There had been no lead-up, no libationary lessons, no warnings, no parental prodding. Just the offering, the virginal esophageal burn, and the irreligious ritual of a shared drink.

I took a gulp and felt the warmth almost instantly. He took one, too, and said nothing. Condolences, the gesture said. We fished in silence until the sun started to dip and the sky went orange, our sign to pack up and drive home along the frozen grey river that looked more like land than water, the life within it rolling quietly and forever on beneath us as we went.

CLIPPINGS (21)

(taken from "Future Olympic Star Loses Duel with Mountain Lion," nearlynews.calm)

"It goes without saying that Vector Sorn was no duellist. Certainly not in a pugilist or swashbuckling sort of way. There is ample evidence from his too-short life to illustrate his pacifist ways. But boy, could he run—that is for certain—and he did indeed win many battles on the track. But there it is: he would not call them battles. If he were with us today and was given the chance he would correct this eulogist. He believed, and said many times, that a race is a communion of effort. Shared pain. A tolling only those who subject and commit themselves fully to can understand. As with the subjection and commitment to anything. Only those who do it know it. On this point, for him, there was no wavering. With respect to being battle-ready, phraseology aside, I will say this about the man who was not a man long enough on this earth: pacifist though he may have been, he never backed down from a challenge. At every turn he met hardship head-on. The loss of his mother and father most notably. Although, again, he would undoubtedly correct my use of the word 'hardship.' He would more likely call the difficulties a person endures something like 'life's inevitabilities' or the 'exigencies of existence.' That was more his style, closer to the diction he tried to command. It should be noted, too, that he never liked to talk about how he did a thing. He just, as the god of victory commands, did it. And he would never recount encounters like the one with the cougar in the mountains unless there were reasons beyond a look-at-me masturbatory sort of reason for telling it. There was never a Vector-the-centre or a Lore-from-Sorn sort of show about him (beyond SL, of course, but that was something very different, he hopes, from the egomaniacal sort of man who talks and talks and talks and never listens). If he was going to talk about himself in any way he needed to be certain there was an audience who genuinely wanted to hear what he had to say. There had to be a reason for saying what he said. As for his time on SL, Valerie Argent was the sole reason and the singular audience. At least for him. She came to be everything. Of course he never told her this or anything like it. And I'm sure that that particular bit of not-telling was, at the moment he realized he was en route to meet his imaginary maker (avowed atheist that he was), among his biggest regrets. Vector Sorn, future Olympic gold medallist and would-be writer of incomparable tomes, is survived only by his maternal grandparents, Stephen and Serra Down of Heron River. The sage-couple on the mountain, he might call them. Two people, in his estimation, who figured out somehow what it means to live a life."

~

The assignment, morbid though it may sound, was to write your own obituary. Five hundred words or fewer. What would you say about you were you the one who was charged with saying it?

Though I hadn't read many exemplars, I figured a good obit should mention the cause of death otherwise it may sound like suicide. Anyway, here's how the cause came to be: I'd been out for a long run trying to work through a problematic plot for another bionarrative assignment, the sun going down, the temperature dropping just enough to be pleasant, blissfully alone on a quiet trail in the middle of the woods, ruminating (thinking while running), when all of a sudden, bam. It hit me. I've been here before. Or at least it felt like I had. The level of déjà vu was other-worldly. When I turned around there she was, two maybe three strides in front of me, this wild, lithe looking cat, staring me down. So what do I do? I mean, really, what do I do? What are my options here? Run? There's no way. Play dead? A lot of good that would do should she decide to pad over for a pre-prandial sniff and nibble. Scream? What if that excites her? Enlivens the blood in her veins. So there I am. Stuck. Nowhere to turn, nothing to do. You always, always have a choice, say the pundits of free will. Well, not me. Not this time. Not at that moment. I was truly and utterly optionless. Frozen. Cock stiff.

It's silly to say I got away. I mean, obviously, here I am. And there was nothing exciting or story-worthy, I have to admit, about the escape. In fact it wasn't an escape at all. The astrologists would call it luck. I don't know what science would call it, if there's even a name. But clearly she wasn't interested. She looked at me, showed me how she could lick her own nose, yawned the way all cats yawn—eyes shut hard, mouth wide open in an unconscious revelation of the dental weapons within—then turned, and slunk away. Not what I expected, to say the least. Not what I remember from my childhood visits to the zoo with Max and Rayn when I'd stand there and watch the muscular pacing, the patience, the unblinking eyes fixed on me as the animal moved back and forth, the low rumble in its throat, all a declaration of my doom were it not for the bars between us.

But there we were: no bars, no doom. Barely a story. Barely an encounter.

Though with a little narrative extension it made for a good cause of death.

As for what I said about myself in the made-up obit, it's what I hope for. That I have been and will remain an enacter of the adage, 'The readiness is all.' That VA at least knows where I stood. Where I stand still. (Which is a problem I suppose—standing still.) That the Olympic gold medal, for what it's worth, will be placed around my neck. Albatross or talisman, whichever it may turn out to be. That I become a good writer. (I've decided that's what I want to do. And be.) That Stephen and Serra know how much I respect and admire them. And that, like them, I somehow figure it all out too.

In the end, what else is there?

Bionarrative Class, Quest University: Squamish, BC

'It's of the utmost importance, in the memoir genre, to tell the truth.' Tutor Karl leaned forward on the seminar table. 'But if the truth doesn't tell the truth lie through your teeth.'

Some of us nodded. Some us laughed.

Tutor Karl crossed his arms and from that point seemed to choose one of us to address directly for each sentence he spoke, saving me—again, it *seemed*—for the last.

'I haven't written a thousandth of what I've read, which could be either understatement or hyperbole. I don't know. But the truth remains.' A grin. 'Irony aside, in terms of sheer volume I'm far more a reader than I am a writer. As we all are, I expect. Except maybe Stephen King.

'My point is, circuitous as it tends to be, that the purpose of this class is not to produce a dozen Frank McCourts but rather to make you better readers of your lives by making you writers of them. And it's okay to make things up to do so. You will neither go to hell for it nor be turned to stone.

'So long as you don't look back when you should be looking ahead. The truth, remember, is not absolute, which doesn't mean it's unconditional. There are always conditions. The truth, and forgive me for sounding liturgical here, is resolute despite its alterability.' He looked at me. 'Just know what you're altering—and why.'

I found myself having lunch with Tutor Karl that day. Which wasn't uncommon. Students had lunch with the tutors all the time. There were relationships—platonic (and otherwise, I'm sure)—as in all universities across the globe. But that's not the point. Here, ostensibly at least, having lunch with tutors was at least in part about creating and maintaining an authoritativeless and egalitarian liberal arts institution. A Socratic arena of shared ideas. An intellectual gymnasium where thought—the construction and articulation of it—were the things laid bare. Instruction and learning for everyone, so the slogan might go. Even for those who would otherwise be at the helm.

We sat down with our trays and talked.

He started. 'Chocolate milk. The modern athlete's go-to drink.'

I shrugged, pulled the cardboard spout open, and took a gulp. 'Someone blogs a pseudo-scientific blurb about the recently discovered nutritional benefits and recovery components of a beverage that until now has been lumped in with the colas and powder drinks as 'bad' for you. The masses, or the few, read what is written and nod at the apparent certainty of the proclamation. The news spreads. And so a truth is born.'

'As simple as that.'

'As simple as that.'

'What about the skeptics?'

'The skeptic by nature'—I put a hand in the air—'is reluctant at first. He takes a carton from the refrigerated unit at the back of the superstore and assesses the bio printed on the side. The ingredients, save the sugar, seem fine.'

'You can't do anything about sugar.'

'It's everywhere.'

'It is.'

'Like the sun.'

He grinned. 'Like the sun.'

'Anyway, the protein-to-carb ratio seems right according to what the skeptic knows from what he's read and so he nods and the truth for him is confirmed. A million and a half runners, skeptics included, boost the sales in the milk industry to such a degree the dairy farmers become overwhelmed by the demand. But it's not in their nature to concede—effort and work being the code farmers live by—and so they wake up even earlier, so much earlier in fact that one day doesn't even end before another begins. They shake their heads at the windfall but like all good God-fearing, down-to-earth folk they sure as hell don't question the windfall. Make hay, so the saying goes. Hallelujah. Blow wind blow.'

'The phrase *sure as hell* seems out of place. Off tone.' He shrugged. 'Anyway, as you were.'

I continued. 'So the ad agencies use Olympians in commercials and employ phrases in their campaigns like *Enduro Grow* and *N-R-G Builder* and *Scientifically Formulated*. The Energy Drink industry raises its pecuniary brow and sets to developing a chocolate milk flavoured version of their own scientifically formulated sugar-water and go head to head with the milk merchants. They're better at lying—experience pays—and so their brand of truth comes out on top and the dairy farmers go back to a manageable, through-the-years-predictable level of supply and demand. Hallelujah. Status quo regained.'

'Sounds Miltonic.'

'Good product name.'

'We could go into business together.'

Like an ad exec pitching an idea I drew my thumb and index finger across the air in front of me in an I-can-see-it-all-now sort of way: 'Miltonic. A tonic for the ages. A tonic for the ageless. Epic.'

'Too esoteric. No one would get it.'

'You underestimate the audience. People always know more than they know they know, however unconsciously.'

'Perhaps.'

'Perhaps be damned.'

He nodded. 'Speaking of the damned, I can't get past your use of *sure as hell*.'

I waited.

'Did you mean it ironically, the *sure as* part?'

'There's irony in all certainty, isn't there?'

He didn't answer.

I nodded.

He grinned.

We stopped talking for a while and ate.

I took the trays away when we were finished and returned with two coffees. 'I read your book. I meant to tell you.'

'So why didn't you?'

'Why didn't I what?'

'Tell me.'

'I'm telling you now.'

'So why bother with the *I meant to* bit?'

I shrugged.

'It's conversational.'

'That's no reason.'

'Okay. I'll start again. I read your book.'

'That's it?'

'What else is there?'

'There's what you thought.'

'You mean my opinion.'

'Yes. Your opinion.'

'Wouldn't that be conversational, too?'

'Of course. But what else is there?'

I folded my arms and smirked. 'Okay then. Here's what I thought. I thought it confirmed a few things.'

His eyes narrowed but I wasn't sure if they narrowed because of the hot coffee or because of what I'd just said. Knowing him, it was an actor's gesture. Always on stage. Always someone other than who he was. That was him. Tutor Karl. Karl Knotold. The Spectre.

'Don't presume to know something, little grasshopper, simply because you read a book.'

'It's not just the book.'

I drank the coffee and waited.

He did the same. 'Is your pause intentional?'

'You told us intention doesn't matter.'

'Are you going to make me ask?'

'I didn't think you'd *have* to ask.'

'You overestimate my intuitive abilities.'

I drank the coffee and waited some more. 'The book alone reveals very little about you personally, if anything at all. You call it a memoir but credit a fictional author. What is written may be true, in the loosest sense, about Karl Knotold. But you're not Karl Knotold.'

'Sometimes I am.'

'Okay, but there's no such thing as sometimes true.'

'Sometimes there is.'

I made a tent of my fingers and leaned back.

'You know, a wise old sage once said—'

'Wise is redundant.'

'An old sage once said—'

'Does it matter if he's old?'

'Okay. A sage—'

'Why not say, *A man once said...?* Let the sagacity be inferred.'

'Semper Professor.'

'Tutor.'

'Sorry. Tutor.'

'Proceed.'

'A man once said, *If context is not everything nothing is.*'

'Smart man.'

'Like I said. A sage.'

'I wouldn't go that far.'

'To get back to my original point: it's the context I have which let's me understand your book in a way I'm sure no other reader has.'

'Is that so.'

'It is.'

He crossed his arms.

'Not to worry. Your secret is safe with me.'

He waited.

I continued. 'I wondered how you and Valerie were connected the moment I met you. To say you were friends was not enough. Valerie's not someone who has friends for the sake of simply having them.'

'No. She isn't.'

'At first I thought maybe you were a Jake Barnes type. In love with her but unable to show it, unable to follow through. And so you didn't mind her having her fun so long as she filmed it for you. An on-screen vicarious sort of love. Agonizing though it may be.'

'You said at first. And now?'

'Now I think you're Oz and she's a knowing Dorothy.'

'Interesting. What do you mean by *knowing*?'

'Oz is in Dorothy's head. He's created by her.'

'Very good. Now consider the etymology of the name Dorothy.'

'You're deflecting.'

'A little.'

I crossed my arms. 'Okay. I'm listening.'

He looked up and gestured with a believer's hand above his head. 'Dorothy, the name, means a gift from God.'

'That fits. I've often thought she's the only evidence any theist would ever need.'

'Vector, my boy. I do believe you've fallen. Struck with your own arrow.'

I leaned forward and looked right at him. 'You're the ghost behind Ghost. Aren't you.'

He nodded.

'Are you nodding *yes*?'

He nodded some more. 'I'm nodding *I'm thinking*.'

'Thinking what?'

'Hard to say.'

He looked over his shoulder, leaned in, and went sotto voce on me. 'Listen. You know what you know. You don't need me to tell you if it's true.'

I nodded.

Not mockingly he asked me what my nodding meant. I told him it meant *Just what I thought*. He said thought was the best verifier and I told him I thought so too.

'So. Now that that's cleared up. What else did the book confirm, as you say?'

'That you are just like her.'

'Just like her.'

'You wanted someone to find out who you were, however unconsciously. It just so happened to be me.'

He folded his arms, leaned back, and sighed. I could see him thinking.

He leaned forward again. 'Presumption, like presentiment, is that long shadow on the lawn.'

He mimed hitting a chess timer. I spoke the next line and did the same.

'Indicative that suns go down.'

'The notice to the startled grass.'

'That darkness is about to pass.'

'And pass it does. Be certain of that. But a ghost casts no shadow.'

I shook my head. 'I don't follow.'

He narrowed his eyes. 'Listen. The poem means that a shadow is a hint of the darkness to come, but you can't know what the darkness is—despite feeling like you do, despite seeing the shadow—until you're in it. What I add—that not everything, like a ghost, casts a shadow—means there are some things that come without warning—and that warning is essential to the understanding—and so it's impossible to know, to understand certain things, even when you're in them.'

Clippings (22)

(a selection of jacket blurbs taken
from the back cover of *Spectre*)

'A masterful memoirist.' (*The New York Times*)

'Knotold makes the reader question the notion of truth at every turn. In the end we're left wondering if the whole world is cloaked in deception.' (*O*)

'Knotold is a magician of the highest order: think Houdini, think Hemingway, think Jesus.' (globeandmail.com/books)

'Part true fairytale, part bionarrative, part existential cartography, *Spectre* is pure spirit.' (*Quill & Quire*)

~

The four appraisals that adorn the jacket of the Canadian edition of KK's memoir demonstrate a thoughtful merger of the popular and the erudite. Cleverly strategical marketing is tantamount in today's publishing world. The way the jacket designer dresses the front and back covers determines the return—as much (more in some cases) as what is written between them—on the publisher's investment in a book. Businesswise it is essential for people to want to read a book or to be seen reading a book. Economically speaking it doesn't matter if they actually read it or not. The number of people who read a book does not determine whether it is a bestseller. How often are books bought only to sit, their spines uncracked, carefully arranged on shelves and coffee tables and desks? The displays that say, Here—see these books?—they represent who I truly am. They are my intellect, my politics, my philosophy. My sense of culture, of humour, of history. They represent for me what it means to be a breathing, thinking human part of this world.

(A snapshot of the names on my desk on any given week while I was working on this keystone project: Richler. Roth. Sartre. Hitchens. Doyle. DFW. Eggers. The OED. Wheelock's Latin. Ondaatje. Gaston. Leonard (surname and given). Harvey. McCarthy. MacLeod. McEwan. McCann. Banville. Strunk & White. Winter. Trudeau Sr. Yeats. And Knotold.)

I don't know exactly how many copies have been sold worldwide (it's not the kind of book to advertise copies sold on the front cover) but I know Tutor Karl has done very well with Spectre. It was shortlisted for the Giller, the GG, the Man Booker, controversially taken out of the running for the Charles Taylor prize, and won the International James Frey Memoir Award. It has been translated into thirteen languages and was on the Globe & Mail's Bestseller list for forty weeks. Sarah Polly has optioned the book for film and asked the author himself to help with the script. In short, Spectre has made Tutor Karl a bit of a rockstar educator and I'm sure Quest is quite pleased to have him on their roster. Everyone—even the strictest STEM students—wants to take his Bionarrative block so that they may learn, as the end of the course description claims, the science behind the art of lying to tell the truth.

Spectre[3]

by Karl Knotold

My name is Karl Knotold and I'm a recovering conjurer.
I've been clean for two years.
This is the spirit of my story.

. . .

The thing about my particular addiction is that it's fairly
innocuous, as addictions go. I'm in no danger of dying pre-
maturely because of it and it's not harmful to others. It affects
them, sure, but it doesn't harm them. Not physically. At any rate,
I was clinically addicted. That's the point. The cerebral, social,
and emotional distress I felt was real. I needed help. Which is
where my decorously debauched angel—Zelda—comes in, with
her irreparably tattered, beautiful wings.

Before I met Zelda I was a soul sapper. A street junkie.
Everywhere I went I tapped into people's souls and made them
appear. Surreptitiously. Overtly. With or without consent. It
didn't matter. I got off on fucking with people's spirits. Like all
addicts I couldn't get enough. I conjured everywhere I went. In
the grocery story, the gym, the library, on the street. Once in
class when the prof was coming to the apex of her lecture I
tapped my desk with a pencil, muttered an abracadabra, and bam,
her spirit was floating right there beside her. She lost it (who
wouldn't?) and I laughed. In the beginning others laughed with

---

[3] For the sake of providing metafictional backstory for VA and KK I'm
including the opening chapter from Spectre with the express consent of the
author who happens also to be the overseas overseer to this particular
bionarrative keystone project. Take it as you will.

me. The thing is I didn't know when to stop. I couldn't. It got to the point where it was impossible for me to look at people without making their spirits rise. (Man of God that I am. Hah.) Then it got so the individual wasn't enough. I'd conjure en masse. Underground when the subway train came rolling in I'd trill both sets of fingers at a particular car and bring out everyone's inner ghosts, muttering to myself, 'Who you gonna call?'

The better I got the lonelier I got, which goes without saying. I was a freak. The tallest man in the world. The bearded lady. The wolf man. Tom Thumb. Frankenstein's monster. I frightened people. It got so everyone knew who I was. They crossed the street when they saw me coming. When I stepped onto streetcars or subway trains everyone scattered. Like startled birds in a field. I found myself alone. I was forced to conjure the spirits of feral cats and birds in trees. I was a vampire sucking on the blood of rats.

And so I sought refuge in the underworld. I went places where people wouldn't know me. Dark places. Places inhabited by other addicts. People who wouldn't know I was conjuring their spirits because they were too consumed with their own compulsions. The drugged. The drunk. The digitally addicted. I stalked afterhours bars, backstreets, alleyways, tunnels, stripclubs, sexclubs, drugclubs. You name it. I went where the downtrodden went. Where total debauchery was the sought-after norm. And the spirits I conjured there were so intense there was no way I could return to the mainstream even if that sort of return were possible.

Soon I was spending all my time in a place called The Sun Never Rises. You had to be a special kind of completely devoted addict even to find it. Off the map. Sub subterranean. Sub subcultural. Sub subversive. Sub sublime. Beneath everything. Beneath hell itself. Alcohol that blinds. Drugs that alter God. Digital devices that are irrevocably hardwired to the brain. Absolutely inescapable. Unless you're saved by the grace of something you no longer or never-in-the-first-place believed in and you wake up one middle-of-the-night-morning in an in-the-country-quiet rehabilitative hospital to find yourself being tended to by what must be angels of a kind and you want to thank the soul who brought you here but at the same time you want to throttle him and yell, What fucking right did you have to pull me from the hellbent spiral I was in? I was nearly there. Holding on only to let go.

The first few months you spend in this too-bright second chance would-be should-be terra firma haven you do little more than scream, flail, shake, shiver, twitch, and sweat. You mutter unintelligible wishes for the end of pain to come, converse with the incorporeal, jerk fistfuls of hair from your skull, knuckle the bedsheets while rocking on the edge, draw bloodless bony fingers down the claylike feeling of your face, and pace around in slippered feet and a pukegreen asscrack-displaying openbacked gown by a window filled with sun and trees and birds and all the unrealistic traits of a dreamt-about earthly paradise. You exist only in the surreality of a body you feel every nerve of and a brain you can't control. Hell is more welcome than heaven. Hell would be heaven. Which is nearly the same state as the downward spiral you were in that put you here to begin with save the presence of an ungodly (or godly) pain.

Then one day you wake up and you're you again. A version at least, remembered from another life, and you don't feel great about it but you don't feel bad either. You feel okay. You feel almost thankful which is a feeling you can't name because it's been so long since you felt it. Emotional amnesia. All the good things will take relearning which means mistakes again will be made. But at least you're in your own skin and you know it and all your senses seem recalibrated, however frayed at the edges. What you see is real and you need no convincing. The taste and smell of your first sober sip of coffee is un-fucking-believable. This is what you say: 'Jesus. This is just coffee? It's un-fucking-believable.' Otherworldly. Almost too good. A faint and distant echo of what put you here in the first place. But you don't think about it. You take everything in like you've been born again.

One day you're drawn to the common room by the purity of a sound you discover is a piano and the sight of the angel sitting at it and the music she plays nearly convert you but then you're brain kicks in and you feel the familiar feeling of your old self's well developed cynicism trickle in. You grin, but guardedly, because the music is heavenly. She is heavenly. There's no other word. And you know you must be fine, you must be okay now, when you realize you're actually contemplating adjectival appropriateness and not the deathly release from the mind-shearing pain of something you cannot name.

In a week you've all but forgotten why you're walking around all day in slippers and a front-opening robe (a sure sign of progress) in a place called Whispering Pines and a sense of the immortal sneaks in. You convince yourself you're in control. Cruising down the oceanside highway of Fully Recovered. An index finger gracing the bottom of the wheel. Straight and clear. Nothing to worry about. A button away from autopilot. Sit back, relax, and breathe in that clean ocean air. Enjoy the ride, Karl. Enjoy the ride.

Here's me talking into the mirror a week plus a day after I woke up as a version of myself again: 'Hey, don't worry yourself. Don't fret, Lady Brett. Don't panic, Yanic. You're fine. I'm fine. We're fine. We know what I'm doing. We do. I do. Seriously. Come on. Do you really think I'd jeopardize our recovery? Of course not. No way. Too much work. Too much heartbreaking neckbreaking painstaking work. Too much pain. I remember the pain. Don't worry. It would kill you—a Hemingway sort of kill you—if you had to do it again. I know that. So no. I'm not going to fuck it up. I promise. Okay? Are we okay? Good. There. So you see. Exactly. Anyway, what could one little spirit do? An ice-breaker. One tiny little spirit. Something I know. Something to put a shot of umph into the old chutzpah. Listen, I'll ask her if she's interested and if she says no I won't push it. One time and one time only. I promise. If a man can't trust himself who can he trust? Am I right? Am I right?'

So one afternoon I pulled up a chair beside her as she played and I sat there like I was the teacher and listened, elbows on my knees, face in my hands. She was playing Moonlight Sonata.

'Not bad for a deaf guy. You can really sense the lunar illumination he was going for.'

She didn't smile. She didn't look up. She didn't respond at all. Instead she leaned over the keys, eyes closed, and held the twohanded final chord until it had been drained of all sound, all reverberation.

'Listen, this might not be the place to say it—or it might be *the* place—but I have to tell you. I've been listening to you play for a week now and, Jesus, I think I'm addicted.'

Ten full seconds after there was no sound coming from the belly of the baby grand she sat up, opened her eyes, and withdrew her hands from the keys. It was ten full seconds. I counted.

At first she didn't look at me when she spoke. 'I can feel his spirit when I play.'

'Really.'

'I can feel his hands on me.'

She bit her bottom lip and closed her eyes. Ran her hands over her arms and shoulders, her neck and face, her breasts, her torso, all the way down to her hips. She made a little moaning sound and opened her eyes.

'Can you feel him?'

I cleared my throat. 'Sure. I mean, well, not like you can.'

She giggled. 'I meant, can you feel his spirit?'

'Oh, right, his spirit. Yeah, I mean, the way you play how could I not?'

'You're sweet.'

I gained a little confidence. 'Tell me you're not in here for theobromine addiction.'

Her eyes darted around and she put a finger to her lips. 'Shh. You're not supposed to say the word.'

'What word?'

Averting her eyes she leaned toward me and whispered. 'Addiction.'

I shrugged. 'Why not? It's not the word that's the problem.'

'It's like saying Macbeth.'

'I don't follow.'

'It's a curse.'

I scanned the room. 'If anyone could handle a curse it'd be the people in here.'

'Hah. What do you know about curses?'

There was no sarcasm or accusation in her voice. She spoke with genuine interest. A natural, sober curiosity.

'I know I have one.'

'You can't mean that literally.'

'Why not?'

'You're serious.'

'There's a hex on me. A blight. A good old-fashioned god-given curse.'

'That can't be true.'

'Anything can be true. If you believe it.'

She folded her arms. 'Show me.'

I checked over both shoulders and leaned towards her. 'You don't want me to say the word but you want me to do the thing that put me here.'

She bit her bottom lip and nodded. 'Would you?'

I felt my heart go.

She took my hands and whispered. 'We can't do it here. Come on. I know a place.'

We stood and left the common room together. We walked slowly, but not too slowly, and did our best not to draw attention to our exit.

'I didn't get your name.'

We spoke without looking at each other.

'Zelda.'

'Zelda.' I nodded. 'I'm Karl.'

We were sitting across from each other in the dark. It was quiet. The risk of getting caught heightened the experience. Which wasn't good. It wasn't good. I take that back. It was good. It was Platonic Form good.

'Wow.'

'I know.'

'That was amazing.'

'You liked it?'

'I don't know if I liked it. Like is the wrong word.'

'I know. The right word is hard to find. It always is.'

'I mean, how could anyone *like* the spirit being pulled from her?'

'I know. I told you.'

'That was really me? I mean, my actual spirit? Hovering there?'

'The genuine artefact.'

'I'm shaken. I feel, I feel—'

'Spent.'

She nodded. 'Yes. Spent. It feels like we just—'

'I know. It feels like that for me, too.'

She sighed and smiled and pulled her platinum blonde hair (a single pink streak down the middle) into a ponytail. She looked over her shoulder at the door and my eyes had adjusted enough to notice the Asian tattoo on her neck. Something like power or control, she told me, when I asked what it meant.

I said, 'Fitting.'

She said, 'So I've been told.'

I looked around. 'What is this place anyway?'

We were in the basement in a room she somehow had a key for.

'A shooting range.'

'A shooting range.'

She nodded and pointed behind me. In the darkness I could just make out the partitioned shooting stations and corridors beyond them.

'Why would a place like this have a shooting range?'

'Experimental therapy.'

'They never experimented with me.'

'They use it for agoraphobics and whatnot. The meek. It's supposed to build confidence.'

'How do you know so much about it?'

She shrugged. 'I just know.'

'I bet it's a wicked release.'

She nodded like she knew from experience. 'It is. That's why they don't let cases like us down here.'

I crossed my arms. 'Do I want to know how you got a key?'

She shook her head.

I checked the door. 'When do they use it?'

'Sundays and Thursdays.'

'What day is it today?'

'Tuesday.'

'So we're okay.'

'We're okay.'

I checked the door again. 'Listen. When we get out of here—'

She put a finger to my lips and closed her eyes.

'Hear that?'

I didn't hear anything.

She stood and started to sway her hips, touched herself as she moved, turned to the inaudible music in her head. She peeled her shirt like a pro and her jeans came off it seemed with the snap of her fingers. A magician in her own right. She danced in front of me. She sat in my lap and moved against me, took me by the wrists, placed my hands on her breasts. She smelled of mango and when I bit the tattoo on her neck she bit her own bottom lip and let out a little moan. She reached into my robe. I stood and turned her against the wall and we stifled each other as we fucked in the darkness. When she whispered she was close I conjured her spirit again and the spectral face, almost like a parody, was openmouthed like the one it copied. The moment she noticed the spirit beside her she shuddered and then fell away from me like a kite with no wind.

Sitting against the wall in the darkness she reached for her jeans and took a package of cigarettes from one of the front pockets. We sat there naked, smoking, taking long deep pulls, and I imagined myself emptying a full magazine onto a target at the end of one of the corridors with a blown-up picture of my own head stuck to the top. I wasn't suicidal but there was no way this was going to be a onetime thing and I was angry at myself for succumbing. I was weak and I knew in my gut that I always would be. I'd never be the story of the man who overcomes.

She was the one to break the silence. Always in control even when she wasn't. 'You were saying?'

I looked at her. She continued.

'You said, *When we get out of here*—you were going to tell me something.'

I shook my head. 'I don't remember.'

'How about this? When we get out of here I'm going to make you famous.'

I snickered. 'Really. How's that?'

She drew an invisible headline with her thumb and index finger. 'Karl the Conjurer. People will pay to see what you can do.'

'I don't think so. People used to run from me.'

'You can't just go up to people and make their wallets disappear or cut them in half. It has to be controlled. There needs to be a stage. There needs to be a safe place for an audience to watch from. There needs to be an understanding.'

'An understanding.'

'Trust me. You'll see.'

'And what about you?'

'What about me?'

'You've got a plan to control what put me here. How will you control what put you here?'

'To be clear my problem was virgins, not sex, and I think I'm done with them.' She put her hands on my shoulders and straddled me. 'Now that I have you.'

And have me she did.

'I'll take care of everything,' she said. 'I'll be Oz. I'll be the ghost behind the ghosts.'

She took me again and I knew in that instant that I was hers for as long as she wanted me to be. She was like this wild, lithe-looking cat staring me down and there was nothing I could do. I was trapped. Stuck. Nowhere to turn. You always, always have a choice, say the pundits of free will. Well, not me. Not this time. I was truly and utterly optionless. Frozen. Cock stiff.

We were finished. This was it. The last time. We were in our final hours together. I could tell the moment she opened the door to greet me. I had had enough experience with the ends of things to recognize the imminence of one. There were no tangible warnings. No subtext in the way she spoke. She didn't look at me or touch me in any particularly portentous way. There were no celestial omens. No apocalyptic images. No coincidental songs of reckoning in the background. I just knew. *I don't do forever*, she said. A clear and tangible end had always been on the touchable horizon. *That long shadow on the lawn*. And now, here it was. I could feel it in my gut. I was filled with the same nervous fusion of fear and relief that knots my insides at the start of a race. Only this time I was holding the gun and it was up to me to pull the trigger.

#305 36 WATER STREET, TERMINUS BUILDING:
VANCOUVER, BC

Slipping on an oversized Beatles t-shirt and nothing else, she padded across the room, slid the balcony door open, and stepped out. I followed. One last time.

Leaning sideways against the rail she struck a match and held the head of her Romeo y Julieta in the flame while she puffed it to life. There was a breeze which took the smoke away like a spirit, and spring, as they say, was in the air.

'I'd offer you one, but—'

I didn't know how the sentence ended but I nodded anyway.

In the wicker chair I'd come to view as one of my spots in her home—as illogical as the notion of such possession is—I stretched out and crossed my bare feet, set my head into the plushly cushioned back, closed my eyes, inhaled deeply, and sighed. The full gesture—the feeling and the thought of it—said this: *I am content. If there is nothing else there is this. And I feel fine.*

The REM song snuck into the moment and as I opened my eyes I found myself humming the chorus.

I was sure this was the last time I'd ever be there—there with her, there this way—and despite the fear and anxiety, despite the extractable pit in my stomach, I felt completely relaxed. I couldn't understand why and I can't explain it now. The best I can do is to say it was like some kind of inner anarchical calm. A private pandemonium peace. With such a conflation of emotions there was no physical way to represent exactly how I was feeling. Tears, should they come, would not do and would be grossly misinterpreted. A tightly drawn mouth and furrowed brow would suggest anger, far too simple a conclusion for and far from what I actually felt. Laughter would be stupid as it too often is.

To be clear it's not that I thought about the physical expression of my feelings in that moment and how best to represent them—that sort of forced countenance is invariably transparent and void of meaning—but now that I'm writing about it I find myself contemplating such body language. Like why I sat there, for example—aware of what I took as an imminent end I wanted no part of—reclined in a wicker chair grinning like a kid waking up a month into summer.

Maybe it was an unconscious acceptance of what I could not prevent or change. I don't know. But what is equally as strange as my demeanour—or perhaps expected, if I really thought about it—is what I said to break the silence.

'Do you have a zoo in this city? I feel like going to the zoo.'

She puffed the cigar and looked at me like I'd just asked her if she'd ever thought about trying to find the end of a rainbow, or if she ever talked to god about heaven and how to get in, or if she believed in the possibility of true and everlasting love.

'The zoo.'

I nodded.

'I *will* miss you, Vector Sorn.'

'You know you don't have to miss me at all. We could—'

'We could what?' She laughed but not condescendingly. 'Get married? Have kids? Settle into the normal adult life?'

Her eyes were bright and open, not narrow and judgemental.

I wanted to say, *Yeah, why not? What's wrong with normal?* but instead I opened my arms. She set the cigar between her teeth and lowered herself backwards into the wicker chair with me. I wrapped my arms around her and kissed her neck. She tilted her head to make it easier for me and puffed the cigar.

I held her tightly (as though for comfort, as though for warmth—as though in fear, as though forever) and she let me.

We spoke without looking at each other, the back of her head on my chest.

I began. 'We don't have to do normal.'

'What would we do?'

'I don't know. This. What's wrong with this?'

'This is part of a show. Without the show this is not this.'

'It's not always a show. We're not on camera right now.'

'No. But we were. And we will be. This is just an interlude.'

'I can live with that.'

'With what?'

'What comes between—in fact it's the perfect way to live.'

'In interlude.'

'In perpetual anticipation. What could be better?'

'On infinite pause. What could be worse?'

'To be in endless *medias res*—to never see the end. I'd take that.'

'The middle of things are only the middle of things when they have a beginning and an end, Vector.'

'Okay, but you can stop. You can choose to stop right in the middle. So why don't we do that. Why don't we stop right now. Right here.'

'Because that would just be a different end. Stopping is the same as ending.'

'You know, you could just agree with me. You could just nod and say, "Yes, Vector, that would be nice.'

She nodded. 'Yes, Vector. That would be nice."'

She smoked her cigar and we said nothing for a while until she broke the silence. 'But imagine sex without orgasm. Imagine a race that never ended. They would cease to be the things they are.'

I nodded. 'So if *this*, what we're doing here, doesn't end then it will just cease to be.'

'Exactly.'

She filled her mouth with smoke, held it, made an O of her lips, and blew the smoke out in a stream. Pushing herself from the chair, she padded over to the rail and, going on her toes, stretched her arms as high as she could over her head. The bottom of the shirt she had on—'Life Goes On' written across the back—lifted as she stretched, like she knew it would.

She turned, threw the cigar down, gripped the rail behind her, and grinned. 'Okay. Let's go. We'll sneak in somewhere and fuck among the animals.'

'You're joking.'

She shook her head and I could see the excitement pulse in her eyes.

Turning away, she crossed her arms and looked over the rail, over Gastown, toward the harbour, where the silent ships moved like toys, where the sun came up every day and made the water shimmer, perilously beautiful. Like Eden itself.

Silver Light

Victor:
Original Sin (Episode 10)

EXT. GREATER VANCOUVER ZOO. LATE AFTER-
NOON.

VICTOR and THE DIRECTOR hold hands as they approach
the ticket booth. They both look happy. By all accounts, a couple in love.

The DIRECTOR carries a small professional-grade video
camera. As VICTOR purchases their tickets, the DIRECTOR
fiddles with the camera's settings.

                    VICTOR
          Two please.

                    TICKET VENDOR
          Just so you know we close in an hour.

VICTOR looks at the DIRECTOR who is busy with her camera. He nods at the ticket window.

                    VICTOR
          That'll do.

INT. VICTOR's MIND. THREE YEARS LATER.

The DIRECTOR is no longer the DIRECTOR. She is
Valerie Argent Sorn. Val Sorn when she extends her hand to

the literati, the press, all the members of the publishing house at the exclusive book-release party for Vector (no longer Victor) Sorn's much-talked-about debut novel *As the Current Pulls the Fallen Under*. She is wearing a silver, backless, ankle-length dress and Cinderella sandals. Each of her tattoos, save the one on her lower back, is visible. The male faction, as she walks by, smiles knowingly and counts Vector Sorn among the luckiest of all men. The ladies whisper and count Valerie Argent among the luckiest of all women. Together they are the couple every other couple and every non-couple wants to be. In his reverie VICTOR is reminded of the way strangers used to look at Max and Rayn.

The night goes on. Drinks and more drinks and smart conversation. At one point the publisher taps a mic and recites a meritorious speech about her latest literary discovery—Vector Sorn—whom she calls to the lectern, amidst the applause, where he opens a copy of the novel and begins to read a selection.

After, there are duties—hands to shake, pictures to pose for, interviewer's questions to answer—but during it all the only thing Vector can really think about is getting Valerie back to the hotel room where the two of them can fall into role and bring to life a scene from Vector's fiction.

EXT. GREATER VANCOUVER ZOO. LATE AFTER-NOON.

VICTOR and the DIRECTOR are outside the cougar exhibit. The animal notices them and—unafraid, perhaps sensing the possibility of food, curious at the very least—moves towards the bars that cage him.

VICTOR watches the muscular pacing—the patience, the unblinking eyes fixed upon him—as the animal moves back and forth, the low rumble in its throat, all a declaration of doom were it not for the bars between them.

Or, VICTOR imagines, maybe it's an expression of envy. A plea. He hears the cougar's anthropomorphic voice in his head: *You don't know what it's like—to be caged—to have nowhere to run—could you imagine nowhere to run?—look at me—the atrophy—skin hangs where muscle used to be—I'm not meant to be weak—evolution made me one of the strong ones—but this cage, this cage has sapped all my strength for the sake of display—I don't know how much longer I can go on—set me free—pick the lock—unlatch the cage door—there's no one here—no one will see—no one will ever know it was you—I'll make no noise—I'll head straight for the bush—I'll bother no one—please—make good on the moments you wish you had back—reach out a hand—don't step away—you can save me—that's something, isn't it?—save me—set me free.*

VICTOR takes a step back.

As though in an expression of disappointment, the cougar releases his gaze and pads away.

                         DIRECTOR
                         (offscreen)
                    Victor. I'm waiting.

VICTOR lifts his head and turns. Like an animal. He follows the whisper—coming at him on the air like a hushed god—dreamy, ethereal, careful, quiet, teasing, dangerous.

He finds the DIRECTOR tucked away in a manmade faux-rock nook meant to look rocky and natural in its terracotta hardness. But there is nothing natural about it. Epigonic at best. Glaringly false in all its efforts to be real.

The DIRECTOR is half-leaning, half-sitting on an edge, her back against the contoured pane of glass set into the fake rock meant for clandestine cougar-gazing, her belt undone, the button of her jeans open, the zipper halfway down.

She sees him and slowly undoes her zipper the rest of the way, slips a hand behind the veil of silver silk. VICTOR glances over his shoulder. They are alone. He looks at the DIRECTOR and watches the prelude. On her whispered command he moves in, kneels as though in prayer. The back of her head pressed against the glass, she closes her eyes. The red eye of the camera she set up in the opposite corner above them blinks. She pulls him up and with the smell of wild earth around them, the pornographic smack of skin on skin and their own breathing are the only sounds in the air. They come together and as he descends—his breathing heavy and slowing, his mouth loose against her neck—VICTOR opens his eyes to see the cougar stretched out in voyeuristic respite only inches away, separated by nothing but the pane of glass between them. Their eyes lock. There is no sense at all of impending doom. There is no appeal in the animal's surveillance. No judgement. No entreaty in its stillness. And VICTOR finds himself contemplating the notions of freedom and of loss. The two things, he figures, in a moment of post-coital clarity, that we, the ones who cage for the sake of preservation, are most afraid of.

INT. #305 36 WATER STREET, TERMINUS BUILDING: VANCOUVER, BC. EVENING.

The door opens and in walks the DIRECTOR whose face (as always in Silver Light) we never see, followed by VICTOR. The DIRECTOR dumps her keys on the table and VICTOR runs a finger along the tabletop as he walks by. To anyone watching, they look like a married couple coming home, a couple who is either just coming out of an argument or comfortable being together in silence. Or both.

VICTOR sighs, falls into his spot on the couch in the living room, and puts his feet up. He takes up a magazine and begins flipping the pages with no apparent purpose. We sense the DIRECTOR entering. As always during the story segment she is

off-screen. She hands VICTOR a glass and they clink an unspoken toast.

Music plays in the background. Ron Sexsmith. The DIRECTOR
has always been a fan. She likes the name. Sexsmith. Like an occupation. Like, in part, what she considers herself to be.

VICTOR looks at the DIRECTOR, at the camera.

                          VICTOR
          This is it then.

The DIRECTOR stands from her chair and comes into full view
for the first time in the history of Silver Light. She sits beside
VICTOR, removes her thick-rimmed glasses, and nods. She is a
woman who never cries but the feeling is that she might now.
There is something in her face that suggests an uncharacteristic
but honest sadness. She is as beautiful as her audience had always
suspected.

VICTOR sighs again and reaches for the backpack he carries
with him always. He pulls out the journal: not his own, from
which he sometimes reads, but Rayn's. The audience will recognize the journal as hers. It is a leatherbound volume. An image
the DIRECTOR has featured in previous episodes. She has done
her filmic best to create dramatic anticipation with respect to
what VICTOR may reveal when he reads from Rayn's journal
for the very first time in his life.

VICTOR turns the journal in his hands, touching it like a
recently unearthed artefact: an ancient tome that may well hold
all the answers. Or none.

The DIRECTOR watches him.

                          DIRECTOR
          Are you ready?

VICTOR nods, opens the journal, and begins reading.

>   VICTOR
> June 21. Paddle the Heron was yester-
> day. Went solo for the first time. God
> was I fast. Even beat dad. In the boat
> he and mom bought me for my four-
> teenth birthday. I've never really
> known sadness so it's difficult for me to
> compare, but I can't imagine ever feel-
> ing happier than I do now.

VICTOR nods, shakes his head. Like the DIRECTOR he is someone who never cries but there is the sense that in these moments to come he might.

>   VICTOR
> I don't know. I don't know if I can do
> this. I don't know if I should.

>   DIRECTOR
> She would want you to.

From anyone else, such a presumptuous claim would incense VICTOR. *Who the fuck are you to say she would want me to?* But instead he believes the DIRECTOR. Like she has some access to truth and understanding otherwise reserved for an unfathomable futuristic replacement species whose omniscience is far greater than any god's.

VICTOR nods and flips to a page he seems to recognize.

>   VICTOR
> July 11. Met the man I will see the end
> of my days with. A cop of all things. I
> always thought I'd wind up with a
> painter or a musician. Opening nights.

> Fancy parties. A house with a studio.
> Sex between sessions. Suppose I'll have
> to settle for sex between shifts.
> Hah. Imagine he reads this one day.
> Hey there, my boy in blue (I like that:
> my boy in blue)—in case you ever do
> read this and because I know I'll never
> tell you (it's a glitch I hope you'll for-
> give): I knew as soon as I saw you. Is
> that crazy?

VICTOR closes the journal, uses a thumb for a bookmark.

VICTOR

> How about a drink?

The DIRECTOR stands and leaves, returns with two highballs
filled with two fingers of Lagavulin each. They raise the glasses
without clinking them. The DIRECTOR takes a sip. VICTOR
takes a gulp.

He opens the journal and flips ahead a couple of years to another
date in the story he recognizes.

VICTOR

> August 1. Happiest day of my life.
> Happiest is not the word. I feel joy.
> Unadulterated biblical joy. I've cer-
> tainly never felt like I needed one, but
> if ever I find myself in need of a sav—

VICTOR stops and looks at the ceiling. He looks at the page and
begins again.

VICTOR

> — but if ever I find myself in need of
> a saviour you will be the one. This

> little bundle of bliss. Stephen Vector
> Sorn.

VICTOR shakes his head. The DIRECTOR puts a hand on his shoulder. He continues to read.

> ### VICTOR
> August 2. You're one day old and already I can't remember life without you.
> August 3. I've decided to make my journal a letter to you. I will write in it every day. Even if it's just a single word.

VICTOR flips through the rest of the journal. At a cursory glance he concludes that there is indeed an entry for every day until there is not. Most entries are only the date and a few words, but there is not one day she missed.

VICTOR reads a few entries at random.

(In the edited down version of the show, VICTOR's reading comes to the audience in voice-over. The DIRECTOR splices in sepia-filtered images of a surrogate Rayn and her newborn. As Victor reads, the images—both still and moving—match what he says. For all intents and purposes the images onscreen augment the truth of what he reads.)

> ### VICTOR
> November 28. Snow. Your first. There will be so many firsts.
> February 10. 103 fever. Held you all night. The most frightened I've ever been.
> May 4. First step. Watch out world. Here he comes.

May 18. "Momma." I swear you said it.
July 3. Asleep with dad. My beautiful
boys in blue.
August 1. One year. Like that.
Everything seems to be happening so
fast.

He flips ahead in the journal.

(A grainy video of a mother and a young boy walking hand-in-hand on screen. They come to a school. She leans down, kisses the top of his head. He looks up, smiles, and waves as he turns and walks away.)

                    VICTOR
September 3. First day of school. You
didn't cry. You didn't even look back.
I was so proud. I was. And I shouldn't
say this—forgive me for saying this—
but it broke my heart. I wanted you to
cry. I wanted you to look back. I
wanted you to turn and reach for me.
But you didn't. You didn't reach for
me. And from that moment I knew no
matter what happened you'd be okay.

(A picture of a seven-year-old boy crossing a finish line, a Terry Fox t-shirt on. The street-lined crowd, cheering. The boy's mother on her knees just beyond the finish, arms out, tears in her eyes, ready to hold him, ready to catch him should he fall, ready to clutch him to her chest and never let go.)

                    VICTOR
September 18. Your first Terry Fox
Run. You insisted on running the
whole thing. Alone. Like mother like
son.

(Snow at night through a living room window. A boy with neatly combed hair in pajamas standing in front of a Christmas tree, presents all around. The father with a hand on the boy's shoulder. For some reason the boy looks sad.)

VICTOR

December 24. Why does he bring me so much and some kids nothing at all? I don't deserve it. This is what you said. Nine years old. I told you that you *did*, you *did* deserve it but I had no answer when you asked me why.

December 25. You hung your head when you came downstairs. You used to get so excited. The weight of the world already on you. I wish there was some way I could bear it for you longer. There's a girl in my class, you told us. I want her to have what I have. Is that okay? Your father and I looked at each other and sort of laughed. What's so funny? you said and I shook my head. Nothing. There's nothing funny at all. I held you for a while and you said, Come on, let's go. She said it's always the worst on Christmas morning. We have to hurry. So we took some of the presents to the girl's house but when we went to the door we heard screaming inside and the smacking sounds of someone being hit. You hung your head again and I hurried you back to the car. Your father intervened. He took the man down and then took him in. He's good at what he does. It was the best present anyone could have given that little girl

and her mother. When it was all over
you looked at me and said, There's no
point in pretending, you know. All it
does is hurt people.

VICTOR closes the journal again on his thumb and rattles the
ice in his empty glass. The DIRECTOR leaves and returns with
the bottle. She tops him up.

He takes a drink, opens the journal, flips ahead, and continues
reading.

(A montage of sepia-filtered images again mirrors what he
reads.)

                    VICTOR
February 14. I watched from the window. You walked across the street
with a rose and a poem I knew you
wrote but never showed me. She
kissed your cheek when you gave her
the rose and the poem. I wanted to
open the window and scream out, Kiss
her back, Vector. Kiss her back. You
turned and came home and never said
a word. Must be love.
June 8. I wanted to come watch but I
could tell you wanted to do it on your
own. When you came home I asked
you how it went and you shrugged and
said, Okay. It went okay. Your teacher
phoned that night and said she didn't
have much experience with such
things but she was pretty sure you were
put on this earth to run. When I told
you what she said, this is what you
said: That's silly, mom. No one is put

on this earth for anything. And if they
were it wouldn't be to run.

The DIRECTOR smiles.

                    DIRECTOR
          Wise beyond your years.

VICTOR closes the journal on his thumb, looks at her.

                    VICTOR
          Cynical beyond my years.

She points the remote at the hidden camera and makes the gun
sound. *Pshew.*

                    DIRECTOR
          I think we have enough.

VICTOR nods.

                    DIRECTOR
          Is it what you thought it would be?

                    VICTOR
          For the most part.

                    DIRECTOR
          It was touching. It revealed things about
          you as a character. There were some
          really good lines. But I thought you
          might uncover something you didn't
          know. Some big secret. To be honest a
          big secret is what I was hoping for.

                    VICTOR
          Sorry to disappoint.

                    DIRECTOR
          Well. A story can't be everything. It
          still works though. I'm glad we waited.
          It'll be a great final show.

VICTOR takes a drink.

                    VICTOR
          I have a secret. Actually, it's not so
          much a secret as it is a lie.

The DIRECTOR folds her arms and waits.

                    VICTOR
          It's about Max. I should tell you. He
          didn't kill Rayn.

The DIRECTOR squints.

                    VICTOR
          He killed a surrogate for the man
          who killed her. And then he killed
          himself.

                    DIRECTOR
          Why are you telling me this now?

                    VICTOR
          I don't know.

                    DIRECTOR
          Yes, you do. You're playing your final
          hand.

                    VICTOR
          Maybe.

DIRECTOR

Okay. When I start the camera, say this: *I hate to have to tell you this. But I lied. I lied about Max. He didn't kill Rayn.* Then go on to tell the story. By the way—nice hand.

VICTOR nods.

She points the remote control at the hidden camera. *Pshew.*

VICTOR

I hate to have to tell you this. But I lied. I lied about Max. He didn't kill Rayn.

(All the trust snuffed out in an instant. If he could lie about something so integral to the story, what else wasn't true?

But the data from Ghost says everyone kept watching. Not one single viewer signed out. There had been a breech of trust but the breech didn't matter as much as the fact that the story had changed and they needed to know why.)

VICTOR

I'm sorry I lied, but I can explain.

He looks away from the camera, then back.

VICTOR

When I was fourteen I was the happiest kid alive. I hadn't known loss. Max and Rayn were the perfect parents and I had the perfect life. But the day I won Nationals for the first time my perfect life changed forever.

(The DIRECTOR slips in a montage of images from past episodes that visually remind the members of that fateful day.)

VICTOR

Baron, my coach at the time, was over
the moon.

(Baron has been highlighted in previous episodes. The audience knows VICTOR doesn't like him—and so they don't like him.)

VICTOR

He'd been training me for a year. He'd
predicted my success on the track.
Guaranteed it in fact. I was young. I
bought in. I listened to him and did
everything he said. But as I lay there at
the finish line that day I watched him
standing over me. Like I was his. Like
he created me—

VICTOR glances at the DIRECTOR who is still sitting beside him. Then back at the camera.

VICTOR

—and I didn't like it. 'This is just the
beginning,' he said. 'You wait. You'll
see.' Like he knew. Like knowing and
being right about what was to come
was more important than what was to
come itself.
I was conflicted. I was thankful for
what he'd done but I didn't want to be
his puppet. I didn't say anything. How
could I? He'd done so much for me.
I should have though. I should have
said something. In hindsight I'd always
known something was off about him.

Rayn never told me how she felt—she wouldn't have wanted to influence me that way—but I knew. The way you know things about the people you're closest to without ever having to hear them say it.

So it's my fault. If Baron hadn't been there that day at Nationals he wouldn't have delayed us. We would've missed Michael Norman Boon. Life would've carried on. Rayn would still be here. And Baron was there because of me. So she died because of me.

He holds the journal up to the camera.

VICTOR

There's something in here I'm afraid to read. If it says what I think it says it'll confirm something I don't want confirmed.

DIRECTOR
(offscreen)

Tell us, Victor. Tell us.

VICTOR

The day before I left Heron River to come out west Baron says to me, *Did your mother ever tell you about me?*

It sickened me. In an instant I knew what he meant and now he wanted to rewrite the story. He wanted to paint the two of them as teenagers in love who might have had a real shot had they met later in life, had the circumstances been more in their favour.

I knew the truth would be written
somewhere in her journal. I couldn't
bear the thought of it, let alone the
thought of reading it in her hand.

But now that it's part of a story. Now
that it's not really her. Now that she's
become a character. Now that it matters not just to me.

VICTOR shows the camera Rayn's journal, flips through the
first part of it until the name Charlie Baron stops him.

(Again, the DIRECTOR finds images to accompany what VIC-
TOR reads.)

VICTOR

March 3. Charlie Baron. Charlie
Baron. Charlie Baron.

March 5. CB & RD. Always and forever.

March 8. C Bear. Chuckie B. Chas.
Oh, Charlie. By any other name
you're just as sweet.

March 10. Went to see Breakfast Club.
Held hands the whole time. He walked
me home and kissed me in the drive-
way. Whispered he loved me. Like John
Hughes was there himself directing.

March 31. Way too much to drink last
night. First time ever. Head kills.
Stomach still churning. Charlie took
care of me though. Said not to worry,
he was there. Said he'd *always* be there.
So sweet. *So* sweet. Even held my hair
when I puked in the ditch. So embarrassed right now. *So* embarrassed. If he
calls I'm not home. I'm not home.

April 1. What a jerk. Phones and says he doesn't think he can be with someone who doesn't know how to hold her booze. Says he can't get the image of me puking on his shoes out of his head. Said even love has its limits and lets me cry for a full minute before saying, Hey, got ya. April Fools. I hung up on him. Slammed the phone down. What a jerk. What an asshole. I'll never forgive him. Never.

April 2. He stood outside my window like John Cusack and held a ghetto blaster over his head. Turns out never's not even a day.

May 22. Paddled to a spot on the river away from all the houses. Took a blanket. A mixed tape I'd made. A six-pack. Made out for what seemed like hours. Like we always did. Then it got a little heavier. All our clothes came off. We were close. I took it in my hand— first time ever—and then he was done. I had no idea that would happen. He kept saying he was sorry. I kept telling him it was okay. I cleaned up and we paddled home without saying a word.

May 25. I can't believe I haven't heard from him. When I call, his mom answers and I can hear her put her hand over the phone. It's muffled but I can hear her talking to him. She sighs and tells me he's not home. I can tell she's upset by it. By the lying. By us. She likes me. She's told me more than once. I don't get it. I don't know what I did.

May 31. Today was the last day. I'm not calling again. Screw him. I didn't do anything.

June 4. He came over and stood outside my window again with the ghetto blaster over his head. I don't know why but I felt sick. When I went out to see him I crossed my arms and stood away from him like there was a wall between us. I asked him why he hadn't called, why he pretended he wasn't there when *I* called. He said he'd been busy. I nodded. I asked him what I did and he said I hadn't done anything. It was him. It was all him. He said he was embarrassed about what had happened. Said he wanted it to be perfect and then he ruined it. I said, I told you it was okay. I wouldn't lie. Why didn't you believe me? I told him he should have just talked to me. He started to cry and I felt sick again. He told me he was sorry. Over and over again. It was awful. I told him it was fine but I didn't move. Something had changed. I didn't know what but it wasn't the same. He stepped toward me and told me he loved me. He kissed me and I let him. But it wasn't the same. Not even close. Ugh. It was awful. Everything about love is awful. I'm never falling in it again.

June 5. School's almost done. I can't believe it. I'm a little nervous about leaving, to be honest. I've never really been anywhere but Heron River. I'm excited though. Laurentian. Capital of the north. Actually, I can't wait. It's going to be so much fun. Charlie's going to U of T for track. Which is where I was going to go but Sudbury's the better choice for me. Especially all things considered. I hope he doesn't get weird when I break it off. He has to see it coming. I've decided to do it after prom. Before the summer. Make a clean break of it. He'll be fine. Girls will love him. I did.

June 8. Charlie won Provincials. Which is a big deal. When he came back he said he dedicated the race to me. Corny but kinda cute. We had a great night. Almost like it was in the beginning. I bet he makes the Olympics one day. He's so determined. That's what I love(d) about him. I don't know. It's funny how feelings change. I don't get it. I doubt I ever will. Does anyone? I guess that's why they're called feelings and not knowings.

June 14. Haven't seen him at all outside of school since the night he got back. It's like he's avoiding me. Like he knows what's coming and thinks he can control it not coming.

June 16. Last day of classes. Prom tomorrow night. He left me a note in my locker. 'Pick you up at six.' The 'i' in 'six' looked an awful lot like an 'e' with a dot over it. Three months ago it would've been cute. I'd have smiled. I'd have blushed. I'd have felt the flutter in my stomach. But not now. I felt sick. Tomorrow's going to be awful. Awful.

June 20. It's been three days and I can't get any of it out of my head. The night was going alright—it was tolerable at least, considering—until we got to the after party where he drank like an animal. I should've left. I could've gotten a ride from someone. But I felt bad. Can you believe that? *I* felt bad. Anyway, we had a tent. Everyone had a tent. Things were assumed. Things were expected. It all seems so unreal when I think about it which I'm trying not to do. Like a scene from a movie or something. It keeps playing over and over and over in my head. God, will I ever not see it? Will I ever not feel it? I've had like twenty showers and I can't get the feeling of him off me. He didn't say a word the whole time. All I can hear is him breathing. It was awful. Awful. He kissed me afterwards and I let him. He touched my face and said he loved me. Maybe it was me. I was drinking too. Not like him, but still. Maybe he got the wrong idea. He must have thought I wanted to. He wouldn't have done it otherwise. Would he? Anyway, I wish I could erase it. There's got to be something you can take to erase it. I know this: I will never ever ever tell another living soul.

VICTOR closes the journal and looks at the floor between his feet, then straight into the camera.

VICTOR
I will kill him.

Suns Go Down

If only I'd been more in tune with her reaction when I came home that first day of high school and told her about the teacher who'd approached me and what he said.

'*Sorn.*'

I turned. He was jogging after me down the hall.

I waited. He caught up.

'*Sorn.*' *He pointed and feigned revelation.* '*Hey, you're the kid whose dad was a big-time swimmer, right? Won two silver medals at the Olympics.*'

I nodded.

He put his hands on his hips and shook his head, beaming. '*Wow. That's impressive. I'd love to meet him some time and shake his hand.*'

I didn't say anything. I was uncomfortable. I looked over a shoulder. I didn't know where to look.

He pointed again, like he was just remembering something. '*Listen. I heard you can run.*'

I shrugged.

'*Not much of a talker, though, eh?*'

He shadow-boxed my midsection and laughed. '*Hey, that's okay. Reticence can be an admirable quality.*'

I could tell he was impressed with what he'd said. Though I'm sure he didn't get the irony.

There was a pause.

'*So. High school treating you alright so far?*'

I half-shrugged, half-nodded.

'*That's good. That's good.*'

The bell rang. I looked up at the clock.

'*Listen, kid. Before you go, I just wanted to tell you. I know a lot about running. I mean a lot a lot. You let me coach you and we could go a long way together. A long long way.*'

I scratched the back of my head, shrugged again, and nodded.

'Great.' He clapped my shoulders twice with both hands and let out a laugh. 'Great. Hey, I can hardly wait. Listen, cross-country starts tomorrow after school. We'll see you then. This is going to be a good fit, kid. A really good fit. I can feel it.'

Jogging away from me he spun around, pointed as though he were just remembering something again, and told me to tell my mom that Charlie Baron says hi. Without missing a beat he spun back around and continued on.

That was my first encounter with him, body language and dialogue pretty well verbatim. But I'm sure I only told Rayn the gist of what he said. I know I didn't relay the last bit.

This is what she said after I told her. *'I don't really know him (sigh), but I've heard he's a really good coach. He was a great runner himself and he knows what he's doing. You have a gift, Vector. It would be a waste not to develop it. I think you should go out for the team. Give it a try. See how it goes.'*

If only I'd paid more attention to what she didn't say.

CLIPPINGS (23)

(taken from "The Quest Begins," runnerspace.com)

'We've been following the Vector Sorn story for six years now, and *following* is indeed the operative word. He is the quiet, unassuming leader and we here at runnerspace.com are his dutiful disciples. He is the son and the father and the purest of spirits and we march in line behind him. He has told us without telling us what it means to be a runner and we have listened with rapt attention. He has written the book without writing a word and we were the first in line to buy a copy.

He runs without a coach and so more of us than ever toe the line unaccompanied by the backpack-wearing, arms-crossed, splits-calling father figure.

We run alone together.

He is Prefontaine without Bowerman. Bannister doing untimed solo quarters on the Oxford grass. He is Morceli on a hot Moroccan night holding 55s for fun. He is Zatopek. Gebrsalassie. Seb Coe unhinged.

He runs alone and so do we. Unfettered and undaunted. The loneliness of the long distance runner incarnate and we hold onto that loneliness like it's a life-line. We know it now. We know what it means and we're better for it. Tougher. Harder. Impervious to hurt. Unyielding. At one with the pain. Addicted to it. For better or worse. Filled with the rush of it. Driven by the push. Fueled by the synergy.

And now the great stage: the heats are set for August
7th, 8:15 EST. The whole country will be watching.
Indeed, the whole world. Go, Vec, go!

So the quest begins.'

~

There has been no mention in any of the media leading up to The
Olympics of Silver Light. I was expecting there to be. I was expecting
someone to stick a mic in my face and say something like, 'Hey, I know
you. You're that guy from that show. The one with the blonde with that
tattoo across her back. What did it say? Anyway, she was unbelievable.
I wasn't much for all those stories about your life. But the sex scenes were
unreal, dude. Un. Real.'

When I thought about it, though, I knew only a man would ever
say anything like this and the audience had been ninety-eight percent
women (Ghostdata). A woman would never talk like that. A woman
would likely never say anything to me about the show at all now that it
was finished. She might look at me in a way that said she knew who I
was and whisper recognition to her friends. But she would never be overt
about it. The odd fan might call out my name. It's happened a few times.
But except for the one time at Hayward Field it's always been from a car
whizzing by or from a highrise window as I run by on the street below.
I wave and that's that. Save for the two in Oregon nothing's ever come
of it. I've been asked for autographs, but I always assume (however pur-
posely naïve it might be)—even when they go on their toes to kiss me on
the cheek—that they're track fans. The point is, I'm as certain as any
man can be of anyone else's future behaviour that no one will ever ask
me about Silver Light in any formal setting. I'm certain. (Oprah might,
if that moment ever comes, but I doubt she was a member.)

I'm sure a few men were able to slip past Ghost's screening process
(like me) and there would have been a few women who let their boyfriends
or husbands watch (more likely their gay friends). But not many. After
every episode there was a survey every member had to complete in order
to gain access to the code, the url, and the airtime for the next show. All
the data from the questions pertaining to viewing patterns revealed that
more than eighty percent of the members watched Silver Light alone. The

community aspect of the show—the place where members could talk—
was in the online chathouse that had multiple rooms dedicated to particular episodes, certain physical and emotional features of the characters,
biorooms dedicated to the life details revealed during the story segments,
fantasyrooms where members dreamt up hypothetical futures with Victor,
fanfiction rooms where members wrote their own episodes. And on and
on. Every room was always full. But the viewing itself, according to
Ghostdata, was more than eighty percent private.

Karl Knotold's revolutionary Ghostware ensured that not one single
bit of data—not one byte—survived beyond the airing of any of the
episodes. There wasn't a single image out there of Victor and Valerie in
Silver Light. Not one line of text. Not a single soundbite. Not a speck
of binary code. There were no hard copy images either. Someone might
have written down sections of dialogue from memory or while she
watched, but it was doubtful. And even if she did, there would be no evidence that what she wrote was said by anyone real. To any non-member
the dialogue would be nothing more than fiction.

The pilot program had worked. Silver Light had been the perfect
platform to test it. Ghost was glitchless and Karl Knotold was on the cusp
of becoming a software tycoon. A billionaire. A global communications
revolutionary. By now every laptop, desktop, tiptop and bottom . . .
every notebook, weebook, bigbook, and skybook . . . every iPhone,
uPhone, yPhone, and tell-a-phone . . . every android, automaton, homo
ex machina, and artificial-intel . . . every microchip, macrochip, subcuta-
neous chip, and bigbrother chip on the planet and beyond will have—
indeed has—Ghost stock-installed.

THE OLYMPIC STADIUM

I'd run in front of large crowds before but nothing like this. It was otherwise, gladiatorial, the roar of the world rolling like a boulder down a hill. Ceaseless, combative soundwaves crashing head-on within the concavity of the Olympic Stadium. Noise you could see. The mash of a million tongues. Not one single recognizable syllable. The din of language beginning. Sucked back into the tower. Babylon recalled.

The temperature inside the stadium was three full degrees higher than the streets beyond: the bodies alone, the excitement they were charged with, the measurable energy they emitted.

The smell of the track—something like home to me now—made me sick and calm all at once. It felt like someone was punching me in the stomach, but not too hard, and I didn't want him to stop: a sensation that keeps me feeling, keeps me grounded, keeps me there.

I'd raced the European circuit for the two years leading up to the Games and so I recognized most of the men on the line but there were a few I'd never seen. They were the dangerous ones, the potential heroes, the unaccounted for.

I was fairly certain it would take nothing more than something in the high 3:30s to advance to the next round. I wasn't worried. I had the fastest seed time in the heat. A new national mark I'd set a month before in a Diamond League race in Oslo. If we went out slow I might even get away with something north of 3:40.

Here's how it unfolded.

The opening lap was, as the pundits of distance like to intone, pedestrian. The leader trotted through in 68. I was tucked in the back and heard 70. I smiled. To put it in perspective, a 70 would be the opening lap in the marathon and their pace for the whole thing wouldn't be much slower. We hit eight hundred in 2:08. First to last was separated by less than a second. Everyone there could hold this kind of pace for twice the distance. Easily.

With six hundred to go I pulled up to the front of the pack. I felt the knees beginning to drive, the heels cycling through. By the time we hit the line and heard the bell there were seven of us who had gapped the rest of the field. Six would make it through to the next round automatically.

The clock read 2:50.

I pushed a button and felt a solstitial calm come over me, a feeling I had put as much time and effort into as the physical work on the track. To the point where I could beckon the feeling without effort. I summoned an image of Val and I in half-sleep in the hemlock-strung hammock down by the water on our ten-acre Vancouver island oasis (the end she had always talked about for us had not yet come). The exact opposite in energy-output that I was about to kick into.

With the next stride I pulled away from the lead pack and continued pulling away for the final four hundred metres. Which I covered in fifty seconds flat.

I touched the line in 3:40 and let myself slow down for fifty metres before I stopped and bounced on the spot. By the time I trotted back to the line the rest of the field had finished and I felt recovered. They cleared us off to the side where I stood with my hands on my hips and answered the interviewers' questions.

Here's how one of the interviews went:

'I'm here with Vector Sorn after winning the first heat of the fifteen hundred.'

Which, syntactically, sounded like *he* had just won the first heat of the fifteen hundred.

'Vector, how do you feel?'

I smiled. 'I feel good, Jim.'

I didn't know him, but he looked like a Jim and he didn't correct me when I said it.

'You really left it close out there.'

I hadn't left it close at all.

'In fact you were trailing for the majority of the race. Is that your usual course of action?'

I'm sure the pun was unintentional.

'Tactics are always at play in the 1500, Jim. It's part of what I love about it.'

'In what way?'

I wanted to say, *In what way* what?

'You see, Jim, in the first round all you need to do to move on is finish within the top six. It's important to conserve as much energy as you can through the rounds.'

Energy conservation between heats at this level is a bit of a myth, especially with the amount of time they give you to recover. It's true the body has only so many truly maximal efforts within it, but after jogging two laps and racing not quite two I'd be fully recovered in two or three hours. It had been far from a maximal effort. Not to brag, but if I had to I could do it all again after a bite to eat and a solid two-hour nap.

What is true is the amount of mental conservation that comes with being able to 'save yourself' for future rounds. There is no doubting the influence of the mind when it comes to the output of physical effort.

'I have to ask you then, why did you finish the last lap so fast? Insurance?'

'There's no such thing as insurance in track, Jim. If you run out, you run out.'

'But if you don't win a medal in the final will it be because you spent too much in the opening round?'

Medals. It's all they care about.

'If I don't win a medal, Jim, it'll be because I wasn't among the best three on the day that it counted.'

He put the fingers of his free hand over the ear that had a chord running from it. He nodded. 'What I'm getting here, Vector, what's just coming through, is that your last lap was the fastest last lap of any fifteen hundred metre race in recorded history. How do you feel about that?'

He put the microphone under my chin.

Hands on my hips I looked straight into the camera. 'I feel good, Jim. I feel good.'

That night I was on the CBC. I was told to wear my Canada gear and say positive things about the Canadian Olympic Committee. My slot was scheduled for eight and a half minutes. The first five would be the bio-bit produced back in June titled Vector Velocity. There were shots of me working out on the track and in the weight room, relaxing at home with Val, looking studious in class at Quest, lucubratory in the library at night, ruminating on trails through the woods at dawn. Bookending the segment were images of me as a fourteen-year-old winning my first national title. The series—whose purpose was meant to highlight Canadian medal hopefuls—was called Canadian Mettle. Very CBC.

Here's how the post bio-bit interview went.

We were in plush, rich-looking leather armchairs. There was an antique coffee table between us on which sat two mugs. There were bookshelves in the background. Besides the four framed pictures of me winning various races, there were volumes of philosophy, Canlit standards, the OED, a Latin grammar, and collections of essays by writers like Richler and Hitchens. There was even a copy of Karl Knotold's *Spectre*. Someone had done their research. I was meant to feel at home. All for three and a half minutes. (More, I suppose, if I happened to become a story worth continuing.)

The interviewer was a man in his late forties. He was tall, fit, and had dark but greying hair. He looked like a former Olympian who the CBC called upon every now and then to do special athlete-to-athlete interviews such as this one. We shook hands and sat in our respective armchairs. On-set hands flitted about: adjusting our tiny clip-on microphones, filling our mugs, dabbing our foreheads. There was a lot of effort, it seemed, to get everything just so. Part of me wanted to say something like, *You know, in my experience all I ever did was show up and act like nothing out of the ordinary was happening. The director wouldn't even say action. When she was ready all she'd do is point this little silver remote at a hidden camera somewhere. Roll film. Pshew.*

I heard someone behind me count backwards from five.

'In five, four, three . . .'

The interviewer smiled, leaned forward, and began his scripted introduction. 'We're here this evening with Heron River native, Vector Sorn, who has in recent years taken the athletics world by storm. Son of two-time Olympic silver medallist Max Sorn and one-time C-1 great Rayn Down, athleticism pumps through this middle distance phenom's body like the oxygen-rich blood that sustains him through the self-developed, self-directed, rigorous regimen of a–hundred-sixty kilometres a week, a regimen which has landed him here on the cusp of Olympic greatness. With the fastest time in the world this season, Vector is seen by many of the most knowledgeable track pundits to be the clear favourite to win gold in the 1500 metre final three days from now. Vector joins us after having taken his opening round heat in history-making style and with ostensible ease.'

On cue he turned from Camera-1 and looked at me. 'Vector. It's a pleasure to have you here. Tell us. How do you feel?'

I sat back, made a tent of my fingers, rested the outside of my right ankle on my left knee, and nodded. 'I feel good, Michael.'

His name came to me as I spoke it.

Michael Miller. He was indeed a former Olympian. He'd competed with Max in Seoul and Barcelona. They were the opening and anchor legs of the medley relay team. I remembered the pictures.

'Well, Vector. Looks like the stage is set.'

I made a show of scanning the bookshelves. 'It does, Michael. It does indeed.'

I smiled and leaned forward for my mug.

'I have to ask, Vector. That last lap today. Why did you run it like that? I mean I can see if it was close, but there was no one around. You could have sauntered in over the last fifty and still qualified. Why spend so much on nothing?'

'The thing is, Michael, I don't think of it as spending and I don't consider it nothing.'

'Fair enough. But still. Some are saying it was a rookie mistake. Adrenalin-charged inexperience. That it might have cost you an Olympic title. Others are calling it showboating. One British correspondent called it an unnecessary act of unprepossessing posturing. What do you say to such indictments?'

I tried to keep my tone light. 'I say since when is winning a mistake? Since when does six years of anything equate to inexperience. I say I'm far more interested in titles of books than titles of men. I say the last time I checked the OED a showboat was a theatre on water and, borrowing from Prefontaine, I don't think there's anything about a race that's a performance. I say negative-construction-reliant, purposefully alliterative, and verbosely condemnatory critics are themselves all three: unprepossessing, posturing, and unnecessary in the first degree.'

He paused for a moment and continued. 'You're a philosophy student—is that right?'

I reached forward for the coffee again, gave a playful wink and a grin. 'We're all philosophy students, aren't we, Michael?'

He smiled and folded his arms, then quickly unfolded them, remembering, I can only assume, that folded arms on an interviewer is bad form. 'I have to tell you, Vector, you do remind me a lot of your father. I hope you don't mind me saying so.'

I kept the grin and nodded.

'We were in Seoul and Barcelona together.'

'Yes,' I said. 'I remember seeing pictures.'

At this point, Michael and I were directed to pause. Someone on the research team had supplied the producers with a series of photographs: Max and Michael poolside with their arms about one another's shoulders, a goggled Max in the blocks, a twenty-year-old Rayn on one knee in her C-1, midstroke. The pictures were filing by onscreen now: a montage of stills with zoom-in, zoom-out, and left-to-right Ken Burnsian effects put on them. The band Whitehorse in the background doing a cool folksy version of Phillip Philips's smash hit Home. Meant, no doubt, to capture the inspirational sadness of a father and a mother lost too young. The last shot was of a fourteen-year-old me standing between Max and Rayn, all of us smiling, the medal from my first national championship victory hanging albatrossly around my neck.

The still scene faded out.

Michael took on a solemn tone. 'It must be difficult, Vector. To say the least.'

I lowered my head and paused. I was familiar with the cues.

When I looked up I touched the corner of my right eye with my right index finger. An idiosyncrasy, an itch, the blotting of a tear. Difficult for viewers to discern for certain, I knew, but effective. 'To say the least, Michael, is sometimes the only way to say the most.'

I noticed someone who looked like a director in the wings. Her arms were crossed. She was grinning.

Michael made a show of scrolling through the notes he had in his phone. 'I have so much more to ask you, Vector, but unfortunately we're out of time.'

'Ah, Michael, we're never really out of time. What would Billy Pilgrim say, we're only ever in different moments of it.'

Michael turned his head to one side without taking his eyes from me. 'You are indeed a character, Mr. Sorn.'

I smiled and folded my arms. Good form, I intuited, on an interviewee. 'So I've been told, Michael. So I've been told.'

'I look forward to continuing our chat after you're through the semis.'

Putting my hands out as if to slow traffic, I made a show of being humble and unhurried. 'Let's not get ahead of ourselves, Michael. If I've learned anything in my short life, it's not to rely on or put too much faith in unfounded, and too often confounded, certainties.'

Michael turned to Camera-1.

'Vector Sorn. The unprepossessing philosophizing phenom of the fifteen hundred. Let it be known that there's no acting here. He is a man on a mission and knows full well what he is doing and what he has yet to do.'

CLIPPINGS (24)

(taken from personal email)

Vector Sorn:
All the best (with words from some of the best):

No race begins at the start line. (Gebrselassie)
All that I am I am because of my mind. (Nurmi)
The training is my secret and I keep the secret in my heart. (Kipketer)
If a man coaches himself, then he has only himself to blame. (Bannister)
Somebody may beat me but they're going to have to bleed to do it. (Prefontaine)
I am animated by an interior force which covers my suffering. (Morceli)
With hope in his heart and dreams in his head. (Zatopek)
I don't find unhappiness if I lose. (Keino)
It is finally complete. (El Guerrouj)

In anticipation & with curiosity,
The Faculty at Quest

~

It's like they somehow knew. What had *happened and what* would *happen. They didn't, of course. I mean how could they? They were among the most intelligent people I'd ever meet but even intelligence has its limits.*

Strangely, though, their 'All the best' message (the irony) reads as though they did know everything and eerily so. Of course it's important to remember that what a message means (and I seem so often to be having to remind myself of such things) has everything to do with who reads it.

No one from Quest—except of course Tutor Karl who had since retired to a life of luxury funded by the windfall that accompanied the selling of Ghost—had said anything. He was now in the same (pardon this) company as Gates, Jobs, Zuckerberg, and all those on the list of unrecognizable magnates whose names and faces remain hidden from the public domain like Karl's himself.

The report (and by report I mean a direct report from him to us, to VA and I) was that he'd sold Ghost to Google for $4.2 billion. He took one of those billion and bought himself a fifty-acre island paradise off the coast of Morocco. (He's now at one with the canaries, he said.) He kept condos in Montreal, New York, Paris, London, and Rome. I hadn't known him to be so clichéd but now he could afford to be, so why not. He kept a place in Vancouver, too, but we hadn't seen him for over a year. We kept in fairly regular contact (messages, I hope it goes without saying, were always filtered through Ghost) and he'd been trying to get us to Innisfree (the name he'd given his little island) since he'd bought it. (I'll send the jet, he wrote. I have a god damn personal jet—can you believe that?) But the year leading up to the Olympics I couldn't afford a sabbatical of any kind. Too much at stake. (Soon, though, I wrote in response. After The Games.)

If a man ever needed one, it would be the perfect getaway.

THE OLYMPIC STADIUM

This may sound like the beginning of a bad joke, but it's not. It's true.

There was an American, an Aussie, and an Irishman who took off at the gun and led us through the first lap in :55. Opposite in tone to the first-round heat I was in. None of the lead three had the finishing speed of the Kenyans (or me—if I'm being objective) and so they were trying to drain the kick from the field by making it fast and hard the whole way through. The thinking was if you made your semi the quicker of the two then even if you didn't finish in the top five automatic qualifying spots you'd get through as one of the small-q next fastest times. Big-Q, small-q—didn't matter. Getting into the final was all that did. Once you were in the final anything could happen. Stories could be written. Heroes could be made.

After one lap the field was already spread out. I was content to stay in the middle, going through in :58.

The lead three were still out front through eight hundred, splitting in 1:52. I was in sixth at 1:56. If I did that twice I'd finish in the low to mid 3:30s. Enough to find the top five, I was sure. Certainly enough to get through with a small-q at least.

Enter ego.

I didn't want to finish in the top five and I didn't want to chance a small-q. I wanted people to talk. I wanted to send a message: I was there to win.

At the sound of the bell I had pulled my way up to the lead three. The clock read 2:38 as we crossed the line.

Coming off the final bend I stepped out into the fourth lane and strode by the lead three with ease. I looked at them as I went by. I wanted them to see how relaxed I was. I looked into the stands, too, and gestured to the crowd. The little hand-raise a golfer gives upon sinking a routine putt.

The fifth and final automatic spot was two seconds behind. Both small-q spots for the final came from our semi. I was four seconds faster than I needed to be. Only three seconds slower than my fastest time ever. One of the top ten fastest Canadian times in history. Don't get me wrong, I had extended myself. I really wasn't sure how much faster I could have gone. But something about having the expectation of winning and then actually winning lessened the pain. I don't want to say it felt easy. Easy is the wrong word. But it felt natural.

Overseas CBC Studio

The CBC invited me to come in for another interview that night. I was given a full ten minutes this time: five for the bio-bit, five for the interview. Walking onto their homey little stage the feeling of expectation came over me again, only it was more dread than anticipation. I could sense that certain questions which hadn't come the first night might come tonight and I didn't know how ready I was to answer them.

The makeup people came flittering through and patted our faces, fussed a bit with our hair. Someone fixed the tiny mic to my collar. I could hear the bio-bit playing in the background. I recognized the music signalling the end.

I heard someone behind me do the backwards count from five.

'In five, four, three . . .'

Michael Miller smiled, leaned forward, and began his script-ed introduction.

'We're here again this evening with middle distance phe-nom, Vector Sorn, who has, as expected, qualified for the Olympic fifteen hundred metre final. Content to run in the mid-dle of the pack for the majority of the semi—'

The camera cut from Michael Miller to footage of my race.

'—Sorn had his fans on the edges of their seats but coming into the third lap he found the proverbial other gear and closed the gap, holding close and easing past the leaders in the final one hundred, effortless it seemed, glancing around as he strode saun-teringly by, breaking the tape in one of the fastest fifteen hundred metre times in Canadian history.'

The camera cut back to Michael Miller onscreen.

'Sorn looked easy in victory and seems to be coming into peak form just at the right moment. The experts, not to mention

his legion of fans, consider him the clear favourite to emerge vic-
torious in two days' time. Middle distance running in Canada is
in the spotlight and Vector Sorn has singlehandedly thrust it
there.'

He looked from the camera to me.

'Congratulations, Vector.'

'Thanks, Michael.'

'Tell us, how do you feel?'

'I feel good, Michael. I feel good.'

Michael Miller crossed his legs and layered his hands on one
knee. 'I wanted to start this evening with the reaction you've gar-
nered on social media. At last count there were a dozen
Facebook pages with over a hundred thousand members each.
Pages with names like Vector the Victor and Sorn in the USA.
Americans think you're one of theirs.'

I grinned. 'I didn't think I was one of anyone's, Michael.'

'Well, I'm sure I can speak for the whole country, Vector,
when I say all of Canada holds you in their hearts.'

'That's a nice thing to say, Michael. Thank you.'

'It's the truth, Vector. Believe me.'

'Okay. I believe you.'

He checked something on his phone. 'Did you know you
have over a million followers on Twitter?'

'The funny thing is, Michael, I've never tweeted a single
tweet.'

'Is that so.'

'It is. I set up an account years ago but never did anything
with it.'

'Hey.' He leaned forward. 'I have a great idea.'

'What's that, Michael?'

'This wasn't planned but I'm sure the producers can accommodate us.' He looked past me and got the okay sign from someone in the wings. 'What's say we have you send a tweet right
now. Here. Live on the show.'

I shrugged. 'I wouldn't know what to say.'

'I don't think it matters. You could write in Klingon and I'm
sure you'd cause a twizzard, Vector.'

'Did you just make that up, Michael?'

'I did.'

'You're quite the neologist.'

'Thank you. I don't know what that means, but thank you.'

As we bantered the producers brought Twitter up on the big screen.

'We'll get you to sign in, Vector, if you don't mind.'

I was given a wireless keyboard. 'I hope I can remember my password, Michael.'

'I have confidence in you, Vector. I've heard you have a photographic memory.'

I grinned. 'Let me tell you, Michael, there are a few photographs lurking in the cobwebby domains of my limbic system I'd like to forget.'

He laughed but I could tell he wasn't sure exactly why.

'There. I'm in.'

Michael looked at the camera. 'He's in, folks. Get ready. Who will be the first to retweet Vector Sorn?' He looked at me. 'Are you ready?'

'There is providence in the fall of a sparrow, Michael. The readiness is all.'

Michael raised an invisible starter's pistol over his head. 'On your mark . . . get set . . . tweet!'

I typed a line and hit enter. 'Greetings from the The Olympic Games. This is Vector Herman Kent Sorn. XO to VA.'

Michael was right. Scrolls of retweets and @VectorSorn tweets came pulsing in.

'I told you.'

I nodded. 'It's a twiluge.'

'Nice one.' Michael snapped his fingers. 'A twinundation.'

I nodded and rattled off three more. 'A tworrent. A twurge. A twsunami.'

Smiling he returned his attention to the camera and the Twitter page faded behind him. 'I have to ask, Vector. Herman? Kent?'

'Nicknames.' I winked. 'Secret identities.'

He nodded like he understood. 'And I'm sure everyone wants to know. Who is VA?'

'She's my wife.'

It was the simplest explanation, if not the truth.

'You're married."

'I am.'

'I'm not sure anyone had the slightest idea, Vector.'

I leaned forward to take up my mug and winked again. 'I hope *she* did, Michael.'

Smiling he flipped through a series of pages on his phone. A finger to his lips, he nodded once. 'Ah. Here it is.' He looked up. His face and voice went interviewer serious. 'I hope you don't mind, Vector, but whenever we profile athletes we like to get to know them on a personal level.'

'Tough to know someone on an impersonal level, Michael, wouldn't you say?'

'Yes. Yes.' He pursed his lips. I'd interrupted his train of thought. 'As I was saying, we like to, you know, delve into who the athlete really is. Find out what makes him tick.'

'My heart, Michael. It's my heart that makes me tick.'

He wagged a finger at me. 'Ah, yes. And in more ways than one, I'm sure, Vector. In more ways than one. I was wondering. Could you tell us about your childhood?' He glanced at his phone. 'About Max and Rayn?'

I sat back in the chair and folded my arms.

Michael opened his eyes a little wider and said nothing. He waited. I wondered how long he would let the silence go. What was the tipping point between a dramatic pause and an awkward silence. Three seconds? Four?

I counted to five and continued. 'Max Sorn was my father. He was an Olympian in every sense of the word. He drowned in Lake Ontario.'

They ran images of Max competing at the Seoul and Barcelona games.

'I'm sorry to hear to that, Vector. Really.'

'But you knew it, Michael. Otherwise you wouldn't have asked.'

He nodded indiscernibly. 'He was a swimmer, isn't that right? A two-time Olympic silver medallist in fact. A terrible irony.'

'Michael. You know he was a swimmer. You were on the relay team with him. We talked about this just last night. They showed a picture of you and him on deck together. I'm sure your viewers will remember.'

'Right. I was just—'

'And to be clear, there is no irony in death, Michael. Irony, like life, is for the living.'

He asked if I might clarify what I meant.

'Take me, for example,' I said. 'I'm struck and killed while out for a run. A neurosurgeon whose mind slowly fades, who loses all motor control and succumbs in his final hour to an inoperable brain tumor. A writer who meets the same tragic end as his eerily autobiographical protagonist. A woman who for years tried to get pregnant, finally does, and dies in childbirth. Or the child dies, or both. Or, as we have it here, an Olympic swimmer who drowns.

'Let's get archetypal for a moment: a figure of pure evil who shoves a figure of pure goodness in front of an oncoming train. The train is an image of progress, of connection, of human innovation. But it's underground, so what does that mean? Here it means nothing more than what it is: a blunt instrument of death. In each scenario I've drawn there is no symbolism in the death event, Michael. Death is death. The only irony is that the living are always trying to find meaning in the absence of life.'

Michael nodded once and looked at the camera. Not what he expected, I'm guessing.

'Vector Sorn, ladies and gentleman. Athlete and philosopher extraordinaire. The long distance existentialist.'

'Let's not get carried away, Michael. I'm middle distance at best.'

He smiled. I didn't.

'And Rayn? Is she the figure of pure goodness?'

I repeated the five-count. 'She is, Michael.'

'She was your mother.'

They were running images of Rayn. Of the three of us.

I counted to five again. 'She was.'

'I bet you wish she were here to see you run.'

Michael at that moment made me think of Baron. He began to look like him. For the first time I understood how Max, when he looked at Lyle Govern, had seen Michael Norman Boon.

The images of Max and Rayn and I continued on screen. I learned later that they had contacted Stephen and Serra who sent them an album's worth. The producers were going for the tearful story. They were trying to make me a character the audience could feel sympathy for, empathy even. Create a fake sort of love: forced and forged. It doesn't take much for a stranger to feel familiar.

When I didn't say anything he glanced at his phone. When he looked at me again he was smiling. 'Tell me, Vector—are you going to bring home the gold?'

'I suppose the good Canadian answer would go something like, win or lose I can plan only to do my best. Or, you know it's really not about the winning, Michael—it's about being here, being part of the Olympic experience.'

'But that's not your answer.'

'No.'

'You're hopeful, then.'

'There is no hope in running, Michael. It's not religion. You don't press your palms together and glance subserviently skyward begging for some invisible puppeteer to propel you to victory. Running is pure action. You either do or you don't. That's it.'

'So it's just a matter of deciding?'

'When the three other variables are even—natural ability, training, and an intelligently designed, tested-for-effectiveness taper—all difficult to measure, I know—then yes, it's a matter of deciding. The Finnish call it sisu. Desire, belief, and a willingness to push are at least as powerful as the body that performs them.'

'You do consider a race a performance then.'

'Ah, you got me, Michael. But no, let me clarify. By perform I mean accomplish, an act which is achieved. Not a play, not a show, not entertainment.'

'Prefontaine said a race was a work of art.'

'He was being metaphorical.'

'You don't agree then.'

'There are similarities. Both are difficult. Both embody beauty. Both resist simplification.'

'How do they differ?'

'Art is hung on a wall, Michael.'

He grinned. So did I.

'When you're finished with the running you should go into politics. You have a way of steering a conversation. You still haven't answered the question and by now I'm sure the audience has forgotten what it was.'

'Am I going to win?'

'Yes.'

'I have not one single doubt.'

'You believe in yourself.'

'To be honest, Michael, I believe in very little.'

'But you *are* going to win.'

'Yes.'

'How can you be so sure? How do you *know*?'

'I don't know.'

I grinned. He waited.

'In all seriousness, I can't say I *know* I will win. That sort of knowledge doesn't exist. It doesn't make any sense. But in the way that I have already explained it I do *believe* I'm going to win which is stronger than knowing I will.'

'Didn't you just say you believe in very little?'

'Yes. Very little. Not nothing.'

'I see.'

'And it's important to note, too, the difference between *believe in* and *believe*.'

'Interesting.'

'Let me explain what I mean by the difference between *know* and *believe*.'

'Okay.'

'Take two simple uninflected sentences. You tell me which is more impactful, more powerful, more affective. In fact don't worry about telling me. You won't have to answer. Your reaction will be enough.'

'Can I know what the context is?'

'Usually context is everything. Here it doesn't matter. Two statements. In and of themselves. That's it.'

He adjusted himself in his chair and rubbed his hands together. 'Okay. Shoot.'

I waited, then spoke. 'I know you.'

He nodded. I paused.

'I believe you.'

He nodded some more. 'I see.' And it seemed as though he did. He glanced at his watch. 'We're just about out of time, Vector, but I do have one more question.'

'Okay. Shoot.'

He grinned. 'What is it you love about running?'

'The assumption in your question is that I love running. The truth is I don't.'

'Really.'

'Really.'

'So why do it then? Why do something you don't love?'

'That's a much better question, Michael. Let me try to answer it.' I looked slightly above his head at the lights and the wires in the ceiling of the studio. I was being filmed, which I hadn't forgotten exactly but hadn't really thought about until now. 'I run for the silence. For the communication in the silence, for what's said without being said. Running is a kind of speaking where nothing has to be explained. If you're part of the run you're part of the conversation. To know it you have to be in it.'

Michael Miller glanced at his watch and nodded. He looked at the camera. 'And there you have it folks. Vector Sorn. Novice tweeter. Expert linguist. Middle distance phenom. Self-certain gold medalist. And philosopher to the stars. To know it, he says, you have to be in it.'

The Olympic Stadium

Pressing the wireless earbud into his head Michael Miller stood trackside awaiting instruction. He nodded as the backwards count came, raised the hand with the microphone to his chin, and smiled at the camera.

'Hello Canada and Olympic fans around the world. We are moments away now from the start of the men's fifteen hundred metre final. The athletes are across the track making their final preparations.'

The camera panned across the track and zoomed in on the twelve of us who strode out in turn, doing fifty-metre accelerations in a seemingly predetermined pattern.

Michael Miller continued offscreen.

'This is it. This is the moment. The three and half minutes Vector Sorn has been training for his whole life. And here we are with him, right here at his side, ready as a nation to be thrust into the spotlight of greatness. Anyone who knows anything about middle distance running says that this race is Vector Sorn's—indeed Canada's—to lose.'

Onscreen were clips from the CBC produced bio-bit which was by now as recognizable to online and TV viewers as a commercial or subway ad: the Vector Sorn brand had become indistinguishable from the man himself.

The images from the bio-bit faded and the camera picked up the present moment across the track. The stadium announcer was introducing the twelve finalists: so and so from Kenya, Ireland, Ethiopia, the United States, Spain, Morocco, another from Kenya, New Zealand, another from Ethiopia, younger brother to the first, the two surprise finalists from Germany and Greece, and me.

The stadium was awash in flashing lights and a rolling spectatorial roar.

The starter called us to the line in a language none of us spoke and a hushed stillness followed almost instantly. A steady white noise of anticipation hovered in the dusk-hot air.

'Runners, take your mark.'

Though we didn't understand the words we understood the command. We responded in unison: one foot forward, toes to the line, knees bent, bodies bowed slightly forward, arms in a mid-stride pose.

When the gun sounded it was like an adrenalin-dripping needle straight to the heart. The stadium erupted. We ripped down the track like an angry swarm. Twelve distinct bodies as one. A band of brothers in arms taking the hill. A pack of den-defending wolves. A skein of sunbound gloryseekers on the wings of Icarus. The catch—the rent in the fraternal fabric—was that only one would forestall falling to the sea. Only one would win. Only one would become Olympic champion. Only one would become part of the myth.

.   .   .

I'll be honest. I thought about stopping here. Partly because none of the end-options I could think of were satisfying (it didn't matter which one was true—I could make any of them true—making something true is not the difficult part—so often all you have to do is say it), partly because I didn't see the point in adhering to convention for the sake of convention, and partly because I remembered hearing and liking this idea: 'The end is apparent. It doesn't need to be revealed.'

But the desire to see it through was too strong. No one has the strength or ability to refrain from revealing the secret if he has it. No one can resist lifting the stage curtains if he finds himself the one holding the rope. Really, there's no point to having a rabbit in your hat if you never reach in, grab him by the ears, and yank him out for everyone to see. It would be selfish and counterintuitive.

Oh, and if it matters, what follows is indeed what really happened. God's honest truth.

'And they're off. Ripping down the back straight they look like an entity sent forth by the gods, one beautiful beast of burden bursting with determined and directed speed.'

Michael Miller finger-pressed the earbud into his head and nodded.

'Forgive me, ladies and gentlemen. I'm excited and when I'm excited I tend to my detriment to be a little verbose. Brevity is the soul of wit, as they say, and so, if you'll allow me the aphorism, brief I shall be. Three-and-a-half-minutes brief to be exact.'

By now we were through the first two hundred and coming down the home straight for the first of four times. I was out front by two clear strides.

'Coming to the line now and Vector Sorn has separated himself from the field. He looks easy in his gait and full of running.'

I had decided at the sound of the gun that there would be no tactics. No sitting and waiting. No pedestrian first half. If this were to be a show, it would be a show from the gun. If it were to be a work of art then every stroke would be purposeful. There would be effort from the beginning. Earned meaning in every stride.

'With one lap in the books, ladies and gentlemen, Vector Sorn is the clear leader, as expected, widening the gap between the field and himself, it seems, with every on-world-record-setting-pace stride.'

I imagined Rayn in the stands. And Max. I pictured them. Not their ghosts, but *them*. Rayn standing, hands like a megaphone, yelling something like, 'Come on, Herman,' oblivious to and unconcerned with those around her, unembarrassed, genuinely excited and nervous and proud. 'That's our son. Our son.' And Max reclined, legs crossed at the ankles, smiling behind his aviators, a program rolled in one hand, the other free to touch her arm. His way of letting her know he was proud and excited too. His way of saying, 'Just so everyone knows, she's with me. She's with me.'

Most coaches would say such thoughts are distracting, point-less, amateurish, evidence of a lack of focus, a great way to become a tourist and forget the purpose at hand, a great way to lose momentum. These are the Olympic Games. Pay attention. Relax and drive. Zero in.

But I didn't have a coach. I was the one to say what I did and how I did it. Why I did it. Me and only me. I was in charge. And for this runner, images—even the sentimental ones, even the emotionally charged and potentially distracting ones, even the unreal and could-never-be-true ones—were fuel for the fire that drove me. Most coaches wouldn't understand. Baron certainly wouldn't.

His voice intruded. *'I've got it on good word I'm in the running for the Olympics, Vec. Get it? In the running?. . . No joke, kid. I'm going to be the distance coach . . . Olympic gold, kid. Ours to lose. Like I always said.'*

I attended the mandatory team meetings and the few minor workouts that led up to the opening rounds. I sat and listened to what he had to say. I ran what he said to run. None of it mat-tered. The few intervals he had us do did nothing for or against us and he knew it. At least three years of thoughtfully planned, personalized training had led every national team member to this point. Everyone played along but we all knew that two weeks under the direction of a figurehead would change nothing. The hay was in the barn.

Twice during workouts he came towards me, grinning like an idiot, finger in the air like he'd forgotten to tell me something really important, like no time or distance had passed between us at all, like he hadn't said what he said about Rayn, like I didn't know what he had done to her, sickeningly spurious sonofabitch that he was. Both times I looked at him, turned, and walked the other way.

They were kids according to her journal. Eighteen at most. What is past is past. Nothing can be done. The focus should be on the present. What's happening now. Unless there is no now, like with Max and Rayn. But really, for me, their now is solid-ified in a then which is as palpable and affective as any present I've ever been a part of. I can see them there in the stands watching me. In a sense they are alive whenever I want them to be. My heart reacts as if they were tangibly there. My mind treats them as though they were real. I can see them and hear them. I can even feel them if I think hard enough. In some ways it's better. There are none of the dull moments which actual life is full of. No arguments. No misunderstandings. Only a quiet, undisturbed presence in distinct and focal relief to everyone around them who blend together in a faceless collection of for-gettable background lives. As though together they are a work of art and I am given free reign to paint them however I see fit. To have such control. To be able to see the endless incarnations of time as one. This is what lets me shelve the inconsequential. This is what gives me certainty. This is what lets me know what I know and do what I do.

'We are coming to the end of the second lap now and Vector Sorn still holds a commanding lead and is right on track—pardon the pun, ladies and gentlemen—for a new world record. A good fifteen metres separate him from the rest of this world class field. He runs as though there is no pressure upon him, as though no one is watching. And it is truly a thing of beauty.'

I split the second lap in 1:48 and felt relatively comfortable doing it.

The third lap is always the toughest. If a miler can get through this section, if he can get to the sounding of the bell, then the end, though still some distance away, becomes, as Val says, inevitable. And what more can anyone ask of an end?

During my third lap, the producers dubbed in an audio voiceover from the Vector Sorn bio-bit, Vector Velocity. (I've watched the footage a hundred times. It never seems real.) There's a closeup of me. It looks like I'm running alone, the pack separate and away. The loneliness of the long-distance runner. You can hear me (or a dubbed-in version of me) breathing and there is a dramatic background heartbeat. My voice has been put through a filter which gives it a manufactured solemnity.

'We've been engineered to do this,' the voiceover begins. 'Not by choice or by happenstance but by evolution. Every anatomically equipped human being can run—opposite arm, opposite leg, one foot after the next—but we are among the few whose muscles fire at a greater rate over time, whose hearts pump more blood more efficiently, whose bodies can withstand more pain because of a brain more willing to push. We are the rats in some god's science lab.'

At the sound of the bell, the camera zoomed out to capture the distance I'd put between myself and the other eleven runners. The bio-bit soundbite was finished and the sound of the stadium resumed. The crowd came to its collective feet. I was the clear and uncatchable leader and I knew it.

With four hundred to go I was ahead by twenty-five metres and I felt my body—muscularly ablaze, gloriously bursting with ecstasy and pain. At the line the clock read 2:30. Olympic gold was mine to lose and the world record was there for me to seize, like the sword from the stone. As though time were something real and touchable, like a rock or a ring or a beating heart.

When I watch the footage now I feel detached from the man on the screen. How effortless his running seems. How automatic. How scripted. Like he could have gone even faster if the director had told him to.

By the time I came round the final bend the noise in the stadium had reached a fevered pitch and Michael Miller's voice matched it. 'One. Hundred. Metres. To go. Vector Sorn is staking his claim on Olympic history, ladies and gentlemen, with every driving, definitive stride. No one can catch him now. Eighty to go and he looks as comfortable here as he did at the gun. The pain he must be feeling. Sixty to go and Canada is on her feet. A hero to the nation. Forty. There is no question. God himself is on his feet, hands in the air in awe of this mortal creation below. Twenty. You're home, Mr. Sorn. Victory is yours. Ten. Come on, Vector—'

The clock stopped at 3:23.23. A new Olympic record by more than eight seconds. A new world record by nearly three.

Ten of twelve men broke the former Olympic mark and five were faster than the previous world standard of 3:26 flat. Imagine breaking the world record and coming fifth.

In every post-race interview, the last being with Michael Miller, the gist of the first and final questions was the same: 'How does it feel to be Olympic Champion?' and 'What's next for Vector Sorn?'

I can only imagine people want to know how someone feels in such a moment because they want to feel it too, which is understandable but impossible. Despite the best intentions, despite the best efforts of the person who does the describing, the transfer of how something actually feels, like winning an Olympic gold medal, is approximate at best and more likely superficial and virtually meaningless. All we really have at our disposal is analogy, which is a flawed way to understand anything, particularly the way something feels. What is there to compare the experience of becoming Olympic Champion to? Summiting Everest, battling and overcoming a storm at sea, having an Atlas-like burden lifted from your shoulders, exaltation, ecstasy, euphoria, celestial ascension, rapture as experienced by an atheist, paradoxical indescribability of the highest order.

I told the audience what they wanted to hear. I tried to describe the feeling. Anything else, however true, would have come across as esoteric and arrogant, like a writer being asked what his intentions were with his latest book—'What were you getting at? What does it all mean?'—who answers with, 'If you really want to know, read the book. If you've read the book but the purpose still eludes you, then perhaps it always will. To be sure, read the book again.'

Part of me wanted to say, *The only way to really understand what it feels like to win an Olympic gold medal and break the world record in the process is to go out and do it yourself.*

But instead I said, 'It feels great, Michael. It feels great. Like summiting Everest. Like battling and overcoming a storm at sea. Like having an Atlas-like burden lifted from my shoulders. Exaltation, ecstasy, euphoria. I'm on top of the world and the view is wondrous good.'

Although neither of us had ever scaled any height of rock or been bounced about on the tempestuous waters of the deep, although neither of us had ever had the world upon our shoulders, we nodded and smiled as though a clear understanding had passed between us. Which is exactly what people do.

I looked at the camera and did my best to achieve genuine sincerity in my tone when I thanked all those who had supported me over the years, a terribly vague statement which had the paradoxical effect of including everyone who believed I was talking to them.

When the red light came on to signal the end of our on-air time Michael Miller passed the microphone to the nearest person and shook one of my hands with both of his. He asked me to sign his Canadian flag which already had a number of signatures on it. He put an arm around my shoulders and gave the thumbs up to the five different cameras snapping shots of us. When he was finished he shook my hand again and thanked me a hundred times. I was there but not really, physically but not mentally. I felt outside the moment. I scanned the stands for Val as Michael Miller continued to talk. I thought she may have made her way down to see me, not to make some show of her affection or excitement but to stand there with her arms crossed, grinning.

I felt someone's hands in the middle of my back. I started walking. The hand wasn't moving me as much as it was guiding me. I looked at the man connected to the hand. A short black spiralled wire connected an earpiece to some sort of device in his shirt pocket. The shirt was white and collared and official-looking. The man's head was shaved. He was muscularly large, taller than me and twice as broad, or so it felt as we moved away from the track. For a moment he reminded me of Danny Mann. Two others, clones of my usher, led the way. I felt like a rockstar or a criminal or both. I couldn't decide. Behind me the cameras had refocussed their attention on the track. Michael Miller had his head down, finger-pressing the earbud and nodding. I was no longer the focal point. I started to regret not posing for a group photo the way we all had after the mile at the Pre Classic. (Even now I rank that as my greatest race. The feeling I get from remembering it surpasses all others. Even this one which was supposed to be the apex of all great things.) I remember shaking someone's hand but I couldn't remember who or what country he was from. I hadn't traded singlets with anyone. I hadn't raised my hands and closed my eyes as I crossed the line. That picture exists nowhere. I hadn't kissed the track. I hadn't fallen to my knees in euphoric relief or joy. I had done nothing, really, to distinguish the moment from all others.

As I left this particular ending I was beginning to feel flooded with a sense of imperfection. I was overcome and rather than feeling elated I felt depleted. Which makes no sense, I know. But it's true, and not uncommon, I think. There it is: truth, for what it's worth, so often contradicts sense.

Clippings (25)

(taken from personal texts)

—Tell us, Vector. How do you feel?

—Funny. I feel like the sun, going down.

—Uncontextualized metaphors are meaningless.

—Dickinson.

—Still.

—I'll be literal then. I feel like I don't know what comes next.

—What comes next is up to you. You're the writer.

—I know. So what if I said I know what comes next but I don't want it to?

—Too often what a man wants gets in the way of what he needs.

—I thought you'd say something like that.

—Technically I wrote it. Which is different. And if you knew why did you ask?

—Sometimes a man needs to be told what he knows.

—I'll see you in a bit then.

—I feel like I should tell you where I'm going.

—Don't.

—What am I going to say?

—You'll know as soon as you begin.

—I've often thought about that first night when you asked me what I was willing to lose.

—And?

—I've never had an answer. Who would ever be willing to lose anything?

MAGNITUDE & DIRECTION

Clippings (26)

(taken from "Confrontation: the Inevitable End,"
thatlongshadowonthelawn.com)

"Later today, Canadian distance coach, Charlie Baron,
will take an ill-fated walk with Olympic Champion,
Vector Sorn. Sorn, one-time star of the subculturally
successful, not to mention explicit, dramatic online
series Silver Light, knew the moment he read his mother's journal on-air during the closing scene of the final
episode that he would exact vengeance on his ex-coach
for what Sorn believed to be the root cause of his mother's tragic death (and subsequently his father's). Not only
did Sorn know that he would one day taste the sweet
elixir of retribution, he knew the very ingredients and
delivery system of the tonic he would concoct and serve,
author that he is of his own life's story. Details to follow."

~

*To be honest, I wasn't sure what I was going to do. Apart from
what was to come, one thing was for certain: I needed Baron to know that
I knew what he did.*

Athletes' Village

After I was finished in the testing room I went to the athletes' village. I knew I'd find him there. He'd been making the rounds since the team had arrived in Rio and now—after my win, which he would no doubt consider and advertise as partially his own—he would be in the mood to celebrate.

If SL were still up and running the athletes' village would have been fertile ground for a storyline. Apples were being offered and eaten from every part of the globe. It was an international garden of flesh and nothing was forbidden. Nowhere is the air more sexually charged and Baron was taking every advantage.

The last time I saw him I was leaving for my semi-final. He was working on a Finnish high jumper: blonde, leggy, beautiful, typical of her event. She was smiling, nodding, running a hand through her hair. I watched him give her a card or something and she took it. He actually leaned in to whisper something in her ear and she let him. He made me sick.

After the testing I found him in one of the games areas. Usually the only athletes in here were the ones who were finished their events, celebrating or trying to forget poor performances.

As I approached his table Baron stood—hand in the air, overblown smile on his face—and met me a couple of strides away. 'Hey. Look who it is.'

Like he'd been half expecting me, like we were good friends, like no time or tension had gone between us.

He put an arm around me and leaned in, spoke so only I could hear him. The looseness at the edge of his words told me he was already a few cups in. 'Listen, Vec. I know you're hooked up with that blonde—what's her name, Val—and I mean, good for you, she's something else, really—but these two Hungarian broads are in the mood for some fun and I don't think I can handle'm both. What do you say? Truce? For old time's sake?'

I raised my brow a little and shrugged, a vague enough gesture to express both indifference and potential interest. Baron slapped me on the back too hard. I stumbled forward and forced a grin.

He pulled out a chair for me and poured four generous rounds from the bottle on the table: vodka with a Russian label. Everything here had an international flavour. He raised his glass and tried a toast in what I guessed to be Hungarian, but was syllabically stilted and, I also guessed, unintelligible. Vintage Baron. '*Eggeh shehgeh tekreh.*'

The girls laughed and raised their glasses in turn. I followed and we all drank. Baron sat and poured four more rounds. 'Rebeka, Rózsa. This here's Vector Sorn.'

They leaned into each other and whispered something I couldn't understand.

They both looked at me, smirking. The one on the right—Rebeka, the blonde one—spoke. 'We know you. You are Victor. The actor in Light Silver.'

I gave them a noncommittal nod, then—confusingly, I'm sure—I shook my head. 'No, no. My name's Vector. Not Victor. I'm a runner, not an actor.'

Baron broke in. 'Runner. Heh. There's the understatement of the century.'

I looked at him. 'Not much of a claim, Charlie. The century's barely begun.'

It felt strange, saying his name like that. I don't think I'd ever called him Charlie. I could already feel the vodka and I was doing my best to be affable.

'Don't let him fool you, ladies. Vector here just became the fifteen-hundred metre Olympic champion and set a world record in the process.' He stuck a finger in his chest. 'And I coached him to it.'

He clapped me on the back twice and clutched my right shoulder, working the muscles like a masseur.

I looked at him, not threateningly, and he took his hand away.

'Victor was runner too,' Rebeka said. 'I think you are him.'

I shook my head. 'I think I am not.'

We all laughed but I'm not sure any of us knew why.

Rebeka persisted. 'No, you are him. You look and sound the same. Exactly.'

I shook my head one more time and played with my phone on the table, watching it spin like a top. I spoke without looking at her. 'Listen. You're not the first person to confuse me with this Victor guy. He must be my Doppelgänger. But you need to know.' I leaned forward and lowered my tone. Looking at Rebeka, trying to remain light and playful, I continued, shaking my head metronomically with each word. 'I am not him.'

Rebeka and Rózsa looked at each other and grinned.

Baron was smiling but not because he understood. In fact he wasn't even listening. I could tell by the way he looked that he was in his head, buzzing from the alcohol and the possibility at hand, the little daydream playing out before him.

Rebeka and Rózsa excused themselves. 'We will return.'

Baron stood and mimicked their rhythm. 'We will be waiting.'

I watched them go. Replicas of each other from the shoulders down. Lowcut white tanktops that revealed every detailed muscle in their backs. Lowriding, asshugging jean shorts they'd have to be cut out of. Calves that looked carved from stone, flexing into upside-down hearts with every bouncy, up-on-their-toes, flirty step. Flipflops that pornographically smacked the soles of their feet as they walked away. The only thing that distinguished them from behind was their hair. Rebeka was blonde. Rózsa, brunette. Flashes of Oregon went through my head like a movie I'd seen. The two girls turned and in unison blew us a Marilyn Monroe kiss. They winked at us and carried on.

He watched them go. 'You believe this, Vec? Top of the world.'

I pictured him standing on a precariously teetering Seuss-styled diving board above a set of wispy clouds, an imagined wind licking the front of his cartoonish hair, six-fingered furry hands on his hips, a clunky stopwatch draped around his neck, exaggerated self-satisfied smile engulfing his face. In the fantasy I'm on the impossibly curvy, rung-twisted ladder below, climbing impishly and stealthily towards him, pure evil beaming from my red oversized eyes. Flip the page and I'm the one standing on the diving board, hands clasped in victory over my head, reveling in the sight of the Seussian Baron falling, face skyward in embellished disbelief, to his certain death.

I looked at him and tried to conceal my seething with humour. 'Geographically, we're closer to the bottom of the world, Charlie.'

He clapped me on the back again.

'Ah, Vec. Always the wise guy. Too clever for your own good.' He sighed and looked at me. 'So—we okay?'

He held out a hand. Like it was that simple.

I shrugged, shook his hand, and told him sure, why not, we were okay. I needed him to believe I was there to reconcile our differences.

He cupped the back of my head, touched his forehead to mine like a quarterback to his wide receiver in the dying moments of the championship game, one last longshot play to win the silver ring. Like a father to his son on the brink of manhood, privately bestowing on him life's greatest secret. Like the coach he believed himself to be to his star athlete moments before the big race. I was expecting him to give me a back-slapping man-hug, the exclamation point to this moment of moments, when Rebeka and Rózsa returned.

Rebeka displayed the bottle of champagne she had procured.

Baron started nodding and gave a little clap. 'Nice. Now where'd you two lovely ladies manage to acquire such a fitting bottle of love?'

Rózsa sat beside Baron and touched his face. He leaned in to kiss her but she pulled away.

'We have our way, Charlie.'

She pronounced his name Zharlie.

'Oh, I bet you do. I bet you do, Rózsa.'

He exaggerated and held onto the *zh* sound in the middle of her name, leaned in again, and rubbed her nose with his. She let him and held his face with both hands.

There I am in my head, the image of me poised on the Seuss-drawn diving board above the clouds, proudlooking, satisfied, bent over a little so that he might see me watching, grinning Grinchily from above the clouds.

Rebeka sat, placed the bottle of champagne in front of me, and handed me a corkscrew. I took the bottle by the neck and started in on the cork. At the pop Rózsa put a hand to her mouth and giggled. Champagne bubbles spilled from the mouth and down the neck. Rebeka ran an index-finger up the length of the bottle to the tip, looked at me with one brow raised, and slid the champagne-wet finger past her pouty lips and out again, sucking the finger clean.

Around the O of the bottle's mouth she circled the same finger and put it to my lips as if to shush me though I hadn't said a word.

I pictured Val in the corner recording.

Slightly aroused, slightly disgusted, I grinned and said nothing. I poured the champagne and mimicked the toast Baron had uttered earlier.

'*Egeh sheh geh tekreh.*'

'You speak my tongue.'

I shook my head. 'I heard Zharlie say it earlier.'

'Fast talker.'

'You mean quick learner.'

She nodded. I wasn't sure she understood the difference.

She looked at me, took my face in her hands, and leaned in. I pulled away—not aggressively—stood, raised my glass, and repeated the Hungarian toast. I sat down again, moving my chair backwards a little as I did. Baron had his hands on Rózsa's thighs. He kissed her arm from elbow to wrist, like a chicken pecking food.

I took Rebeka's hand, innocent but suggestive enough to make her think I was interested, and spoke to Baron. 'Hey—I know a place.'

He looked at Rózsa and spoke to me. 'I know a place, too, Vec. And I'm close to fuck'n getting there.'

He ran his hands up Rózsa's thighs, fingers splayed, and squeezed.

She giggled and squirmed, swatted at him playfully with both hands.

He buried his face in her neck and made little foraging noises. She held the back of his head with both hands and closed her eyes, which encouraged him.

Rebeka had left her chair. She was in my lap, nibbling on an ear, as practiced and delicate a skill as a tip at the net. I bit my bottom lip, enough for a shot of pain, struggling to let Rebeka continue, struggling not to throw her from me, grab Baron by the neck, and drive a knee right through his skull. Finally I managed to manoeuvre Rebeka so that I could slip her from my lap and stand without offense. She held one of my hands with both of hers as I grabbed Baron by the shoulder and squeezed. He pulled away from Rózsa, a snorkeler breaching the surface for a few deep puffs of air, and looked at me, eyes partly shut.

'You believe this, Vec?'

'Top of the world, Zharlie. Top of the world.'

He laughed. 'Top. Bottom. Fucked if I care.' He took his glass and drank off the champagne in one long swallow. 'Fucked is *all* I care right now.' He leaned in, kissed Rózsa, and stood all in one motion. Throwing an arm around me, again he touched his forehead to mine. 'What's say we blow this pop stand?'

I nodded. 'Like I said. I know a place.'

He looked around the room as he spoke and threw a hand out like a magician, almost hitting me. 'He knows a place, ladies and gentlemen of the village. He knows a place.'

I caught his wrist and set his arm at his side. I could have sent him to the ground right then. I could have knelt into his chest and filled his face right there.

You fucking raped her.

Smack. Smack. Thump.

You fucking killed her. She's gone because of you.

Smack. Thump. Smack.

How do you like me now, asshole?

Smack. Smack. Thump. Suh-mack.

I imagined Val saying 'Cut,' lowering the handheld camera, nodding approval. I let the imagined scene fade. I bit my lip again: deep, quick, searing pain to keep me in the moment. I could almost taste the blood.

When I spoke I tried to sound cheerful. 'Up for a little adventure?'

He twirled and dipped Rózsa like a ballroom dancer. Touching his nose to hers he spoke in a low tone. 'Ah, adventure. What more could a man who has everything ask for?'

Let him stand there, I thought, above the Seussian clouds with that stupid grin on his face, wind-licked hair, arms akimbo, oblivious. Let him stand there while I climbed, implacable as I was, the final few rungs, loading all the hate and fury I could summon into one last step up, one last push, one summative story-ending act. Let him stand there while the sound of the distant train grew, that long steel bullet curving into sight, blotting out the sun, chugging slowly in, bringing with it the sort of apocalyptic darkness and mythical vengeance worthy of the most sinister craftsmen of the underworld.

Smack. Smack. Thump.

Nighty night.

A Subway Station

All the details are gone. It's like my mind's a harddrive that's been run through Ghost. I can't remember the colour of the walls or if there were buskers with violins or guitars. I have a vague memory of flipping a coin into someone's case. I cannot put down with certainty whether there were any cultural icons on display or whether the Olympic rings announced the coming together of the world amongst a congregation of international flags flown from the ceiling. In fact I cannot even say with certainty if there was a ceiling or if it was the sky above us. I don't remember the heat or the glare of the sun. I don't remember if there were clouds or rain coming down. I cannot say with any accuracy how many dozens of people were standing on that particular platform on that particular afternoon. I know only that on the small arms' reach stage where we stood we—Baron and I— were the sole spotlight players. Rebeka and Rózsa had gone to the washroom. Or maybe they had gone to seek out another bottle of some kind. Or maybe they had gone for food. Maybe they had ditched us. I don't know. Again, I can't say for certain. But I do know I never saw them again. If they did indeed return it would have seemed like their two leading men had vanished. They would have shrugged, no doubt, and carried on, the course of their lives unaltered in any real way. If they wanted to they would have replaced us in a heartbeat with a wink and a smile. If nothing else we are all replaceable. Who was Baron to them? Who was I? A character they thought they knew and were curious about because my physical presence had blurred for them the line between invention and reality. But there was no way of checking the manufactured details against the actual ones. There was no text to go back to.

And so there we stood, two men waiting.

Ineffectually, he scuffed the concrete with the sole of his shoe. Like an aging bull snorting at the red flag for the routine of it rather than rage. 'Listen, Vec. I gotta say. When I saw you walking toward me back there in the village I didn't know what to expect. I thought you'd never speak to me again. I thought you hated me. You can't know how relieved I am that you finally put the past behind us. Really. I've missed you, Vec. You're like a son to me.'

My hands, like two caged animals, were in the front pocket of the hoodie I had on. I squeezed them with everything I had into fists. I did my best to keep an even tone lest he grasp too soon the weight of what was to come. 'You give me too much credit, coach.' I elbowed him, a little too hard, and he stumbled on the spot. 'I can't put the past anywhere but where it is.'

He rubbed his arm. 'Always the clever one, eh, kid?' He looked at me like he knew me. 'You get that from Rayn. Your old man was sure no genius.'

He laughed but not maliciously. He was trying to be genuine, trying to create a moment of fraternal if not paternal-slash-filial closeness. Somehow—incredibly, mindblowingly—he thought enough time and forgiveness had passed that he could joke about Max and Rayn, as though he knew them, as though they had been friends of his, as though their loss had genuinely affected him and he was honouring them with an instance of reflective humour the way the bearers of memory and love sometimes do.

I heard the train coming.

Baron: 'So, where's this place you know?'

I tensed and my heart went. 'Not far.'

He went on his toes and craned around the station. 'Where'd those two go anyway?'

I shrugged. 'Maybe they ditched us.'

'Hah. No way. Those two are goers for sure.' He elbowed me a bunch of times and went 'Heh-heh-heh' the way he did. Then, 'Where *are* they?' He went on his toes and looked around again but to no avail.

I listened to the train. I could see the nose of it in my periphery, snorting. There would still be plenty of speed.

Like a seasoned orator of the stage I raised my chin a little as I spoke. 'Once not long ago there was a woman among us named Rayn who kept a journal of all her thoughts.'

Too focussed on the whereabouts of his conquest Baron didn't respond.

I continued. 'I came to have that journal but because I did not want to discover the truth of what I feared it contained I refrained from reading it for a long long time.'

He gave me a passing look, eyes furrowed.

I felt myself stop thinking. Like in a race everything became unhurried, automatic. I was certain, clear, and every word I uttered, every movement I made, was beautifully fluid.

'When I finally did read it I discovered the ending of a story that had remained to me unfinished for years.'

He looked at me, eyes a little wider. Something clicked. He understood, which is all I needed to know.

I flipped my hood up like a boxer, took one step back, and loaded my two hands like the double hammer of a gun. The moment stretched out as though time didn't exist. I saw flashes of Max and Rayn in the story of their meeting. I saw them in the stands, cheering. I saw her in her canoe on the river at home. I saw him on the podium in Seoul, the grainy image of him in the pool the moment before touching the wall. I saw him in the story of Lyle Govern. I saw him washed up on the February shores of Lake Ontario. I saw Rayn on the tracks the moment before impact, smiling, her eyes telling me not to worry, everything will be okay.

I saw Val in the wings pointing her silver remote: *pshew*. And as though on cue I shoved Charlie Baron with the force of a god and he fell from above the Seussian clouds. I looked down on him, grinning, and in a puff of smoke, like a trick with a camera, he was gone.

Without incident I turned and stepped away.

AFTER WORDS

As unlikely as it may seem I was soon touching glasses with Valerie Argent in a whiskey bar peopled with patrons who had no idea who we were.

The next day we were on a private jet to an island off the coast of Morocco, Karl Knotold on the runway like Jay Gatsby in a white suit and scarf, silver aviators reflecting the sun, tanned and smiling, arms crossed and waiting. With him—leaning into him on either side, as though frozen in portrait for a larger-than-life hovering-above-the-city billboard proclaiming 'Imagine the Freedom'—were Veronica and Vanessa Redhill. Together an image of absolute languor and luxury. As unreal as heaven itself but there, nonetheless, in plain view. Val and I disembarked and joined them as though it were as natural a place to be in this world as home.

Acknowledgements

Chris Needham, for everything he puts into publishing.

Mr. (Richard) Borek, for all the time & the close reading & the thoughtfulness.

Di Brandt, for the kind words & for continuing to be a teacher more than a decade after our last class.

The NA, for the company & the conversation, for the books & the beer.

Shelley Macbeth & Blue Heron Books, for the continued support.

Friends, distant & returning. The core of the original Rebels Track & Field team, for the heart & the grit & the early morning workouts. They taught me more than they can know and continue even now to inspire.

The Kuchmaks, for all that they do.

The Koubas on Eighth (Stacy, Justin, Carys, & Brynn), for reasons that would take a whole book to impart.

The Madills on Seventh (Patty (Mom), Hazel (Gramma), William (Poppa)), not to forget Fourth, for reasons a whole book could not begin to impart.

The Sneaths.

Dad.

Ethan. My best buddy old pal.

Penelope. My little Penner Grace.

Abigael. My little Rosie Girl.

And Tara, as always, for everything.